"Ben's been spoiled all his life," Luke said. "That's what his behavior is all about."

"How do you know? How do you really know what his life has been like up to now?" Kat asked. "He's only nine. You need to let him learn to love you, Luke."

Their faces were so close that Kat could feel his breath on her cheek.

"That's just it," he murmured, his eyes soft with a vulnerability she'd never seen in him before. "What if he never forgives me and never grows to love me? Perhaps I've already lost my chance with him."

On impulse, Kat moved closer. Cupping his jaw with gentle fingers, she touched her lips to his, and when his arms wrapped around her, it felt so right. His lips closed over hers, soft and yet demanding, and for an endless moment it felt as if they were one being, a part of the vast space and beauty that surrounded them...

But they weren't alone. With a surge of guilt, Kat pulled away in panic, looking for Ben. What were they thinking?

Dear Reader,

Thank you for picking up my book, I do hope you enjoy it. There is just something timeless about the sea that draws us in. At times serene and breathtakingly beautiful, it can also be awe inspiring in its ferocity—dangerous, wild and untamed. A bit like life, really, I suppose.

I am so enjoying writing this series, Songs of the Sea, and I would love to hear your comments. You can contact me at info@holmescalesridingcentre.co.uk.

All very best wishes,

Eleanor

HEARTWARMING

A Father's Pledge

—

Eleanor Jones

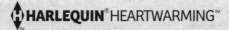

HARLEQUIN® HEARTWARMING™

Recycling programs
for this product may
not exist in your area.

ISBN-13: 978-0-373-36853-2

A Father's Pledge

Printed in U.S.A.

www.Harlequin.com

Eleanor Jones was brought up on a farm in the north of England and learned to love animals and the countryside from an early age. She has ridden all her life, and after marrying her husband at just eighteen years old and having two wonderful children, they set up a riding center together. This is still thriving over thirty years later, doing hacks, treks and lessons for all ages and experiences. Her daughter competes at the national level, and she is now a partner in the business and brings her adorable three-year-old son to work with her every day. Eleanor's son is also married with two children, and they live nearby.

Eleanor has been writing for what feels like her whole life. Her early handwritten novels still grace a dusty shelf in the back of a cupboard somewhere, but she was first published over fifteen years ago, when she wrote teenage pony mysteries.

Books by Eleanor Jones

Harlequin Heartwarming

Creatures Great and Small

The Country Vet
A Place Called Home
The Little Dale Remedy
Shadow on the Fells

Songs of the Sea

Footprints in the Sand

Harlequin Everlasting Love

A Heartbeat Away

I would like to dedicate this book to my dear sister, Catherine, who lives by the sea.

PROLOGUE

NEVER HAD LUKE TRAVIS felt such guilt before—guilt that sat so heavy on his heart it weighed down his every movement. Waiting there for Ben, *his* Ben, the nine-year-old boy he had abandoned so many years ago, to arrive at Flight—the special school where Luke worked—was both the best and worst experience of his life. He'd never expected and was totally unprepared for this. And the sad thing was that he had no excuse to give his son. Luke had just been young and selfish and irresponsible, simple as that.

He sat rigid on the wooden chair, drowning in memories. Ben's mum, Carly, so wild and so beautiful. *When you're young and impulsive*, he told himself, *sometimes you make crazy decisions, blame other people and just walk away.* He knew he had and he wasn't proud of it. But now he'd been given a chance to make amends, to prove that he could be a good dad. He intended, despite the self-doubt that haunted him, to do the very best that he could for his son.

Luke glanced at the clock again and again as the time crept nearer, three thirty on a sunny afternoon. At any moment his son, the son he barely knew, the son he had left behind by persuading himself that it was the best decision for the child, would walk through the office door. And Luke had no idea what to say to him.

Then the door opened, and there he was, walking determinedly behind his grandma, Mollie, his smooth, young face an echo of Luke's own, but was filled with anger and aggression.

"Hi," Luke said awkwardly, offering his hand.

Ben just stared straight through him, as if he wasn't there. The boy was right to hate him because that was what he deserved.

And then for one solitary, fleeting moment, Ben's mask of anger slipped. His jaw quivered as his head dropped forward, revealing his vulnerability, and Luke swore to himself that from this moment forward his son would come first. It was time to make amends, to come to know him and to earn his love, no matter how hard it would be.

Luke understood now, without a shadow of a doubt, that walking away from his son had been the worst mistake of his life.

CHAPTER ONE

A LOUD SCREAM took Kat Molloy's attention and she ran across to where Tammy Nelson was rolling on the ground, clutching her knee. Huge tears rolled down the little girl's cheeks as Kat gave her a hug. "It'll be okay in a minute," she promised. "Look, it isn't even red."

Tammy carefully stood up, testing her weight on her injured joint. "See," Kat said. "It's better already."

Tammy smiled happily, rubbing away her tears. Then she pointed in horror toward the sea, her blue eyes wide beneath their frame of ginger curls. "Miss!" she cried. "Ben's gone right out into the water!"

Kat's heart leaped into her throat.

"Ben!" she yelled, spotting the boy's slight figure heading out into the waves. "Get back here...now!"

Tammy and the two other children in Kat's care, nine-year-old Johnny Cartwright and seven-year-old Angel Dunn, stood ankle-deep in the rushing foam that shimmered onto the sand, watching in awe as the blond boy with a wicked grin waded out until the water was to his waist.

Ben had been at Flight for only a couple of weeks, arriving just a week after Kat herself, but he had always been in some kind of trouble since day one. Unfortunately, it had made him quite a hero to the younger ones. With a sigh, Kat stepped deeper into the water, dragging her legs against the current as the boy waded out even farther, waving cheekily. A prickle of alarm set in. The cool water might look enticing, but the undercurrents here were strong, and beneath the waves lurked quicksands, which could catch waders unaware.

Ben splashed around, grinning mischievously as he lowered his shoulders into the rushing tide. "It's okay, Miss. I can swim," he called, his voice blowing away on the wind. "It's easy—watch!"

Kat struggled toward him. "No, the current is way too strong. Get back here, Ben! Just paddling, I said."

For a moment, the boy defied her, propelling himself through the water with flailing arms as the other children looked on in awe. Kat waded deeper into the rippling foam, calling his name with as much authority as she could muster, ignoring the icy water soaking her jeans.

When a tall figure splashed by her, she was surprised to see Luke Travis making a beeline for Ben. The waves he made as he passed knocked Kat off balance, and suddenly the sand seemed to give way beneath her feet. The water closed over her head, taking her breath, and she felt a rush of raw panic before she lurched back up into the sunlight, swallowing seawater and coughing.

Luke had grabbed hold of Ben and was dragging him back to shore. The boy struggled angrily as Luke dumped him on the sand, and Kat hurried across to check him over, ignoring her wet clothes. Her relief quickly turned to indignation when she realized that Ben was okay.

"I could have drowned," she yelled at Luke. "And I had everything under control."

Her voice was lost amid the cries of the gulls that circled above them. This wasn't the first time Luke had intervened in one of her sessions. He seemed to show up at every one of her sea- or nature-therapy outings, watching her with the kids and butting in at every opportunity. Yes, he was Ben's dad, and the assistant general manager at Flight, but *she* was the child therapist, and she knew what she was doing. Just because Luke was struggling to be a proper father to Ben didn't mean he had a right to keep questioning her ability to look after his son.

And now, of course, he could justify his hypervigilance with this incident. It was just what he'd been looking for. Luke Travis didn't believe she was capable of doing her job, and today had given him even more fuel to fire that belief.

Kat pushed her wet hair back from her face and headed toward Ben and Luke. Even though Ben seemed all right, she needed to check on him. She had no excuses; this was her fault. She was in charge of the children and she should have been watching them all more closely.

Luke was standing slightly apart from the small group of excited children, his arms crossed. She ignored him as she walked up to Ben.

"Sorry, Miss," he said, his cheeky grin belying his apology. "But I did tell you I could swim."

Kat glanced sideways at Luke; his frown of disapproval made her suddenly aware that her heavy pink sweater was clinging to her body. She clasped her arms across her chest self-consciously, realizing with a sinking heart just how unprofessional she must look.

"Are you okay, Ben?" she asked. "You didn't swallow too much water, did you, being dragged through the sea like that?"

"I told you," he insisted. "I can swim and I didn't swallow any water."

"Well, I'm glad to hear that, Ben, but there are going to be consequences for not listening," Kat went on in what she hoped was a stern voice. "Right now, we're all going to have to go back to school so that you and I can get changed."

"Seems like that's a good idea anyway," Luke interrupted. "Before one of the children drowns."

A red flush crept into Kat's face as she turned to the children, who were giggling behind their hands. "Why don't you all go and see who can find the nicest stone," she suggested. "But don't go too near the sea… or out of my sight."

"I'll win," cried Tammy, already running off. Angel followed close behind, and the other kids joined the search. Ben, however, hovered within hearing distance of Luke and Kat, pretending to look at the ground.

"I had everything under control," Kat told Luke. "Things could have gone much worse with three of us in the water. If you had to insist on monitoring my class, you could have stayed on shore and made sure the other kids didn't run off."

"I have every right to monitor all the children's classes," Luke said drily. "And to be honest, it seems your classes need more than just monitoring. You shouldn't be left in charge of children if you can't watch them properly."

Kat fought to contain her anger. The last thing she wanted was for them to have a full-blown argument with the kids nearby. "What you are obviously trying to insinuate," she eventually said in a low, steely tone, "is that you don't think I'm capable of caring for *your* son. Who is clearly out of control. Do you think you could have stopped him from going into the water like that? I have a long track record of caring for kids and keeping them safe."

"All I know is what I saw here today," he

responded. "And I will be reporting the incident."

Kat bristled. "What did happen here today? As far as I'm concerned, Ben took advantage of the fact that I was helping Tammy after her fall and broke the rules by going for a swim. I reacted as quickly as possible to that, and I'd soon have had him back to shore if you hadn't butted in."

"I was only messing around, you know," Ben said, surprising them both. "What's the big deal? I was just having fun."

Kat and Luke turned to him and the other children, who had returned from their rock hunt while the adults were arguing.

"It's true," agreed Tammy. "He likes having fun. Don't you, Ben?"

"I like Ben's fun," added Angel with a gap-toothed grin.

Luke held Kat's gaze.

"Nothing wrong with having a bit of fun," Ben announced in a sulky voice. "You should try it sometime."

At that, Luke's face hardened. "Well, it looked to me as if you were in a very dangerous situation," he said, resting a hand on the boy's arm. "Having fun is one thing, but you must learn to obey the rules or you could get hurt. Miss, here, needs to apply a little more discipline, I think."

"What?" Kat asked. "To myself, you mean, or to the children?"

"To both, actually," he said. "Now come on, Ben. I'll make sure that you get back to school in one piece."

"We'll all go back together," Kat said, ushering the children toward the path.

"I hate you," Ben muttered under his breath, pulling away from Luke to catch up with the other kids.

Kat's heart went out to both of them. She knew Luke had only just met Ben, and it had been a difficult adjustment. For father *and* son. But Luke throwing his weight around like this was not going to help build their relationship.

Water dripped from her clothes, and she shivered. "Look," she said, falling into step beside Luke. "Why don't we just take a step back on this. No one got hurt and all you're doing now is upsetting poor Ben."

"Upsetting him?" Luke's voice was cold. "You're the one who's upsetting him by not doing your job properly. Children need boundaries and discipline, and you don't seem to know the meaning of either."

Kat's cheeks burned. She was not going to be drawn further into this dispute. Most of the children here had already endured too much conflict in their young lives. They might come across as tough, but they were so vulnerable.

"If you feel that strongly, maybe you should bring it up with Tim Ellison or Mike," she said. Tim was the principal at Flight, and Mike was head of care. "They asked me to come here to run my sea-therapy course. I think you'll find they'll back me up."

Luke glared at her. Determined not to be intimidated, she stared ahead and kept walking. "Look," she said, "I'm just trying to do the job I know I'm good at, Luke, and that is to try and help Ben. Perhaps you *should* talk to Mike, though. No one understands the kids and their situations like him. He can probably help you—"

"What do you mean, help me?" Luke cut in. "With what?"

"With Ben, I mean—he can help you with Ben."

A flicker of emotion momentarily clouded his features, and Kat thought Luke was about to lose his cool. For a second, his eyes held hers and she saw such pain in their depths that it suddenly occurred to her that maybe Luke Travis was scared…but scared of what? His steely demeanor returned and he looked away.

"Don't get too far ahead, children," she called, increasing her pace.

They all waited for her and Luke to catch up before heading onto the narrow pathway that ran up the cliff to Flight. To her surprise, Ben fell in beside her, his small hand shyly clasping hers. She closed her fingers around his, then glanced back at Luke. He was watching them intently, his mouth set into a grim line. She felt a jolt of sympathy for him. She couldn't help thinking that perhaps beneath his tough exterior was a man who was more than a bit out of his depth.

WHEN THEY ARRIVED back at Flight, squelching in through the imposing front door of the large, converted country house, Hilda, the pleasant, round-faced care worker, was horrified by the state of them.

"You go and get a shower, and I'll see to the others," she told Kat. Luke had stalked off somewhere the moment they'd stepped inside. "It's nearly teatime, anyway. And Ben needs a shower, too, by the looks of him.

What happened—did you fall in the sea or something?"

Ben squirmed, shamefaced, and Kat smiled. "Something like that," she said. When the little boy flashed her a grateful glance, warmth flooded her heart. Luke Travis might be his dad, but he was wrong about Ben. It was love the boy needed, not discipline. Shame he couldn't see that.

Kat went to shower and change, unable to get the day's events out of her mind. What had happened between Luke and his son, and how come they'd had so little to do with each other up until now? She knew the basics of Ben's behavioral problems—he wouldn't be at Flight at all if he hadn't had issues at home with his grandparents, who were his official guardians. She just wasn't sure where Luke came in or why he hadn't been involved in the boy's life until now.

Hot water warmed and soothed her. She stretched up her arms and closed her eyes, raising her face to the deluge, trying to relax. But Luke Travis's angry expression wouldn't leave her mind. His brown eyes had been so dark and fierce. What if he did complain about her to Tim or Mike?

Well, just let him try, she decided, as she

piled her wet hair on top of her head and reached for a towel. She had done nothing wrong. She was here to do a job and she wasn't about to let him interfere with her courses. She'd already proved that her sea therapy worked; getting children to understand nature, the constant, timeless rhythm of life and the tide's ebb and flow helped give them a sense of belonging to something bigger than their everyday lives…helped them heal. Luke Travis should be attending her courses as a student, not as a critic; it might do him a world of good to stop and take stock of what really mattered in life.

It wasn't until much later, curled up in bed with the moonlight streaming in through her window, that Kat's thoughts went back to her own issues. Her past was always there, waiting for a chance to remind her why she'd started working with troubled children in the first place. And as she drifted to sleep, her subconscious took over, taking her back to the day when her whole life turned on its head, ripping away her childhood…

She was trying to hurry, but her legs refused to do as they were told, as if she was wading through water. Ahead of her the cottage she'd called home for almost fifteen years seemed to loom out at her, its windows strangely sad and empty when normally they shone, bright and inquisitive, as if enjoying their glorious view of the sea that stretched out before them to meet the sky. She had always felt that the cottage had its moods and today it was angry with her; she could feel it in her bones. And all because she'd stayed late after school for once, to play in the park with the normal kids who didn't have to rush home every day to care for their sad, crazy mothers.

The song of the sea filled her ears with its familiar, rhythmic swish as she stepped through the front door. Her heart thudded loudly in the silence of the small sitting room. Her mother's lumpy figure was slumped on the sofa, eyes wide-open, gazing into nowhere...

And then the screaming started, the screaming that went on and on and on...

Kat sat up in the darkness with the screaming still ringing inside her head. Guilt and horror seemed to pin her to the bed. She forced herself to breathe; it was a dream, just a dream.

Moonlight slid in through the window, calming her, bringing back reality. She'd never truly escape that nightmare, though; it was a memory. Her mother had died because she had left her all alone, upsetting the routine that kept her sane and sending her over the edge.

Thanks to all the counseling she'd had afterward, Kat understood that it wasn't her fault and that she had to stop blaming herself. She'd been barely fifteen, a child who should never have had the responsibility of caring for a mother who was suffering from depression. There were times, like tonight, however, when the dreams came back to haunt her, casting out her common sense and forcing her to relive the agony of that day.

She tried to look on the bright side. The dream always reminded her why she'd followed the path that had finally led her here, to Flight. For she had been one of those lost, confused kids who had no stability in their lives. By becoming a child therapist, she'd been able to give something back. It had helped to ease the sorrow and guilt that she knew would hang over her forever, no matter what anyone said.

CHAPTER TWO

AFTER HER DISAGREEMENT with Luke, Kat felt relieved to be off work the next day. Determined to put their unpleasant incident out of her head, she decided to head down to the shore, hoping to get new ideas for her sea sessions. Despite her positive attitude, however, as she wandered along the line of flotsam and jetsam she couldn't help but remember the threats he'd made about reporting her incompetence. She needed to see Mike and explain what had happened before Luke gave his version…assuming he hadn't already done so. Even if he had, she could still share her side of things.

Kat turned her face into the wind and breathed in its salty tang, listening to the sounds and smells and waiting for them to smooth away her troubles. Today, though, her "seaside fix" just didn't seem to work. In fact, it had the opposite effect, taking her back yet again to the bleak and empty phase of her life she'd tried so hard to forget.

Her mother used to tell her that she was selfish and irresponsible, and sometimes, deep down, Kat couldn't help wondering if it was true. The familiar guilt gnawed at her gut. What if Luke was right? What if she had been too lax with Ben? Perhaps she *should* have been watching over the children more stringently…and perhaps she should have watched over her mother better. The thought made her feel fifteen again, and she shuddered.

The voices inside her head that had shouted at her then, blaming her for her mother's death, were now mostly just a whisper in her memory, except when the dreams came to haunt her as they had last night.

Those voices had been stilled by the soothing song of the sea on that awful day as she'd waited down on the shore for someone to answer her emergency call. Her quickly fading footprints in the sand had made her feel invisible, bringing comfort. But she hadn't truly been invisible because the paramedics had soon found her, speaking in quietly caring, low, soothing tones that held a hushed urgency. *How long have you been your mother's carer?*

Do you have any other relatives? Where does your father live?

She'd screamed at them to shut up, her hands clamped tight across her ears. They'd shared concerned glances, raised their eyebrows and whispered behind their hands. She'd been totally ignorant about the world, totally ignorant about death and totally unaware that her mother had been suffering from depression for over five years—since her father left.

Today, the bay was sparkling and serene, so beautiful that it took Kat's breath away. She'd been afraid of the sea for a while after her mother died, for it was so closely linked with the day she'd found her body…and yet, deep down, she'd yearned for it, too.

It had taken five years for her to finally pluck up the courage to visit the coast again, believing that just being back in its awe-inspiring company would rekindle all her heartache, guilt and anger. She couldn't have been more wrong. As soon as she'd gazed across the sweep of the bay to where the sea and sky became one, and breathed in those familiar scents, with the buffeting wind in her face and droplets of water on her skin, she'd known that the sea was still her friend, wild and beautiful and sometimes dangerous, but always dependable. And then she'd known that she should never have been afraid of going back to the coast, for her mother's illness had had nothing to do with this place at all.

Jenny Brown's Bay shimmered ahead of her now, serene and tranquil for once; it felt all-forgiving.

"I'm sorry, Mum," she cried out into the gentle breeze, raising her hands to the sky. "I let you down when you needed me, but I will make up for it, you'll see."

Trying to put the past behind her, Kat carried on walking. The memories clung and it occurred to her that perhaps she should be thanking her mother, for Kat's childhood experiences had led her to become what she was today, someone who could, hopefully, make a difference in the lives of children who needed support and guidance.

She took a deep breath and studied the flow of the rippling tide. Its changeless rhythm intrigued her, for although the ocean could often be terrifying in its ferocity, it was also consistent. No matter what was going on in people's lives, the tide continued rushing up to the shore and flooding back out right on time; the sun still shone, the rain still fell and all the creatures in the world went about their daily lives following nature's call without question.

That was what she loved about nature and animals: durability. Which was what had made her decide to develop her specialized therapy. Children who had no stability in their lives gained strength and confidence from their seaside sessions. She'd seen it time and time again, and Kat firmly believed that nature could teach most people a thing or two, if they only took note. Pity Luke Travis didn't spend more time taking note of what her courses were about, she thought, instead of being so negative and critical.

It was late afternoon before Kat arrived back at Flight. The big, stone-built house must have once been some wealthy person's country residence. As she approached, it stood tall and square against the brightness of the sky, its windows sparkling in the sunshine. It was a beautiful house, a wonderful place for the children here to call home. For many of them, Flight was the only true home they'd ever known. It was well run, too, with a great team. Tim Ellison, the principal, had a cottage on the grounds, while Mike Thomas, head of children's care, lived on-site with his wife, Gwen, who worked alongside him.

Most of the other carers, therapists, teachers and cleaners lived locally, including the general manager, Wayne White. Luke was Wayne's assistant and he lived on-site, as did Kat, though she was on the lookout for a place of her own.

Kat deeply respected Mike and Gwen, particularly since they often spent time with the children in the main house. She liked the way they went above and beyond their job descriptions, helping make Flight feel like a real family home. The layout also helped with that, featuring single and double bedrooms for the kids and a large, comfortable communal living room, two smaller sitting rooms, a dining room with one huge table and a massive kitchen, where anyone could eat or snack or just sit near the stove. Alice, who came in daily to organize the cooking, was usually to be found there, along with one or two of the other kitchen staff.

Kat and Luke had small apartments in a new annex at the rear of the house, but as they both had private doors into the garden, their paths rarely seemed to cross. Apart from a brief, cordial conversation when she'd first arrived at Flight, Kat hadn't had much to do with him. A brief nod as they passed in the hallway or the odd polite comment was about the only interaction they had had... until Ben arrived. Ever since, Luke seemed to have taken it upon himself to interfere with everything she did.

Kat had been working at Flight for just over a week when Mike had called her to his office to tell her that a new pupil, Ben Jackson, was arriving that afternoon and would be assigned to her for counseling. As usual, Kat had wanted to know as much about the boy's background as possible and she'd spent time before he arrived looking through his notes and questioning Mike. Ben's grandparents were his guardians, but his grandmother, Mollie Jackson, had been struggling to care for him properly after his grandfather had fallen ill. Ben had become cheeky and disobedient, as well as regularly skipping school or refusing to go at all. The elderly lady had been at her wit's end, so when Ben's social workers had suggested sending him to a special school, she'd agreed. She'd selected Flight because that was where Ben's father worked. The father he had hardly ever seen.

Mike had emphasized the importance of

treating Ben like any other child at Flight. The plan was for him to get to know his father gradually without making a big deal of the relationship. They didn't want the other kids to sense favoritism or feel excluded, but preventing Ben from getting to know his dad could be detrimental to him as well.

When she'd found out that Ben's father was Luke Travis, Kat was surprised, to say the least. Luke was thirtyish and single, as far as she could make out. Not even the staff, who had known him since he first came to Flight as a general office lackey, had a clue that he had a son. Apparently, he'd never mentioned the boy to anyone in the years he'd spent working up to assistant manager.

Kat's first meeting with Ben had been unproductive; he had refused point-blank to answer any of her questions and he exuded anger, an anger that she knew hid loneliness and fear. One thing was for sure: Ben Jackson was one very mixed-up little boy, and the more she could find out about his background, the easier it would be to try to help him.

She'd even tried to talk to Luke, shortly after Ben arrived, but it had been like talking to a brick wall. Luke didn't seem to know anything about his son and he'd flatly refused to discuss how they'd become estranged. Perhaps now, though, after yesterday's fiasco, she should approach him again. If she asked for Luke's help, maybe it would break the ice a bit. What Ben needed right now was calmness and stability, and his father arguing with his counselor was definitely not the way forward.

Kat tapped on Luke's apartment door, trying to appear professional and in control even though her heart was fluttering in her chest. It swung wide open at once.

"Oh, it's you," he said drily.

"Look," she began, pulling back her shoulders and lifting her chin, "I'm really sorry about yesterday, and I wondered if perhaps we could have a chat…about Ben. You know, so we can get on the same page about what's best for him."

Luke towered over her, a deep frown etched across his forehead. "No offense," he said, "but I'm not sure I want us to be on the same page where Ben's concerned. It's your job as his counselor to find out why he's been behaving as he does. I'm his father and I don't have to answer to you."

"Well, no…obviously, I understand that."

Kat squirmed. "I just thought that if we had a proper chat about Ben's background and his relationship with you up until now, it might help me understand his situation a bit better."

"We don't have a relationship," Luke retorted. "That's the whole problem. And we are unlikely to ever have one if you don't stop putting him in crazy situations that encourage him to get into trouble."

Kat tried to keep her cool, but heat flooded her face. "He was not in a 'crazy' situation yesterday—he just took advantage of me being distracted to have some fun. I'll be the first to admit that I should have kept a closer eye on him and maybe reined him in earlier, but he was never in any danger, and the situation was not crazy. In fact, his behavior was typical of many young boys. Or perhaps you've forgotten what that's like. In my experience, when children behave badly, it's for a reason. Usually it's a cry for help… or a way to channel their anger at the world. Children need stability and love in their lives if they're ever to get back on track."

"So now you're telling me that I don't love my own son?"

"No, of course not!" Kat felt as if she was going around in circles. "I just want to understand him better, and I thought you might be able to help with that."

"Look…" Luke gave a slight shake of his head as if summing her up as stupid and exasperating. "I agree that Ben needs stability, and he has that here. The other thing he needs, though, is discipline—ground rules he has to learn to follow. I don't believe your airy-fairy method of counseling is giving him that. Yesterday proved it. It seems to me that all you're doing is letting the kids run wild."

"Well, it seems to *me* that you and I will have to differ on that," Kat said, holding her head high. "Oh, and by the way, I do happen to be the only one of us who is qualified to decide what a child needs."

"You don't need qualifications to bring up kids, just common sense."

"And exactly what part has your 'common sense' played in your son's life up until now?"

Luke paled, and Kat wished she could take back what she'd said. He glared at her then turned on his heel and slammed the door in her face.

Regretting her decision to talk to him, Kat walked slowly through the large gardens, needing time to calm down and think things through. As she reached the cliff top where the beautiful old house was perched, she stopped for a while to look out across the wide vista of the bay, breathing in the crisp, clear air before heading toward the front door of the school, feeling much calmer and more in control of her emotions.

As she stepped into the spacious hallway, she smelled the comforting aroma of roast beef and the fragrant lilies that stood on a side table beneath the window. She hesitated, listening to the sound of children's laughter floating through from the kitchen. Despite the troubles that most of the children here had faced in their lives, Flight was in many ways a happy house, and she was very grateful to be a part of it. She just hoped Luke Travis would allow her to help his son thrive here.

Kat still had to talk to Mike, so she headed toward his study to see if he was still there. As she approached the half-open door, she could hear him speaking to someone. Could it be Luke, fueled by the confrontation they'd just had? She paused in the hallway, feeling guilty for listening in on a private conversation but unable to resist. If it was Luke, she needed to hear what he was saying about her.

"I think you just need to give her a bit more time," Mike said. "She does have a lot of experience, and I'm sure that she knows what she's doing. I'll have a word with her, if you like."

Kat didn't wait to hear the other person's response. It was obviously Luke complaining about her. She knew where she stood with him now and she definitely didn't want eavesdropping added to her list of misdemeanors. When she met Gwen at the end of the hallway, her heartbeat increased tenfold; two minutes sooner and she'd have been caught red-handed.

"Hi," Kat said in what she hoped was a bright, calm tone. "If you're looking for Mike, I think he's in the study. I heard his voice as I walked past."

"Thanks," Gwen responded with a puzzled frown. "Is everything okay? You look a bit flustered."

"Yes…" Kat took a deep breath. "Of course, everything's fine."

"And your sea and nature sessions are going well?"

"Really well. I'm looking forward to expanding to animal therapy."

"Good luck with that," Gwen said. "Though it may take a bit longer to set up than your sea therapy."

Now, what did that mean? wondered Kat as Gwen carried on down the hall. Had Luke already managed to put a spoke in the wheels? Well, her previous work with children and animals had been a huge success, and once she got this program all set up and running, it would succeed, too. Gwen was right that it would take some organizing; she needed not just the right animals, but a place to keep and care for them, plus feed and bedding and everything else they required. Not to mention risk assessments for absolutely everything. She'd better start making plans right away.

CHAPTER THREE

IT HAD BEEN ALMOST half an hour since he'd slammed the door on Kat Molloy and Luke was still seething. What did she expect, anyway? Obviously, he was going to watch out for his son, and if her sessions were in any way unsafe, he was going to interfere. She might be competent enough as a counselor, but her ideas about sea and animal therapy were something else. And now their disagreement had probably pushed Ben even further away from him.

All Luke really wanted was to make things right with his son, but everything he tried seemed to go wrong. And how she'd had the gall to turn up at his door and ask for help when she'd caused so much trouble was beyond him. He did feel a prickle of guilt for the way he'd ended the conversation, but she'd pushed him too far. How dare she insinuate that he didn't love his own son?

With a heavy sigh, Luke went into the

bathroom to shave and freshen up before dinner. He stared into the mirror and soaped his chin, his mind drifting over the past few weeks.

Since the moment he'd heard Ben was coming to Flight, Luke's life had turned upside down—not that he'd have it any other way, of course. He remembered Mike calling him into his office and questioning him about Ben. Luke had tried to be totally honest, but as far as he'd known, Ben had been living a privileged and secure life in the care of his wealthy grandparents, Mollie and Jim Jackson, and his mother, Carly—Luke's exwife.

Mike had frowned slightly, waiting for him to go on, and Luke had found himself making excuses for not being in his son's life. When Ben was born, Mollie had promised him that she and Jim would make sure their grandson would be well taken care of, and he and Carly would have done nothing but argue if he'd stuck around. He'd believed he had nothing to offer Ben and that the boy didn't need him, either.

"Did you want to be in his life?" Mike had asked, and he'd hesitated before replying. He wasn't proud of that.

"I didn't even know about him at first," he'd said. "Carly and I were only married for a few months, and I hardly knew her family. Her mother called me a long time after we split up, totally out of the blue one afternoon. I was working down south. 'I think it's only right that you should know about Ben,' she said."

Luke genuinely hadn't known that Carly was pregnant when they split up. Apparently, she'd insisted that she didn't want Luke in her son's life, but that hadn't sat well with Mollie. After that initial call, Ben's grandmother had promised to keep in touch and let Luke know how the boy was doing. And she had phoned him occasionally. When he'd moved nearer to where they lived, though, and pushed to have more contact with his son, maybe even get to see him, she had dropped what at the time felt like a bombshell.

Mollie had asked him to meet her at a tea-room on the outskirts of Lancaster one Saturday afternoon, a smart upmarket place that served proper English afternoon teas.

She'd already ordered when he arrived, but after she'd said her piece, the crustless egg sandwiches and fruit scones had turned his stomach. "Look," she'd said kindly, placing her hand earnestly upon his. "I know that you and Carly were no good together, and it was right that you should split up so soon. No point hanging on to something that wasn't working."

"Our whole marriage was a series of impulsive decisions," he'd agreed.

Mollie had nodded wisely, understanding. "I know that. The thing is, he's never met you, Luke. He is almost two years old and you are a stranger to him. I thought it only right that you should know you have a son, but I honestly believe it would be way too confusing for him to have you turn up in his life now… One day, perhaps, when he's old enough to know what he wants, he'll probably ask to meet his dad and we would never stop him, but for now—for now we think that you should stay away, for Ben's own good. He has a life, Luke—a happy, secure life filled with love, and he lacks for nothing. Your life's not settled right now—you told me that the last time we spoke. You don't have a steady job, and who knows where you'll be next week, or next year. Do you really think it would be fair to let Ben get to know you, only to maybe have to leave him again?"

Everything inside him had screamed with objection. "But he's my son. I need to know my own son."

Mollie had clutched his arm. "Look, you've had nothing to do with him up until now. He's happy and loved, a lovely, bubbly, content little boy, and you just want to pull his life apart for your own satisfaction."

"But I'm his father."

"Please, Luke. Think about Ben, not yourself. We can give him everything he needs to become the best that he can be. So please, if you care about him at all, just walk away. It will be the most unselfish and noble thing you could ever do for your son… Maybe when your life's more settled and secure and you can guarantee that you'll always be there for him, we can reconsider."

He hadn't agreed; he'd never agreed. He'd walked away from her that day with his emotions laid bare. Was she right? he'd asked himself again and again. Was he really being selfish in wanting to be in his son's life? Ben didn't need him; that was for sure. The boy had everything, so maybe he should just back off as Mollie had suggested, until he could walk back into Ben's life and make him proud to be his son. He'd always felt like a failure to his dad and he didn't want to be a failure to his son, too.

He'd done as Mollie had asked, but still tore himself apart over his decision, until he'd seen the job posting for a handyman position at Flight and it had seemed like a sign. Working around kids who needed help seemed like a good way to make a difference, since he'd been totally unable to have an impact on his own son's life…yet.

Of course, he hadn't given Mike all the details in his office that day, but he hoped he'd said enough to make it clear that he regretted not being in Ben's life up until now.

Splashing cold water on his face, Luke grimaced at the spot of blood on his chin. It seemed he couldn't even shave now without losing concentration.

Luke made himself a strong coffee and sat at his desk, his mind still spinning. It was seven years since he'd walked away from that meeting with Mollie, and he hated himself for agreeing to do as she had asked. He'd been wrong to stay away—he should have fought to see his son. He should have moved heaven and earth to be in his life… He'd known it the minute Ben had stepped through Mike's office door just a few short weeks ago. And if he'd been around to spread the load when things started to go wrong for the Jacksons, maybe Ben wouldn't have needed a special school at all. And maybe not having a dad in his life was partly what had caused Ben's emotional issues in the first place.

The information they'd been given by the social worker was that Ben had been becoming more and more difficult for his elderly grandparents to handle. Jim was ill and Mollie had to spend a lot of time looking after him, so Ben had been left to his own devices most of the time. He'd been missing a lot of school, wandering around town until supper. Ben's school had gotten the social worker involved after a local store had contacted them about one of their students stealing candy.

Apparently, things had first begun to go wrong after Carly had died several months earlier. That unexpected piece of information had left Luke shocked and angry. Mollie should have told him about Carly; he would have stepped in. She'd obviously kept the news from him because she was worried that he'd want to play a part in Ben's life…and he would have, if he'd known the whole story, but he'd never have tried to take him away from them, if that was what she was worried about. The boy had been allowed to run wild and lost his way, and now it was up to Luke to try to instill some discipline into his son's life, to teach him right and wrong. It was one of the few things from Luke's own childhood that he could impart. He wouldn't be where he was today if it wasn't for the rules and structure he'd been made to follow when he was young.

In that first awkward meeting, just before Gwen had taken Ben to settle him in, Luke had tried to talk to him.

"It's so nice to finally meet you, Ben," he'd said. "And you don't need to worry because I'll be looking out for you."

Ben had met his eyes then for the first time since he'd walked into the room; his brown eyes were dark with hurt and anger.

"I don't want you!" he'd shouted. "And I don't want to be here."

The boy's slight body had seemed to crumple, and when he'd rubbed his eyes fiercely to keep the tears at bay, Luke had taken a step toward him, needing to do something, anything that might make his son realize that everything was going to be okay. Ben shrank away from him, though, and instead of just following his instincts and giving him a hug,

Luke had hesitated and glanced helplessly at Gwen.

"Right, Ben," Gwen had announced briskly, trying to defuse the situation. "We have a lovely room ready for you, so why don't you and I go find it and meet some of the other children here. You'll see your gran again before she goes, don't worry."

Ben had jumped up to follow her at once. Anything, it seemed, to escape from the stranger who had just walked into his life, the stranger who they'd told him was his dad.

"Why don't you and Mollie go somewhere private to catch up," Gwen had suggested. "Then perhaps you'll understand the situation a bit better."

"Good idea," Mike had agreed. "Lily and I will do the necessary paperwork."

Lily was Ben's social worker. Luke remembered how shocked he'd felt in that moment. Paperwork! It had seemed so wrong to talk about forms in the same context as planning the life of a child.

"A necessary evil, I'm afraid," Mike had remarked, noting his expression. "We have to follow the paper trail. Now, why don't you get Mollie a hot drink and a sandwich before she heads back. You can talk in the small sitting room."

It had been both strange and strained, being alone with Mollie. She was obviously trying to keep the lid on her emotions. She'd told him what she thought he needed to know: Carly had died in a car accident in London, where she had been working. Jim was ill and without him around their car sales business had gone rapidly downhill and started losing money. Mollie was overwhelmed. Basically, she'd admitted, as she twisted her wedding ring on her finger, she had gotten to a point where she just couldn't cope anymore, and it was Ben who'd suffered. Taken up with her own worries about business, Jim's illness and grieving for her daughter, she'd neglected Ben, giving him none of the attention he'd been accustomed to. He'd become cheeky with her, moody, and gone out of his way to cause trouble in any way he could. Once the social worker got involved after Ben's shoplifting incident, they'd suggested giving her some respite by sending Ben to a school for children who needed help.

"I just hope that I've done the right thing," she'd murmured, breaking down. "But what other choice did I have?"

That comment had set off Luke. "You had me!" he'd cried. "You should have told me what was going on, let me help."

"But that's why I asked if he could come here, to Flight," Mollie had explained. "Now you *can* help him."

After Mollie left, Luke had tried to digest everything she'd told him. Why had she kept him in the dark about Carly's death? And she'd talked about Jim being ill…diagnosed with what, cancer?

Still, he was glad for the opportunity to keep a close eye on his son and finally have some input into his upbringing. And maybe one day… Maybe one day Ben would be able to forgive him for abandoning him. Luke had told himself that he'd done the right thing by leaving his son in what he'd believed to be a stable and loving environment—an environment he didn't believe he'd been capable of providing—but he'd been wrong. He just hoped that it wasn't too late to make things right.

Which was why he couldn't let someone like Kat compromise his son's well-being. Ben was his responsibility now, and Luke didn't intend to let anyone put him at risk. He was sorry for slamming the door in Kat's face, but everything she did was out of order. Ben could have drowned trying to swim in the sea, and who knew what might happen if she was allowed to go ahead with her animal-therapy idea. He'd talk to Mike tomorrow, he decided, and try to make him understand just how dangerous some of her sessions truly were.

Ten minutes later, with a surge of fresh determination, Luke headed outside across the garden to the dining room, hoping he hadn't missed dinner. The large room was almost empty and the tables were clear, apart from one at the very end of the room, where three children were still eating. Recognizing them at once as Ben's classmates, he headed across to join them on impulse.

"Any food to spare?" Luke asked brightly, sitting down. "I'm a bit late for dinner, I'm afraid."

Dennis Baker, a skinny boy with a shock of red hair, just shrugged. "Help yourself. We've just about finished anyway."

"Seen Ben around?" Luke asked casually before biting into a grilled cheese sandwich.

They looked at each other and giggled. "Ben's never around, at least not with us," Dennis said.

Luke frowned. "Oh, and why is that?"

"'Cause he's weird," explained Dennis.

"He doesn't go around with anyone," Dan Kent, the boy on Dennis's right, blurted out. "Or talk to anyone."

Luke held back a rush of anger. It was hard not to get emotional when it came to Ben. "Dan, do you remember how you felt when you first came here? You have to try and help new children fit in here, not put them down."

"We'll try and help him, then, Mr. Luke," Dennis agreed. "If you give us a fiver."

All three boys, including Johnny Cartwright, who'd been silent until now, broke into a fit of giggles. Luke's frustration surged again. What chance did Ben have of becoming a well-adjusted boy with kids like these around to goad him?

CHAPTER FOUR

THE AROMA OF coffee filled the air as Kat headed along the hallway. Tempted, she followed the scent to the dining room, surprised to see that it was empty, apart from a few boys sitting at one end of the table. Luke was with them, she noted with surprise.

Dennis and Dan were giggling together, while Johnny looked on in awe. She could see by the set of Luke's shoulders that he was angry about something; when wasn't he angry, though?

Wondering if she might have to intervene, she strode toward the small group. She knew Dennis only too well, and Luke's face was dark with contained fury.

"What's going on here?" she asked in what she hoped was a breezy tone.

Luke swung around, and for a moment, she thought she saw a flicker of relief on his face. "This young man," he announced, "is trying to bribe me."

The giggling stopped as quickly as it had started when the children saw Kat. "Wasn't me, Miss," Dennis quickly announced.

"He told me he would only look out for Ben if I gave him a fiver," Luke said.

Kat frowned. "Is that true, Dennis?"

"Ben's weird," Dennis responded. "So why would I want to look out for him, anyway?"

Kat pulled out a chair and sat down. "You know why, Dennis. We all look out for each other at Flight. A lot of the kids here have had troubles, including you. You were very unhappy when you first came to Flight, remember? Didn't people help you?"

Dennis stared at the table and shrugged. "I guess."

"So hasn't it occurred to you that maybe Ben is unhappy and homesick, too?"

"Dunno," he muttered.

"Well, did people help you when you needed it?"

"Might of."

"There you go, then," Kat said, smiling. "So you'll help Ben?"

"I guess."

"Thanks, Dennis. That's really kind of you. Isn't it, Mr. Luke?"

Put on the spot, Luke nodded. "Yes, thank

you, Dennis. I guess you were only joking about the fiver?"

Dennis pulled a face. "I guess so. Come on, you two. Let's go."

As the three children raced off, Kat laughed out loud. "Bribed by a nine-year-old!"

Suddenly Luke was laughing, too. "Want a sandwich?" he asked, handing her the plate.

"Don't mind if I do," she said.

They ate in silence for a minute or two. "You're good with kids," Luke said eventually.

"It's my job," Kat reminded him. "Surely you must understand children, too, though, having worked here for ages."

Luke shook his head slowly. "Not really. My job description covers everything from mending fences to placing orders for school supplies, but I haven't had much contact with the kids. That's more yours and Mike's department…and Gwen's, of course."

"I'm sorry for insinuating that you don't love Ben," Kat said abruptly. "I crossed a line."

"And I apologize for slamming the door in your face," Luke offered.

Kat held his gaze. "We're never going to agree, you know."

Luke nodded. "At least not when it comes to your therapy courses." He pushed the plate toward her. "Have another sandwich."

Kat picked up an egg salad sandwich and nibbled at the edges. "You wait until I start with the animal therapy," she said.

Luke stood, scraping back his chair. "We'll have to agree to disagree about that. Anyway, I should get going."

"Before we have another falling-out?" Kat asked, raising her eyebrows.

"Something like that," he said with the hint of a smile.

KAT WAS STILL thinking about her conversation with Luke twenty minutes later as she walked along the cliff-top path to the village. Flight was set up high, way beyond the risk of high tides. Kat looked out across the bay, which sparkled in the evening sun. The sea shone with crimson light, and a few late gulls were circling, screaming out their lonesome cries before settling down for the night. It was heartrendingly beautiful here, she thought with a sudden rush of emotion, feeling happy about her decision to take this job, despite her problems with Luke.

Perhaps his reaction earlier—and his attitude toward the sea therapy—boiled down to fear. Maybe Luke was just scared—scared of the responsibility that had been thrust upon him.

Kat was good at understanding what made people tick and why, and not just the children in therapy with her, either. In her view, most adults were still affected by their childhoods and how they were raised. She'd seen it again and again in the foster homes she'd lived in as a teen, observing the ways people reacted and dealt with things. Her own childhood had taught her a lot about life, once she'd come to understand it, or at least tried to. Luke was angry because he was out of his depth with his son, but he should be letting her help Ben, not going against her.

As she followed the path down toward the shore, she considered her plans for the animal therapy. At her last placement, she'd virtually run the unit. The kids helped care for the animals while learning to understand their behavior and needs. The way the animals depended on them gave the kids a sense of responsibility, and the animals' resilience and trust often gave them a whole new perspective on life. She hoped to start something similar—with fresh ideas, of course—here at Flight. Getting past the red tape was the biggest obstacle, especially when narrow-minded people like Luke Travis were raising objections at every turn.

A row of cottages stood next to the shore and were set on a limestone outcropping just above the high-tide line along a narrow track named Cove Road. She'd noticed the cottages before, but tonight in the half-light their brightly lit windows drew her toward them. Terraced and small, they were each two stories with neat front doors and welcoming windows. What a wonderful place to live, Kat thought: to wake up beside the sea each morning, staring out at the glorious, restless and ever-changing view.

The first of the three appeared to be occupied. Clothing flapped on a line at the back, a child's bike lay discarded on the front walk and a light shone from somewhere inside. The second cottage was dark; it appeared closed and empty and kind of sad, its exterior pebble-dashed and a dull, weathered gray. The one at the very end, however, was painted a bright, fresh shade of white. It looked loved, she thought. A sign in the front window caught her eye and she went closer to read it. It was handwritten with For Rent in bold print.

Excitement prickled as an idea took root and grew. The cottage was close to Flight. It was by the sea. It was perfect.

Unable to wait, Kat dialed the number on the sign. The call went to voice mail. "Hi, it's Elsa. Sorry I'm not here right now…"

The voice was clear and warm with a slightly melodic accent, but Kat's heart sank. What if the cottage had already been rented? Pushing her phone back into her pocket, Kat walked cautiously along the pathway to the bright red front door and tried the number again.

She decided to leave a message. "Um… I was just inquiring about the cottage for rent in Jenny Brown's Bay…" Kat left her contact information then clicked End.

Certain that there was no one inside, she walked around the side of the cottage and peered over a door in the fence that led into a small backyard. Everything looked spick-and-span, obviously recently redone. She had to have this cottage; she just had to.

Night was settling in as she headed back toward Flight, wondering how long it would take this Elsa person to reply to her call. The wind rose in her ears, whipping through the crooked bushes that lined the path, and she gazed out across the bay, remembering.

Sandston, the place where she'd spent her early childhood and the place where her mother's sad life had ended, was not unlike Jenny Brown's Bay. It felt right to be here.

Suddenly, her phone began to ring and she dug it from her pocket.

"Hi, you were asking about Number Three Cove Cottages."

"Oh, y-yes…" She felt stupid, childish, stuttering. This meant so much to her. "Is it still available?"

"It might be. I did have someone interested, but they weren't one-hundred-percent sure."

"I'm a hundred-percent sure. Please. It's exactly what I'm looking for."

"Well, the thing is," Elsa said, "I won't just rent it to anyone. It has strong emotional ties for me and, to be honest, I'd rather just live there myself."

Kat instantly liked the woman's honesty. "Why don't you, then?" she asked.

"I intend to one day, but my husband, Bryn—" the name rolled softly off her tongue "—has a lot of commissions in Cornwall, so we need to stay around there. Our children,

Emma and Mick, are settled in schools here, too, and we don't want to uproot them unless it's absolutely necessary. But tell me more about yourself."

"Well, I'm a child therapist working at Flight," Kat explained hopefully. "And I really do love the cottage."

There was a pause on the other end, but when Elsa spoke again, she sounded like she'd made up her mind. "Call me back tomorrow with all your details, and I'll sort out a lease."

Kat was ecstatic. "Thank you so much! I'll call you first thing."

She was climbing the steep track to Flight, her head in the clouds and her whole body aglow with excitement about her new home, when she heard footsteps coming up behind her. She carried on, trying to hurry, but the footsteps grew closer.

"Do you deliberately turn up wherever I happen to be?" Luke's deep voice made her jump.

"I could say the same to you," she responded, turning to see his tall figure striding toward her.

"I've been helping Mel with Wayne's birthday present," he said. "It's a secret, though, so don't say anything."

They fell into step together. "As if I would," she objected. "I don't really know Mel, anyway."

"Well, I've worked with Wayne a long time and I want to make his birthday special. Even if he is my boss." Luke laughed, and she was amazed at the way it transformed his features.

"You should laugh more," she said. "It suits you. He seems nice, Wayne," she added when he didn't respond.

Luke nodded. "He organizes everything around here. I just help him make it all work. At the moment, he's trying to get funding for an adventure trail on the grounds. You know, like an obstacle course. I'll help build it, but money's tight for things like that."

"That sounds great," Kat said, though she wondered if she'd have the same problem getting funds for her animal therapy. She'd need buildings and feed and enclosures.

"Yeah, he's the best. And so is his wife." Kat had only met Mel in passing, but she seemed sweet. Luke continued, "In fact, all the staff here are great. The place wouldn't function without Mike and Gwen, and Tim has the classes running like clockwork. You'd think this was just an ordinary boarding school if you didn't know better."

"You get difficult children in every school," Kat agreed. "I've worked with children from private schools who appear to have every advantage in life."

Luke slowed down. "Ben isn't bad, though, not really. He's just lost his way."

"No child is bad. Their problems usually stem from their upbringing and circumstances."

"He just needs some boundaries," Luke insisted. "I learned that very early on in life. Discipline's important, don't you think?"

"Not necessarily." Kat chose her words carefully. "I mean, it is to a degree, but respect is more important…and love. Children need stability in their lives to build their confidence. They need to know that they are loved."

Luke frowned. "Love is important, obviously, but my dad was very strict and it didn't do me any harm. A child could have all the love in the world, but do you really think it's going to solve behavior issues? Is that why we send criminals to prison—to love them?

That's the problem with your courses, Kat—you let the kids run too wild."

Kat saw red. How dare he lecture her on something she was highly trained for.

"Says the man who abandoned his son." As soon as the words left her lips she regretted them. "Sorry, I shouldn't have said that."

"No kidding."

He took off without another word, running ahead of her with huge, loping strides. She watched him go with a lurch of regret. No matter, she decided, increasing her pace. She had confidence in her work, and she wouldn't let him interfere with it.

TRUE TO HER PROMISE, within two days of Kat's phone call, Elsa May Malone Evans, the owner of Number Three Cove Cottages, emailed Kat a lease and Kat responded by sending her new landlord two months' rent, sealing the deal. She had arranged to pick up the keys in the village later that afternoon, from a man named Ted, and she couldn't wait. She'd already done some online shopping and had ordered several items. The cottage was fully furnished, but she wanted to make it feel like her own as soon as possible.

During her lunch break, she stopped into

Mike's office to let him know she would be moving out.

At first he just laughed. "But won't you miss Luke?" he asked, raising his eyebrows. "I know how well you two get along."

"Very funny," she responded. "He's obviously been complaining about me."

"Actually, no, he hasn't said anything about you personally. It's general knowledge that you and he aren't exactly the best of friends."

"He's against my therapy methods, that's all."

"Luke just worries about Ben. It's a big deal, suddenly being introduced to the son you've never met. You should give him a chance, Kat. He's a decent bloke."

"I'm sure he is, but I'd love it if he could back off and let me get on with my job."

Mike frowned, and his tone grew serious. "You and Luke really must try and put your differences aside. You have to cooperate with each other for Ben's sake—you, of all people, should understand that. I couldn't care less about your petty arguments. This is about the life and future of a vulnerable young boy."

"Well, yes, of course it is," Kat said, her cheeks growing hot. She hadn't meant to sound churlish in front of her boss. "And that is what I care about more than anything—helping the children."

"So figure it out," he said. "Ben isn't in a good place right now, and it's showing in his behavior. To be honest, he seems to be getting worse rather than better. I'm sure you heard about the incident with Mr. Mather yesterday, when he refused to do the work he was given then ripped his notebook up. You're a professional. Talk to him, Kat. Gwen tells me Ben listens to you. It's what we hired you for."

"I hadn't heard about that incident yet," Kat admitted. "The report from his teacher doesn't come in until this afternoon. I'll discuss it with Jed before my session with Ben later. I've seen him improving in the sea-therapy course, and his sessions have gone well. Frankly…"

Mike waited for her to go on.

"Frankly, I don't think Luke is helping. He interferes all the time, criticizing everything I do. He's been complaining about my therapy sessions and I think it's because he wants all the funds he can get for the adventure trail he wants to build." The idea had been percolating since their encounter on the path the other evening.

"Well, Luke hasn't said anything to me about the way you run your courses. You're right that it's not his place to criticize you—you're the expert, after all—unless the kids are in danger." Mike leveled her with a stern look. "And I sincerely hope I won't hear anything like that. But if he's worried about the animal therapy using up valuable funds, that's quite understandable. We only have so much to go around here for special programs. As I've said before, I'm open to the animal-therapy idea, but I'll need to see a full proposal, including costs, before I can approve anything."

Feeling suitably scolded and unprofessional, Kat apologized. "I'll talk to him," she promised. "And I'm really sorry. I know it's up to me to make the effort."

"Then we'll say no more about it," Mike said, smiling. "I don't like to interfere but you do have to try and get on with him…for Ben's sake."

CHAPTER FIVE

AFTER THE HEATED conversation between him and Kat, Luke kept on running until he reached his apartment. Her words rang in his ears. *Says the man who abandoned his son...* Truth was, she was right: he had abandoned Ben. But for her to put it so bluntly was...harsh, to say the least. Okay, so she'd apologized, but that wasn't the point. And she was wrong about him being against her courses; this fatherhood thing was new to him, and the responsibility was overwhelming.

A hot shower and a change of clothes made Luke feel more objective about the situation. Surely there was a way to work around the issues between him and Kat. A knock on the door shook him out of his thoughts. "Kat!" he cried when he opened it. "What are you doing here?"

She stood her ground, but appeared slightly uncomfortable. "I thought I'd... I mean, I just wanted to let you know I'm moving out."

Luke frowned. "Okay…thanks for letting me know."

"And I wanted to talk to you about Ben. To explain myself, I suppose."

He nodded. "Go on…"

"I believe what Ben really needs is attention, and more than anything, to know that he's loved. I don't have all the details about his home situation, but there's clearly some underlying cause for his insecurity. All we can do is talk to him and make him feel wanted."

Luke tried to be straight with her. "Look, I respect your role as Ben's therapist, but he's *my* son and I worry about him. It irritates me when you go on about love—of course I love him. But I also believe boys his age need discipline as a first priority, an awareness of what's right and wrong and consequences for their behavior."

The expression on her face told him she was about to make some sarcastic comment, but instead she turned a bit pink and nodded. "Okay, why don't we just agree to disagree…again. We both want what's best for Ben, don't we? I can tell you that my methods are tried and tested, but you are his dad and I respect that. For now, he just needs to settle in here and feel safe. Of course he needs discipline in the long term, but if you step back a bit I think you'll find that my nature and animal therapy really puts kids in touch with the reality of life, makes them aware of what really matters and teaches them to love unselfishly...to care."

Despite his reservations Luke had to admit that he was touched by her intensity. "I'll keep all that in mind."

"No more arguments?" she said with a shy little smile that he found quite intriguing.

"No more arguments," he agreed.

As she walked away, he couldn't help but notice her strong, determined stride, which belied the sensitivity she'd just shown. Maybe he should sit in on her next sea-therapy session, not to be critical but to try to understand where she was coming from. And who knew; getting involved might even help to break the ice a bit with Ben.

Feeling good about his decision, Luke headed for Wayne's office to see what jobs were on the list for today. Wayne was sitting at his computer, frowning at the screen, his graying head tipped forward in concentration. He glanced up with a smile when he heard Luke come into the office.

"Oh, good. You're here," he said. "I need you to put in an order at the suppliers. Just check with Gwen first to see if there's anything she needs. After that, can you make some calls to get the best price for rebuilding the fence at the back of the grounds? It could probably do with a temporary fix, too, if you have time. And the TV in the small sitting room is on the blink."

"Not too many problems, then," Luke said, smiling. His job was to support Wayne in any way he could and he'd come to realize that being assistant manager at Flight meant being up for almost anything.

When Luke had arrived at Flight in his early twenties to work as a general handyman, Wayne had taken him under his wing. In fact, Luke had lived with Wayne and Mel at their house in the village for the first few weeks, until the new staff annex was ready for him to move into. Since then the couple had taken it upon themselves to watch out for him. The assistant-manager position had actually been created for him. That was why he felt so guilty about keeping Ben a secret; Wayne and Mel had never said anything, but he could see that they were disappointed in him. He intended to make it up to them by helping make Wayne's impending birthday the best ever.

Thinking about the smart little boat tucked away in the corner of Tanners' boatyard, Luke couldn't help but smile as he went off to complete the day's tasks. It was Mel's present to Wayne, but he'd helped her find it and spruced it up with some fresh paint. She was convinced that Wayne would love it; Luke hoped she was right.

KAT SPENT THE morning with the children's therapy group for five-year-olds. She always found it hard when children so young had problems; it just didn't seem right. How could anyone neglect or be cruel to such little kids?

Lucy Bell was a particularly heartrending case. She'd been taken from a squat in the northwest because her mother had been too spaced out on drugs to care for her most of the time. Left to fend for herself, she'd had little communication with others, and according to her social workers, she'd lived off scraps and leftovers and was rarely washed or dressed properly. Kat worked with her most days, just trying to get her to communicate, and this morning Lucy had smiled for the first time ever when Kat walked into the room. It felt like a breakthrough.

"Hey, Lucy," Kat called. "Want to play a question game with me and Aaron?"

Lucy looked up from the pile of colored blocks she was playing with and nodded, her big blue eyes shining. "I like Aaron," she said.

"And he likes you, too, Lucy," Kat told her. "We all do. Now, who wants to be first?" Aaron put up his hand. "Okay, Aaron, what's your first question?"

Aaron looked at Lucy for a moment; he knew this game well. "Which toy do you like best?" he asked.

"I like my dolly," Lucy said, cuddling her lifelike baby doll close against her chest.

"Your turn, Lucy," Kat said.

Lucy frowned. "Where's your mummy?" she asked Aaron.

"She's in heaven with the angels," he replied, unfazed.

"My mummy's sick," Lucy told him. "That's why they're looking after me here."

"Let's play building," Aaron suggested.

"We'll use the blocks," Lucy responded. "Come on. We could make dolly a house."

Watching the children interact and develop confidence and positive social skills made everything worthwhile for Kat and reconfirmed why she loved her job so much. Spending time with the kids—talking to them, playing games and encouraging them to engage in the world around them—was how she spent most of her sessions. Her goal was to get to know each of them: what they liked, what made them laugh…and what made them cry. That was the hard part. Some of the kids had had such a hard time in their short lives that it made her mess of a childhood seem almost charmed.

When the session finished and the children went off to their classroom, Kat spent a few minutes tidying up the toys. Later this afternoon she was taking the six-to-ten group, and colored blocks weren't as useful in getting them to open up.

Before that session, she wanted to give Ben a book about the sea she'd been promising to lend him; hopefully the book would capture his imagination and give him something to talk about. In one-on-one counseling he tended to be withdrawn and sulky, which she attributed to him having seen so many well-meaning social workers and therapists over the past few months. On the other hand, he'd been full of energy during the more informal sea sessions, winding up the other kids and causing trouble, but laughing, too.

Kat's heart ached for him. It was clear to her that Ben just didn't know who he was. His whole life had been turned on its head, and it probably seemed like everyone he thought he could believe in had let him down. Not to mention his dad's appearance after nine years of silence. It would be hard for Ben to learn to trust again, and building a relationship with Luke was going to take a lot of forgiveness.

She glanced at her watch; he'd be out of class any minute. Kat grabbed the book and headed over to the new, chalet-style classrooms across the grounds, arriving just as the doors burst open. A stream of children came running out, but she couldn't see Ben. When the crowd of kids had thinned and he still hadn't appeared, she walked up the steps and in through the half-open door. Mrs. Selby, the math teacher, was standing by her desk, her cheeks flushed with anger, while Ben glared up at her. Kat noted his closed expression, which was more concerning than a tantrum or display of anger.

"What's the matter, Mrs. Selby?" she asked.

Chris Selby turned her attention away

from the boy, bristling with indignation. "It appears that Ben does not like math and he's flatly refused to do any work at all today. All he has done is scribble all over his textbook. I've told him to take his workbook with him and finish his arithmetic questions before tomorrow. You can go now, Ben."

Ben stood still, staring into space. "I said you can go," she repeated.

When Ben ignored her, Kat stepped in. "I can deal with this if you like, Chris. I've brought him a book he wanted to borrow. I'll make sure that he does his math—don't worry."

"Well, if you're sure."

"I'm sure. You get off to your next lesson."

After Chris left, Kat turned to Ben. "Now, what was all that about?"

"I hate math and I hate her," he mumbled without looking up.

"Mrs. Selby just wants you to do well, Ben. And if you're really struggling with math then perhaps I can have a chat with Mr. Ellison about getting you some extra help."

"Don't want extra help. Don't want to do it at all."

"Well, if you grow up not even knowing how to multiply and divide, you're not going to get very far. Anyway, let's not worry about that right now. Come on—it's a lovely day and you have a break now, so why don't we go out into the garden and I'll show you the book I've brought."

Ben followed Kat outside, dragging his feet.

"It's so beautiful, isn't it?" she said, gesturing at the smooth green lawn spread out before them like a large patch of velvet surrounded by a vivid splash of colorful blooms carefully nurtured by Ned, the groundskeeper. "Don't you think it's a beautiful garden?" she asked Ben.

"We used to have a nice garden," he responded quietly.

Ben had never mentioned his life before Flight to her. Kat crafted her response carefully. "If it was as nice as this one, you must have been very lucky."

"Granddad used to do it." Ben's voice sounded wobbly. "He loved gardens. I helped him."

"Your granddad must be a very nice and very clever man."

"He used to be," muttered Ben, grabbing the heads of some big red flowers and ripping them off.

"Ben!" cried Kat as he threw them onto the lawn. "Don't do that."

Ben looked at her then took off at a run, trampling the flower beds and darting in and out of the trees. Kat followed at a distance, keeping an eye on him but letting the boy let off steam.

Kat had never heard him mention his granddad's illness before, and his condition obviously bothered Ben much more than she'd realized. She knew Mollie had to spend all her time caring for her husband, but it was more than a lack of attention from his grandmother that seemed to be at the root of Ben's problems.

Like a lot of troubled children, Ben was far more sensitive than he let on. He was very susceptible to nature; she'd seen it in the sea sessions and again today when he'd finally let out some of his feelings in the garden. She would have to harness that sensitivity to find out more about his situation and help him regain some kind of balance.

Eventually, Ben made his way into the main house for lunch, so Kat headed to Mike's office, hoping to get more details about Ben's past.

"Hi," Mike said, glancing up from some paperwork. "I could do with a distraction."

"Not going to give me a hard time today?" she said, smiling.

"Look," he responded, putting down his pen, "I know you're totally professional and I believe in you and your methods—that's why you're here. You have to see my point of view, though. Luke is, understandably, in a strange place right now. The son no one knew about has turned up on his doorstep and he doesn't quite know how to deal with it. You'll probably say that he should have been in the boy's life from the start but—"

"Of course he should," Kat interrupted.

Mike shook his head. "No one's perfect. Have you always done everything right in your life?"

"No," she admitted. "I've made lots of mistakes in my life already."

"Well, there you go, then," he said. "All I ask is that you and Luke make an effort to get along for Ben's sake. Or at least make an effort when he's around."

"Ben is the one who matters in all this," she agreed. "By the way, while we're on the subject, do you know anything about Ben's background, anything about his granddad's illness, perhaps, that might help me understand him better?"

"To be honest, our information is much briefer than I'd like," Mike said. "You know as much as I do. Mollie and Jim Jackson brought him up while his mum, Carly, went back to finish her studies. When she was killed in a car crash a few months ago, I can only presume their grief and loss turned their lives upside down. Grief can change your whole world in an instant, completely uproot your perceptions, priorities and ambitions.

"Ben must have been, or felt, neglected by his grandparents. He'd lost his mother suddenly and then he lost the attention of his grandmother. He reacted by becoming withdrawn and lashing out when he was put under pressure, according to his social worker."

"But what about Luke?" asked Kat. "Why didn't he step in when his ex-wife died?"

Mike shrugged. "Who knows… Maybe no one told him he had a son. Or no one told him what had happened to Carly."

Kat shot him a skeptical look.

Mike raised his hand. "Obviously I'm bi-ased. I'm fond of Luke, I've known him a long time and I trust him. What's important now is that he and his son develop a stable

CHAPTER SIX

KAT PULLED THE keys for Number Three
Cove Cottages from her pocket, her fingers
shaking with excitement. The key ring had
a metal fish attached to it, and it shone in
the sunshine. As she approached the front
door, she glanced behind her, sensing someone watching. But she didn't see a soul and
was met with silence. It wasn't silent at all,
though, she realized. Jenny Brown's Bay was
lonely and beautiful and bleak, perhaps, but
never, ever silent.

The waves crashed onto the shore, rushing back out into the sparkling sea in a fizz
of foam. The wind moaned softly, bringing
with it a salty tang that lingered on her lips,
and the cry of seagulls rose into the clear
blue sky. She turned back to the red door.

Ted, the old man who had given her the
keys, had talked a lot about her landlady,
Elsa May Malone Evans. He thought very
highly of her and Bryn, and of their daugh-

ter, Emma, but Kat got the impression that he hadn't had much to do with Mick, their little boy. The history of the place intrigued her, and she longed to know more about the Evanses and what they'd done in Jenny Brown's Bay.

She pushed the door open and stepped into her new home, her body alive with excitement. Light filled the whole house, beaming in through the front windows. She liked that; it felt as if the house and the glorious, endless sea and sky were one. In Sandston, she had lived right on the shore, too, but the cottage had been dark and sad, or at least that was how she remembered it.

She placed her bags on the wood floor and walked through to the small but cozy kitchen. It smelled faintly of food and…paint, that was it. Elsa had mentioned that her husband was an artist. She stepped back into the hallway to study a painting she'd passed on her way in; a man throwing a stick for a yellow dog way out on the shore, and a woman with an abundance of wild, gold-streaked hair walking toward him, waving. The sea and the sky looked so real Kat could almost hear the waves. Something about the scene made her heart fill up. It seemed so full of love and yet sad, too.

She looked at the signature in the bottom right corner: *Bryn Evans*. So this was one of his pieces. That must be him, too, playing with the dog…and was that Elsa? The woman's hair seemed to glint and glimmer as if it was real.

Smiling, Kat went back and carried her bags to the kitchen and started to unpack them.

Kat spent the morning trying to make the cottage her own by putting up a few pictures and carefully positioning the bright cushions she'd bought online on the well-used leather sofa. She arranged flowers in all the downstairs windows and made up her bed, too, with her pretty new sheets and duvet, and filled the fridge and cupboards with the items she'd bought in the village shop.

With a satisfied sigh, she cut a large piece of the freshly baked cake Alice had given her and sat down at the kitchen table feeling as if she was finally home.

She'd asked for the day off to move in to her new home, but she'd scheduled a sea-therapy course in the early evening. She hoped to run it right here on the shore. Only three children would participate, which was a bonus: Ben, Tammy and Millie, a withdrawn ten-year-old girl who would be attending her first sea session.

After lunch, Kat intended to wander along the shoreline in search of interesting items to inspire and captivate the children, particularly Ben. At least when he'd tried to several days ago, he'd laughed and shown some emotion other than the sulky attitude he so often adopted. And he'd taken hold of her hand; that had felt like a real breakthrough.

After she'd talked to Mike yesterday she'd thought a lot about the way Ben had behaved, ripping the heads off the flowers. That had revealed a deep anger, and she was sure that it stemmed from his relationship with his granddad. Whatever the cause, she had to try to understand what was going on in Ben's head if she was to help him come to terms with it and move on.

The shingle crunched beneath her feet as she followed the waterline. Higher up the beach was the trail of flotsam and jetsam left by the tide. That would be a good place to start searching for something to spark the children's imaginations.

Her search proved surprisingly successful

as she came across a toy sailboat tangled up in the seaweed, several glass bottles, a shoe and even some pieces of pottery. With a satisfied smile, she headed back to the cottage. She'd enjoy showing the children her new home and she'd give them each a piece of Alice's cake at the end of the session.

Kat set off for Flight just before five. She was due to collect the children at six, but wanted to catch up with Mike first to see if he'd thought any more about her meeting up with Mollie Jackson. She approached the house with a lingering sadness. She'd enjoyed living here for the last few weeks, right in the hub of things; maybe she should have stayed a bit longer. But she hadn't wanted to miss the chance to rent the cottage on Cove Road. It was the perfect home.

With her mind full of ideas for the sea session, she ran up the steps and in through the huge front door. Turning right as she entered the hall, she collided with someone, lost her balance and staggered back in confusion, breathing in the spicy scent of a man's cologne. A strong hand grabbed hold of her arm.

"You!" she gasped, looking up to meet

Luke's warm brown eyes. They sparkled with humor as she tried to pull away.

"You just can't stay away from me, can you?" He laughed. "Joke," he added when she stared at him in horror.

Kat put a hand to her face, embarrassed by the heat flooding into it, and he dropped her arm as if it was burning his hand.

"It's okay," he told her, stepping back. His tone was brusque and businesslike. "No harm done. Not to me, at least. Tell you what—you can make amends by letting me sit in on your therapy session tonight. I'm prepared to give it another shot if you are."

"No, I…" How dare he even suggest it after the way he'd acted last time? Nothing had changed; her methods obviously weren't up to his standards then and they wouldn't be now.

Noting her reluctance, he smiled awkwardly. "It'll be fine," he insisted. "I promise not to interfere, if that's what you're worried about."

"I'm not worried. Do what you like. I need to go see Mike first and grab a bite. Then I'm picking the children up."

"What time?"

She hesitated. "Just after six," she finally said, feeling guilty about stretching the truth.

The guilt still niggled when she met up with the three children in the dining room at six and Luke hadn't arrived. It was his own fault, though, she told herself; he was the one who'd caused the problem. And she needed to have Ben to herself if her therapy was to have a chance of success. He'd never let down his guard if his dad was there, watching his every move with his misplaced, overprotective attitude. That day in the sea was the first and only time Kat had seen Ben relaxed and having fun, even if he was trying to wind her up. After Luke had interfered, he'd switched himself right off again.

"Are we really going to the seaside again?" Tammy asked eagerly.

Kat tousled her hair. It was hard not to tousle Tammy's mass of bright red curls. "Not only that," she told her, "you're going to come see my new house and have cake."

The little girl's brilliant blue eyes were as wide as saucers. "By the sea? You really live right by the sea?"

Kat nodded. "Nearly on the shore."

"Are we all having cake?" Ben asked, butting in.

His gruff little voice hid a hint of excitement and Kat felt relieved that Luke wasn't here to spoil it.

"Come on, then," she said, eager to get going. Tammy grabbed her hand while Ben tried to appear nonchalant, as if he really didn't care either way. The new addition, Millie, who was quiet and well behaved with short brown hair and a sweet, sad smile, followed in their wake.

As they rounded the corner, leaving the house behind, Kat glanced back. Flight seemed to smile at her, she thought, as if they shared a secret. She suppressed a smile. Luke Travis would think she was quite irresponsible if he knew what sometimes went on in her head. One thing he definitely did not have was an imagination, though she probably had too much of one, if that was possible. Well, she decided, she needed her overactive imagination. Her career depended on it.

"Come on, kids," she called. "I'll race you to the path."

LUKE GLANCED AT his watch and grimaced. He'd gotten caught up talking to Mike and lost track of time. Apparently, Kat had been pushing him about the animal therapy and she'd also asked for a meeting with Mollie Jackson. He should be the one talking to Mollie; Ben was *his* son, and Luke was desperate to make things right between them. Somehow he had to make amends for being missing for nine years…if that was even possible.

Reaching the front hall, he looked around for any sign of Kat or the children. It was only ten past six; surely she would have waited a few minutes. By twenty past, he realized he must have missed them. But he wasn't giving up that easily. Luke strode out into the evening sunshine, deciding he'd go down into the bay and try to catch up with them. Mike had told him about Kat renting one of the cottages right on the shore, so he guessed they'd be headed in that direction.

He jogged down the narrow cliffside path, scanning the wide expanse of sea and sand. The tide was coming in, rushing round the perimeter of the bay. Prickles of alarm ran along his spine. Jenny Brown's Bay was renowned for being dangerous, and these were the exact conditions that could cause serious problems. Apart from the undercurrents that were capable of dragging even strong swimmers out to sea, there were also quicksands.

Kat had been here for only five minutes; did she even realize what could happen? The smooth stretches of sand might look harmless, but they could set around an unsuspecting wader's feet and legs like concrete…and if the tide came in, they'd be trapped in rising waters. He increased his pace. Where were they?

KAT HEADED ALONG the shoreline with the children running ahead. When the tide began to rush in, she settled them safely on the rocks to watch.

"It's called the bore," she told them. "It's a wave that rushes around the outside of the bay just as the tide starts coming in. Unsuspecting people who have gone out too far can get trapped by the water on the sandbank in the center."

Ben looked up with interest. "Will we get caught?"

She shook her head. "No, because we understand the dangers. Eventually the tide will rise, almost to the edge of the track if it's a high tide. Today, though, it will probably be lower than the flotsam and jetsam that we're going to look at in a minute."

"What's flotsam and jetsam?" Tammy piped up.

Kat gave what she hoped was a mysterious smile. "It's things cast off from life," she said. "Things that people have let drift out to sea."

"What kind of things?" asked Ben, obviously intrigued by the idea. He looked at her with his father's eyes and her heart tightened. How come Luke Travis always managed to rattle her, even when he wasn't here?

"Who knows," she said. "Bottles, perhaps, from the other side of the world, maybe even with messages in them. Or toys or pottery, just objects from people's lives. You can depend on the sea. It comes in every day and goes out again right on cue. No matter what's going on in the world, the tides never change. You can depend on lots of things in nature—trees and animals and plants just do what they do, year after year. Grow, blossom, bear fruit…and have babies if they're animals, of course."

"Can we see the flotsam and jetsam now?" Ben asked.

"Of course you can." Kat smiled. "As long as you promise not to try and go for a swim this time."

"*He's* not here this time, though, is he?"
Ben said quietly.

For a moment, Kat felt a flicker of sympathy for Luke. He may have done wrong by Ben, but maybe it wasn't right of her to judge him too harshly. She didn't know all the details. He was Ben's dad, after all, and it must hurt to see that the little boy wanted nothing to do with him. "Come on, then," she urged. "Let's go see what treasures we can find."

She watched in delight as the three children searched for treasure among the rubbish and seaweed that made up the flotsam and jetsam. It was Ben who found a bottle; he picked it up carefully, holding it out to catch the rays of the sun. Despite its time spent being battered by the sea, the glass sparkled.

"Where do you think it came from?" he asked her, turning it to and fro.

"Could be anywhere in the whole wide world," Kat told him. "Spain, perhaps…or France or Scotland."

They all peered at it with excitement in their eyes, as if expecting the bottle to suddenly reveal its secrets.

"No message," Ben announced sadly.

"Maybe not," Kat said. "But it does have a picture on it."

The sailing ship embossed in the glass immediately caught the imagination of all three children.

"What if it came from a pirate ship?" Ben suggested with awe.

"You never know," Kat said. "Here…" She held out the bag she'd brought to collect their treasures. "I'll look after everything until we get home."

Twenty minutes later, after Millie found the battered wooden dog that Kat had seen earlier and the kids had gathered several pieces of brightly patterned pottery, Kat began leading them toward her cottage.

Now that the tide had settled, she gave them permission to wade into the water— just up to their ankles.

"Look for shells and fish and any other sea creatures that live here," she suggested. "And beautiful stones, too. They can bring you good luck, you know."

Kat was thrilled at the way the three children got into their task, but Ben was the most enthusiastic; Tammy and Millie didn't want to get their feet wet. Ben found more stones than the other two, and by the time Cove Cottages came into view, Kat was weighed down by all the items in her bag. She was just about to tell them that that was enough for today when Ben started yelling.

"Look! Look!" he called, waving her over. "What is it, Miss?"

He was a little farther out in the water than the others, ankle-deep in foam and still wearing his running shoes. Kat waded in to join him while Tammy and Millie stood wide-eyed on the sand.

"Why, it's a crab," cried Kat. "A big one, too. Watch your toes."

"Can we keep it?" he asked hopefully. "We could put it in a big bucket with sand and water."

"It wouldn't be happy anywhere else but in the sea. This is its home. Let's just watch it for a while and see what it does."

The crab scrabbled sideways, burying itself in the muddy sand, and in an instant it had disappeared.

"Where is it?" Ben demanded. "I want it back."

He glared at her, but she ignored his display of anger. "Look, Ben," she said quietly. "It would have been cruel of us to take the crab away from its home. This is where it belongs, and we need to respect that. We'll find other crabs, lots of them, maybe even bigger ones."

The little boy just looked at her, his golden-brown eyes, so like Luke's, suddenly sad. "They took *me* away from *my* home," he said. "And that was cruel. They took my grand-dad away from me, too. So why couldn't I keep the crab?"

"Sometimes people do get new homes, for reasons they can't always understand," Kat said. "It might feel bad, at first, but in the end, it's a good thing. Keeping the crab because *you* want to wouldn't be fair, and it wouldn't be good for the crab. You know, hermit crabs get new homes all the time, too. Ones they choose. They find empty shells to live in and have to adapt to new surround-ings every time they switch homes. Change can make anyone feel a bit lost at first, but after a while people, and crabs, get used to it. Sometimes it works out even better than before."

"I don't *want* to get used to it and it can never be better than before!" he yelled. "I want Granddad back how he used to be. So leave me alone!"

When he took off running along the shore, Kat's heart sank. "Well, we're going to my new house to have some cake now," she called, keeping her tone casual with no trace of anger. "It's just over there if you want to come and see it… If you don't feel like it today, then I'll see you when we get back to Flight. Be careful walking up the track on your own."

"Aren't you going to chase after him, Miss?" asked Tammy. "Or yell at him?"

"No," she said determinedly. "He'll come back in a minute.".

She led the girls toward the row of cottages, heart in her mouth, keeping Ben in her peripheral vision. The little boy kept on running until he reached a clump of bushes and then he stopped. She heaved a sigh of relief and opened the bright red door, ushering the other two children inside. "Go through into the kitchen, kids," she said. "I'll be there in a minute."

Ben was walking slowly in her direction, his shoulders rounded. She called out to him, smiling warmly. "Oh, good. I'm so glad you decided to come back. It would be a shame for the cake to be wasted."

Just like the last time, when Luke had shouted at him for swimming out too far,

Ben took hold of her hand. "Come on," she said, her heart turning over. "I'll show you my new house."

CHAPTER SEVEN

LUKE WAITED, TAKING in the wide expanse of clear blue sky and breathing in the sounds and scents of the seaside. Before he came to Flight he'd rarely been near the ocean, but over the past few years he'd come to love its changing faces, coupled with the dependability of the tide. The sea could be dangerous, of course, even frightening at times, and behind its glorious beauty lurked so many dangers—quicksands, sudden storms and the bore. Only a few weeks ago, a tourist had become stranded way out in the bay, stuck in the quicksands. He would almost certainly have drowned if someone hadn't called the coast guard.

Luke moved impatiently from foot to foot. Where were Kat and the kids? The sun was sinking slowly down toward the horizon, where sea and sky became one; the water was calm and quiet now, shimmering with a hint of crimson. Surely it was getting late to still be playing by the sea.

Suddenly, he saw them: Kat, laughing out loud, her dark hair blowing around her face and the three children bouncing along beside her, alight with excitement. They were walking right at the edge of the sea; in fact, pushing the boundaries as usual, Ben was actually in the water wearing his sneakers. He yelled in excitement, waving to the others, and they all went across to see what he wanted to show them. Kat spoke to him and he squared his shoulders, obviously objecting. Luke had become quite familiar with that stance since Ben had arrived at Flight, and as usual it ended the same way. One minute he was talking to Kat and the next he was running down the shore. So much for her *special* courses, Luke thought. This one certainly didn't seem to be doing Ben much good.

Luke watched with concern as Kat and the other two children headed for the cottages. Was she just going to let him go off by himself? He started to increase his pace, but Kat sent the other two children into one of the cottages and turned to Ben, who was standing still now. He started to walk slowly toward her, shoulders hunched and expression impassive. Then she spoke to him and he walked beside her to the cottage. When he took hold of her hand, Luke felt a sudden, irrational lurch of an emotion bordering on jealousy. Of course Ben was going to turn to her when she let him do whatever he wanted; his elderly grandparents had obviously spoiled him, too. He'd had no discipline in his life and no motivation to improve his behavior or do things for himself. Kat's methods weren't going to help. If anything, she'd probably just make him worse by letting him have his own way all the time. Ben would play her like he had played his grandparents.

Luke continued along Cove Road. Kat spotted him as he approached and he could tell by her slightly daunted expression that she wasn't pleased. Ben was far more obvious.

"What are you doing here?" he blurted, his face dark with anger.

"Thought I'd come and find out how it was going," Luke said, forcing a smile onto his face. Kat stared at him, and he thought, for a moment, that she was going to tell him to leave. Her eyes, framed by her dark hair, were so blue against the light tan of her skin...and so unfriendly.

"It's going great," she said. "Isn't it, Ben?"

The little boy nodded, unable to hold back his restored enthusiasm. "I've got treasures," he said. "Lots of them."

"We're going to eat Alice's cake now," Kat said. "You can have some if you like...can't he, Ben?"

Ben hesitated, indecisive, and Luke gave him what he hoped was a friendly smile. "I guess," Ben eventually said, but the scowl on his face said otherwise.

KAT HAD BEEN of two minds about how to react when Luke appeared. She wanted to make an excuse, maybe tell him that he was too late for this session and could join in with her next one. Something about the way he stood, though, shoulders slightly rounded and expression bleak, made her change her mind. He looked so like Ben, right down to the slightly confused and troubled expression in his golden-brown eyes. She just hoped Luke didn't interfere again and destroy all the good work she'd done tonight—and she *had* done good, she was certain of that, no matter what Mr. High-and-Mighty Luke Travis might think.

Her plan was to gain Ben's trust in order to find out what made him tick. Only then could she start to work out his problems. It was becoming clear to her that Ben's uncontrollable behavior couldn't just be attributed to his grandparents spoiling him. He was hurting; she could see it in his every move, apart from when he'd been searching for treasure. That had made him forget his worries for a while. She'd promised Mike that she'd try to help Luke and his son to heal their rift, but if Luke kept interfering with her sea therapy, she wouldn't have a chance to help Ben at all, let alone their father-son relationship.

The chocolate-and-white cake was huge, with stripy icing on the top and chocolate butter icing in the middle. How Alice had expected Kat to eat it on her own was a total mystery. Perhaps she'd guessed that Kat would share it with the kids.

The children sat side by side on the bench seat overlooking the bay. They drank juice from the colorful plastic cups Kat had bought and wolfed down large slabs of Alice's cake.

She and Luke sipped coffee in slightly awkward silence.

"Hey, kids, why don't you try and count the seagulls while Kat and I have a chat?" Luke suggested after a few moments.

They started chanting in unison, "One, two, three, four, five," while Kat squirmed.

"Well," she said, straight to the point as always. "What is it?"

"Do you think the sessions are going well?"

She nodded. "Very well."

"Good. It's just… Well, if you don't mind me saying… I couldn't help but notice that Ben tried to run away, and that could have had serious consequences."

"It could have but it didn't," she retorted. "Is there anything else you'd like to add?"

He held her blue eyes in his and somehow she couldn't seem to look away. No man should be that handsome, she thought; in fact, in a way she found it disconcerting— she much preferred quirky-looking men with character.

"The thing is," he went on after he made sure the kids were still preoccupied with their counting. "If he had run away or gotten hurt, you'd have been liable."

When a flood of pink colored her cheeks, he held up his hand. "Please don't take this the wrong way. I don't want to get at you. I just worry that with three children to watch, in that situation, it could be difficult."

"So what you are actually trying to tell me," she murmured crossly, not wanting the children to overhear, "is that you still don't approve of my sea therapy. And you think I'm irresponsible."

"Not disapprove," he answered quickly. "Just…"

"Yes?"

"I just want Ben to be safe."

They moved a few steps away from the bench. "Well, Ben's safety hasn't concerned you for the last nine years. Why now?"

His eyes darkened. "I had no choice then," he told her. "He wasn't my responsibility."

Kat's thoughts went back to her own childhood. Parental responsibility was a subject way too close to home. Her mum had made the ultimate rejection, and Kat knew how it felt to be unwanted. "He's your son. Shouldn't you have *made* him your responsibility?" she asked.

He looked down at his hands, clasping his fingers together. "I wasn't given the opportunity," he said quietly. "And now that I have—"

"Is there any more cake?" Tammy interrupted. She was standing right in front of them, a pleading expression in her huge blue eyes.

"All right, just a small piece," Kat agreed. "Anyone else want some more cake before we set off back to Flight?"

Kat was glad of the distraction and she busied herself with the children, deliberately not looking at Luke. When they'd cleaned up their plates, she dropped them into the sink and announced that it was time to go. Ben had taken off his wet shoes and she could sense Luke's disapproval when he realized what a state they were in.

"He had fun," she said pointedly. "I'll lend him some clean socks and his shoes will dry overnight."

IT WASN'T UNTIL they all set off along Cove Road, toward the path that led up the cliff to Flight, that Luke found his moment. The children were racing on ahead, and he took hold of Kat's arm, pulling her back.

"Now that I have the opportunity to be Ben's dad..." he began. He wanted to say "I don't think I'm up to the job," but his pride wouldn't let him. "Now that I have the opportunity," he began again, "I want to make sure that Ben grows up knowing the difference between right and wrong. At the very least. He's been spoiled all his life by his grandfather and grandmother, drowned in love, I guess. He needs to learn acceptable behavior or he'll never succeed in the real world."

She glanced sideways at him. "Having fun is acceptable behavior," she said. "And being loved too much doesn't make anyone bad. He does have a lot to learn—I agree with that. My therapy sessions can teach him about caring for others, but I need to know what skeletons he has lurking in his past. Anyone can see that he's confused."

"He just needs right and wrong to be black and white," Luke insisted. "That will help his stability and build up his confidence."

At that point they caught up with the children.

"Are you going to Wayne's birthday bash?" Luke asked, wanting to change the subject.

"I heard about it," she said. "But I don't know if I'm invited."

Luke laughed. "Everyone's invited. Even the children are going to be allowed to come down for an hour or two. Wayne and Mel's house backs right onto the sea and she's planning a surprise barbecue for his fiftieth."

"I guess you must know them both well," she said.

Luke nodded. "They're like family. I stayed with them when I first came to Flight, and it was Wayne who insisted on making me his assistant manager."

"And did *they* know you had a son?"

For a moment, Luke was lost for words. It sounded so bad to admit that he'd even kept his son a secret from his friends...as if he didn't care or was ashamed. "No, they didn't," he admitted. "And I'm not proud of it... To be honest, I have a lot of regrets, but what's done is done, I guess."

Kat looked at him for a moment, really looked at him. "It's what you do now that counts," she said quietly, before turning to the children. "Come on, kids. We're home." Flight loomed up before them. Impressive and yet also homey, it seemed to call out a welcome. "Let's get you kids inside. Gwen will be wondering where we've got to."

Luke reached out and touched her arm. "Thanks," he whispered, and then he was gone. Kat watched until he disappeared from sight.

AFTER AN EVENING spent outside and all the excitement of moving into her new home, Kat expected to sleep like a log. She snuggled down beneath her duvet, breathing in the aromas of new bedding and the salty air blowing in through the open window. But she couldn't stop herself from trying to make plans for her animal venture. Tomorrow, she decided, she'd ask Mike about using the old outbuildings in the garden to house the animals. Just rabbits and hamsters to start with, creatures that were easy for the children to handle and care for.

Her mind wandered and her thoughts strayed to Luke. It seemed that he was just as much in need of some counseling as his son. He was even more difficult to understand than Ben. How could he have kept his own son a secret for all these years, even from his best friends?

Who loved Luke Travis, anyway? He had Mel and Wayne, but he seemed...lonely. He'd had a wife, albeit briefly—Ben's mother—but according to Gwen and Alice, he'd never had another girlfriend. At least not since he'd been at Flight. Kat wondered if his wife had broken his heart.

And even now, with his son here, a boy obviously desperate to be loved, Luke was still struggling. It was as if he was all closed off inside, sharing himself with no one. The thought made Kat sad.

Bringing her knees up to her chest, she closed her eyes. She'd been like that once. After her mother died, Kat had clung to the guilt, keeping herself to herself; it was only by being fortunate enough to have some brilliant counselors and carers that she'd found a way through it. That was what had motivated her to train as a child therapist herself, so that she could give something back and hopefully make a difference in other children's lives. Here at Flight, she finally had the opportunity to make her dream come true by running her own courses, the nature-therapy sessions she'd been specializing in ever since she'd qualified.

If Mike expected her to help Luke and Ben develop some kind of relationship, he needed to know her professional opinion of Luke, too. It seemed that it wasn't just the children who needed therapy at Flight.

CHAPTER EIGHT

KAT WOKE EARLY, confused, and then she remembered: she was in her new home by the sea and her life was looking good. Today she hoped to start planning her new course, and she'd decided to set out some rules about parents—one in particular—getting too involved in what she was doing.

She had a couple of counseling sessions this morning. One was with Millie, the girl who'd been in her sea session the previous evening. Millie needed one-on-one counseling, as she was very withdrawn. That was one of the reasons Kat had wanted her in sea therapy—to pull her out of herself—and she was sure the animal therapy would be good for her, too. Animals had a way of getting through to even the most troubled children; she'd seen it again and again.

The tide was in when Kat headed out of the cottage for a quick morning walk before she had to be at Flight. The water lapped right up to the edge of Cove Road, and she had to stay well up on the rocks above the tide line. The sky was a rumbling gray with slashes of deep purple hovering near the horizon as she set off along her rugged route. The sea, however, was calm, apart from the waves that gently buffeted the rocks, and the wind in her face was pleasantly warm. She gulped in the salty air, feeling thankful; never had she imagined that she might find somewhere as wonderful as this to live. Her landlady, Elsa, must really miss it.

By the time she headed back to Cove Cottages, the tide was on the wane. Flotsam and jetsam lay in heaps, harboring no end of treasures—for the kids, at least. There was even a bright red football sitting on a pile of seaweed and a silver, heart-shaped necklace; surely it couldn't be real silver. She picked it up, untangling it from the debris that had carried it here. It certainly hadn't lost any of its luster, so perhaps it was real silver. It felt like a sign. This was a lucky place, and all she needed now was a dog to keep her company. *Where did that idea come from?* All her life, she'd wanted a dog, but it had never been practical. Perhaps it was time.

Kat returned to her cottage for a light break-

fast before walking up the path to Flight.
Patches of blue sky were clearing out the gray,
allowing the sun to peep through. Her first
appointment wasn't until nine thirty, so she
had plenty of time to try to catch up with Ben
before his lessons started—not for a therapy
session, but just for a friendly chat. She had to
get to know him, and it was important that he
started to feel comfortable about living here.
She wanted to find out more about his granddad, too.

As it happened, she was too late to catch
Ben. Gwen had sent him to tidy up his room
before lessons started.

"There are some things we just have to insist on," she told Kat. "All the children are
taught to take responsibility for their own
rooms, and it's important he gets into good
habits from the start. Ben seems to take a
real delight in trashing his room. Rather than
telling him off, I just make him sort it out
himself. Yesterday he sulked and missed
breakfast, but today he's gone off to do it
quite happily. He has gym class first thing,
mind, and he does seem to love sport."

Kat went by the kitchen to get a coffee and,
to her dismay, Luke was already there, doing
the same. Short of rudely walking away, she

had no choice but to say good morning. He was wearing faded blue jeans, she noted, and a pale blue shirt with the top two buttons undone. He looked cleaner cut than usual, as if he'd made a special effort.

"You going somewhere fancy today?" she asked, trying to keep her tone casual.

"And are you?" he asked, looking at her outfit pointedly.

When she was doing formal therapy sessions at school she always felt she should at least try to look professional. Today she was wearing a pencil skirt with a bright floral blouse and mid-height heels. "I only do casual for the nature-therapy courses," she explained.

He gave her a warm, slightly crooked smile, his eyes sparkling with amusement. "So this is you looking serious, is it?"

"I *can* do serious, you know," she retorted.

"I'm sure you can," he said. "Unfortunately, though, when I watch your sessions you are invariably wading around in the sea or losing control of my son."

She froze, forcing back an angry retort; she mustn't let him get to her.

"I'm sorry," he said suddenly, taking her by surprise. "I'm sure your serious sessions are very professional. I just want what's best for Ben, and I believe that children have to learn to stick to the rules."

"So were your parents strict?" she asked on a hunch.

"Parent," he replied. "My mum died when I was small. My dad was in the army, so yes, I guess you could say he was strict. Rules and regulations were his life."

"What about now?" she asked.

"I haven't seen him in years," Luke said matter-of-factly.

"That's sad," she said quietly.

He shrugged, pouring boiling water into his mug. "You don't know my dad."

"He's still your dad, so you must have some regrets. Now you have the chance to make up for what you missed by making sure you and Ben get a proper father-son relationship going."

He held her gaze briefly, and then he thrust his broad hand forward. "Okay. Truce? You have your ways and I have mine, but the one thing we can agree on is that we both want what's best for Ben."

Kat took hold of his hand; it was warm and strong and tanned, and her heart raced.

For one wild moment, she wondered what it would feel like to be in his arms.

"Truce," she managed, pulling her hand free and turning away.

"Oh, and for your information," he called, as she picked up her cup and headed for the door, "the reason I've dressed up today is because it's my day off and I was thinking of going into town to buy Ben a bike."

Kat stopped and turned. "Don't you think it would be a good idea to take him with you? So that *he* can choose? Now, that really would be building bridges."

Luke hesitated. Then he gave her a wry smile. "Actually, I mentioned it to him and he refused point-blank. Nice, eh—real father-and-son stuff."

Moved by the sadness in his eyes, Kat almost reached out her hand in sympathy, but held back. "You just have to work on this. You can't expect him to come around overnight. He's lost his mum, his home and his grandparents—everything familiar. And suddenly the dad, who in his eyes hasn't wanted anything to do with him for years, has stepped right back into his life. You have to earn his trust, Luke."

"It wasn't because I didn't *want* to have

anything to do with him. He needs to know that. It was for the best at the time, that's all."

"And how hard did you actually try?" Kat asked.

Luke shook his head sadly, and this time she did take hold of his arm. "Just be his friend," she urged. "He's here at Flight now. He doesn't need you to worry about discipline."

"You don't understand," he objected. "I know what his grandparents are like. They're very wealthy and they've ruined him with kindness, totally spoiled him."

"Well, you're talking about buying him a bike, so how is that different?"

Luke narrowed his eyes, his jaw tensing. "Every boy should have a bike," he said. "That's not spoiling him."

"That's probably how his grandparents felt," Kat suggested. "Especially after he lost his mum."

"What do you know about that?"

"I'm his therapist. It's my job to know what's been going on in his life. I'd like to find out more about his granddad, too. Ben's upset about his illness, but I think there's more to it."

Luke shot her a sharp glance. "What do

you mean? What about Jim? I know he's been unwell, but Mollie just told me it was old age catching up with him."

"Maybe I got it wrong," Kat said, doubting herself. "Ben said something about losing his granddad, that's all. He was very upset about it."

"Yes, you obviously got it wrong," Luke said. "That's what happens when you jump to conclusions. I think I know my son and his business better than you."

"Are you sure about that?" Kat asked, hating herself for the low dig.

Luke's face reddened, and he seemed to be working something over in his head. "Okay," he said finally. "If Ben wants a bike, he'll have to come with me."

She nodded. Maybe she was getting through to Luke after all. "That'll give you a chance to bond. You could take him to McDonald's or something. All kids love McDonald's."

Luke's mouth quirked into a smile. "Perhaps I'll ask you, too," he said.

"No…thanks," Kat responded. "I think it should be just the two of you." Why on earth would he ask her something like that?

As he walked away, after giving her an exaggerated salute, she noted how much more confident his strides were, as if he had a goal now. *What a strange guy.* Just when she'd thought she couldn't stand him any longer, he'd dropped his arrogance and revealed an almost vulnerable side to his character.

Feeling more optimistic about the whole situation, she headed off to the bright, airy room just off the new annex that had been allocated for her counseling sessions. Afterward, she'd go and find Mike to try to persuade him to organize a meeting with Ben's grandmother, along with discussing her animal-therapy plans.

Her first session, with sixteen-year-old Robert Bevis, left her beaming. It always felt good when she made real headway with a kid, and she'd seen such a change in the lanky, dark-haired teenager since they'd started their sessions. He'd shown a huge interest in athletics, so she'd had talks with Graham Brown, head of sports at the school, to see if the field held any future for Robert. Graham had sung his praises but said that with his attitude, he would never be able to make any kind of career. But with her help and support, Rob had started to build up his confidence in himself, which was the only thing holding him back.

Today he showed her a letter from a sports academy that was offering him a place when he left Flight later that year. She couldn't take credit for that as she wasn't even at Flight when he'd applied, but he'd talked to her about it, opening up and asking her advice. That was the best reward she could ever have.

"If you ever have doubts or setbacks, you can always call me," she told him. "The only person who can hold you back is you. You just have to believe in yourself."

"I'm going to try really hard to do that," he said. "If you'll help me."

"Of course I will. It won't always be easy, though."

He nodded determinedly. "Yes, I know that, but at least I'm getting the chance to try. I'm going to give it my best shot."

"That's all anyone can do," Kat said. "You are as good as anyone else."

The young man smiled with a newfound confidence. "I'll remember that always," he told her.

When Millie Summers came into the room just after Rob left, Kat was still glowing about his news. She focused her attention on the quiet young girl, who sat down with her hands linked in her lap. "Well, Millie, how do you feel about maybe going for a home visit soon?"

Millie glanced up at her then looked away nervously. "Dunno," she said.

"Do you feel excited...or scared, maybe?"

"I want to see my mum, but only if Bob has gone. I hate him."

"Bob has gone far away, Millie. He can never hurt you or your mum again, I promise. Your mum is living in a new house now and it will be just you and her and maybe, before long, your little brother, too."

Millie brightened at that. "Dominic?" she cried. "Dominic's coming home?"

"Well, it's early days. We'll start with a few home visits to see how it goes, and who knows—before long you might be able to go home full-time and help your mum look after him." The idea brought a glow to Millie's usually deadpan features.

"I'd like that," she said. "And Bob's really gone?"

"He's gone," Kat assured her. "I could come with you if you like, for your first visit."

"Will you, Miss? Will you really come?"

"If you're sure it's what you want."

Millie nodded.

"You can do a few visits, and you don't have to go back to live there until you're sure it's what you want."

Her face said it all.

Today, thought Kat, as she gathered up her notes and books after Millie's time was up, she felt good about her work. It wasn't often that both her sessions went well; sometimes she came away sad and depressed after being unable to get through to the child she was trying to help. Both Robert and Millie had been at Flight for a while, and she had just taken over from their previous therapist, so she couldn't take all the credit for their improvement. Still, it was satisfying to think that she'd been a part of helping them get their lives back on track.

Buoyed by her rewarding morning, she went straight over to Mike's office.

To Kat's disappointment, Mike was less than hopeful about the possibility of her seeing Mollie Jackson. "I did mention it to the social worker," he said. "But she didn't think it was a good idea. Mollie is under a lot of strain, and she couldn't see it being very helpful for Ben, anyway. Ben's grandfather had surgery several months ago, and his recovery has been poor. Caring for him takes up all Mollie's time."

"I just need to understand what Ben's been going through a bit better," Kat pleaded. "If you give me her address, I'll go and visit her myself."

Mike shook his head. "I couldn't let you do that. It would be very unprofessional to turn up on her doorstep. Look, Kat, why don't you let Ben tell you what's bothering him in his own time."

Disgruntled, Kat bit her lip. He was right, of course; there were codes of conduct to follow, but it had been worth a try. "I understand. While I'm here, can we talk about my animal-therapy idea?" she asked, changing tack.

She could practically hear Mike's inward groan. Obviously she'd caught him on a bad day. "I've been thinking about that, too," he began.

"And?"

"And I think you need to concentrate on your sea and nature exercises for a bit longer before we embark on the new project. There are a lot of health and safety issues to consider."

Disappointment clawed at her insides.

Mike had been so enthusiastic about the idea when she'd first suggested it, so what had happened to make him change his mind?

"Luke has been trying to talk you out of it, hasn't he?" she said, realizing at once that hurling accusations was the wrong approach.

"This is coming straight from me," Mike remarked in a cool tone. "As I said, there are a lot of issues to consider first, and the children's safety has to be a priority."

"But I was only going to have rabbits and guinea pigs to begin with," she objected. "Maybe pet lambs in the spring—gentle, harmless creatures that will encourage the children to be kind and caring."

To her relief, she detected a softening in Mike's unexpectedly harsh expression. "I'm not saying never," he said. "And I suppose you could start small by getting some rabbits and the like, as long as you make sure that they're well-handled and won't bite or anything."

"Can I use the old outbuildings in the garden?" she asked eagerly. "I'll clean them out on my days off."

Mike raised his hand. "Whoa, steady on. I'm not going that far yet. Can't you keep them at home for a while? And in a few weeks when they've settled in, you can introduce me to them and we can talk about keeping them here at school. That will give us time to do the safety checks and get parental permission."

Kat sighed. This was as good as she was going to get for now. "Okay. It's a start at least." She stopped and turned on her way out the door. "It *was* Luke who made you think twice, though, wasn't it?"

Mike smiled, his good humor restored. "He didn't really object, just made me realize that I have to take the health-and-safety side of it seriously…and he's right."

"Of course. But I'd already considered all that. I have run these courses before, you know."

"I know you have. I think Luke just worries about Ben. The idea of being a dad scares him—you can see it from a mile away. He's floundering and he doesn't want to fail. Don't tell him I said so, though… And, Kat!"

"Yes?"

"I really am still enthusiastic about your animal therapy. We just need to get it right."

"We will," she promised. "You'll see. Luke getting it right with Ben may take a little longer, though."

"Don't be too hard on him," urged Mike. "Luke, I mean. I think he feels guilty about neglecting Ben up to now, but he's trying to make amends."

Kat couldn't help a sharp retort. "He should feel guilty. He took the easy option when Ben was small and now he's paying the price. A child's trust is difficult to win—you have to earn it—and as far as Ben is concerned, his dad is a total stranger who has never wanted anything to do with him before."

Mike nodded and sighed. "I'm well aware. On a lighter note, are you going to Wayne's party?"

"Luke mentioned it… Do you think I should?"

"Of course you should. They'd be disappointed if you weren't there. It's a surprise party, though, so not a word to Wayne. He doesn't want a fuss. Fat chance of that with Mel in charge."

"Mel seems nice," Kat said. "And I love the way everyone here is so welcoming. I feel as if I've been here for years rather than just a few months."

Mike raised his eyebrows. "Despite the situation with Luke?"

"That's simply an obstacle to be overcome.

We both have Ben's best interests at heart—
that's the main thing."

"But different methods."

Kat laughed. "Yeah…something like that."

CHAPTER NINE

BEN SURVEYED HIS room in dismay. At home, he'd never had to clean up his own mess because there had always been a cleaner to pick up after him. Later, when everything went wrong and all the staff left, he'd just left it in a mess. His grandma had kind of stopped noticing; she didn't notice anything anymore… certainly not him, not even when he did things to try to get her attention. He didn't like to think about it because it made him sad, but the mess in his room had brought it all back to him.

He closed his eyes tight, trying not to cry and trying not to remember the way his grandma used to love him, before Granddad… Rubbing his hand across his nose, he ran down the stairs and out into the sunshine. He refused to think about Granddad.

As he headed toward the garden, he saw that man, Luke. They said he was his dad, but that was stupid; he didn't have a dad. And the person who'd come closest was gone.

Ben didn't like Luke. He was bossy and fussy and he was always getting at Kat. Kat, he did like. She was nice to him, but that didn't mean she'd stay. No one ever stayed, and sometimes even when they seemed like they were still there, they weren't. Like Granddad.

Everything used to be so good. Then his mum died and everything changed. His grandma had sent him here because they didn't want him anymore; he knew that. She'd warned him again and again that she would send him away if he carried on being loud and refusing to do as he was told. But no one even noticed he was there when he was quiet; at least he knew when they were shouting at him that he had everyone's full attention.

Ben ducked behind a tree before Luke saw him and started to run, clenching his fists tight and going so fast he got a pain in his chest. He liked that because it stopped him from thinking about Granddad and home.

Ben stopped running when he got to the wildflower garden, his favorite place at Flight. His granddad had a wildflower garden, and Ben used to help with it. After Granddad changed, no one took care of it anymore…or of the smooth green lawns with their beautiful borders.

"Pretty, isn't it?" a voice behind him asked and he spun around in shock to see Luke. "Do you like flowers?"

Ben shrugged, donning his couldn't-care-less cloak; he'd worn it a lot before he came here.

LUKE TRIED AGAIN. "It's nice here, isn't it?"

Ben shrugged, and Luke gave up on the small talk. "Actually, I've been looking for you. I wondered if you'd like to come to town with me and choose a bike… Every boy should have a bike."

"I did have a bike."

Ben's tone was angry, and his stance held aggression, but as far as Luke was concerned, any response was progress. "Come with me. It'll be fun," he suggested brightly.

Ben shook his head. "No, I don't want to."

"Oh, well…" Luke turned on his heel. "Your loss."

"Is Miss coming?"

A surge of irritation made Luke want to keep on walking. But he was the adult. The dad. He had to be a good role model for his son. "Miss who?" he asked, turning around.

"Miss Kat," said Ben. "The sea lady."

"Do you want her to?"

Ben scowled, rounding his shoulders in the way that was becoming quite familiar to Luke. "Not really bothered."

"And will you come if she does?" Luke asked him.

"I might."

"So I'll ask her?"

Ben walked away, head down and shoulders hunched. "Can if you like," he muttered.

Luke let out an exasperated sigh once Ben was out of earshot. How was he going to go about asking Kat? They were hardly best friends. The opposite, if he was honest with himself. And did he really want to spend an afternoon in her company? Perhaps he should just forget the whole idea. But no, he reminded himself. This was for Ben's sake. If he needed to invite Kat along in order to interest his son in spending time with him, he'd do it.

Luke saw Kat later as she was leaving the school to go home. She came out the front doors just as he was about to go in.

"Hello," she said with a brief, impassive

smile. He nodded, noting how she'd neatly tied back her sleek, dark hair with something blue and floral. It matched her eyes. He struggled for words, and when they didn't come, he wondered if it was a sign. If Ben wanted a bike then he could have one, but taking Kat along was something else.

As usual, Kat felt awkward when she saw Luke. She smiled determinedly with no hesitation in her step, but just for an instant their eyes met and her heart thumped a little harder in her chest. He opened his mouth and closed it again, as if he'd wanted to say something but changed his mind. No, she decided, she was just being overimaginative. Anyway, there was nothing he could say that would be of any interest to her. They didn't see eye to eye about anything, and Mike had admitted it was Luke who'd persuaded him to stall on her animal venture. The man was nothing but a thorn in her side.

She walked quickly down the pathway to Cove Road. As soon as she reached her bright red door and pulled her shiny fish key ring from her pocket, a sense of peace settled over her. She paused for a moment to look out across the bay, feeling blessed. The sea was sparkling and calm and the sky was a clear, pale blue. Way out near the horizon she could see a tiny boat, and along the shore, where it was less secluded, a dinghy was just casting off at Tanners' boatyard. A young man with dark hair jumped into the dinghy while his companion, a slim, young blonde woman, hovered cautiously on the jetty. He laughed, urging her to step in beside him, and when she eventually plucked up the courage, he pulled her to him, wrapped his arms around her and kissed her tenderly.

Kat turned away, feeling uncomfortable to be watching such a private moment, and not sure what to do with the longing it had unlocked inside her. What would it be like to fall in love, to have that certain someone who knew your every thought? She stepped into the cottage, suddenly lonely. Her job had always been enough for her, and the boy-friends she'd had along the way had had to take second place to fulfilling her ambitions. Now, though, she had time on her hands, and deep down, if she was honest with herself, part of her longed for what her poor mother had never had—someone to love who would truly love her back. Someone to share her whole life with.

Luke's face sprang into Kat's mind; there was something about him that drew her in, but there were far too many issues between them for it ever to go anywhere. He was against everything she did, for a start, and as his son's therapist, she had to keep things on a professional footing. Getting too friendly with Luke would compromise both her career and Ben's healing.

Before she closed the door behind her, she couldn't resist another glance at the young couple. They sat side by side, his arm flung around her shoulders as the dinghy headed out into the smooth, sparkling sea. The girl's hair blew in the breeze as she threw back her head, laughing at something the young man was saying. Their closeness was so apparent, even at this distance, and Kat was once again beset by loneliness.

She closed the door firmly behind her and leaned against it, taking a breath. She had her own place now, her independence and a worthwhile job that she loved; that was what she needed to focus on. Today had been a mixed bag, but there was always tomorrow, and Mike hadn't said no to her animal-therapy course. She would start doing risk assessments, she decided, to show him she was serious. And she'd do as he suggested and begin acquiring some animals. Perhaps she could bring the children here, to Cove Road, to get to know them. In understanding and caring for the animals, the children could learn to be responsible, to care and nurture and immerse themselves in the realities of nature: its stability and its cruelty. They could learn to love with nothing to gain but fulfillment. They could learn resilience and adaptability.

The idea of getting a dog came back into her mind. If she did decide to find one, it would have to be a dog, or pup, that loved attention…a Labrador, maybe.

BY SEVEN THIRTY the next morning, Luke was already out at work, carrying fence rails across the garden. The property backed onto open fields, where milk cows grazed, and the thought of them rampaging around the smooth green lawns and flower beds had been quite enough to inspire him to make a start on fixing the fence.

Last night all he'd been able to think about was whether or not to ask Kat to come to town with him and Ben. Of course, Ben still hadn't agreed to go, but surely he wouldn't refuse the opportunity, especially if Kat came with them. Having her along would be tough for Luke, though. If he was totally honest with himself, it hurt to see Ben getting so close to Kat while adamantly rejecting him. And that thought, in turn, made him feel guilty. He should be happy to see his son showing an emotion other than anger, even if that emotion didn't include him. And he could see why Ben was drawn to her; there was something about Kat, something real and appealing, something that would appeal to him, too, in different circumstances.

Fixing the fence proved to be harder than he'd expected, and the weather was uncomfortably hot. By lunchtime, Luke was dripping with sweat and his shoulders were aching. Still, he was determined to get the job done, so he worked through his usual break.

At two o'clock, he stood back in satisfaction, surveying his handiwork. The cows, interested in the goings-on, ambled over to the fence, poked their huge heads into the garden and mooed loudly.

"Too late, girls," Luke called. "You won't get in now."

Their big brown eyes stared back at him inquisitively, reminding him of Kat's animal-therapy plans. Animals accepted you for what you were—he got that. Maybe her ideas weren't quite as out there as he'd first thought.

CHAPTER TEN

AT EIGHT THIRTY Kat left the cottage. It was only a five-minute walk to Flight, and her first session wasn't for another hour, but she liked to get to the school in plenty of time. She walked slowly, taking in the glorious view and thinking about the young couple the night before, setting off in their dinghy, basking in each other's love. Again came the pang of loneliness and she increased her stride.

Today was her last session with Millie before she went back home for a trial period. Instead of the short visits Kat had proposed, after a discussion between Mike, Kat and Millie's social worker, it had been decided that the best way forward was for Millie to go back to her mum for a trial period under constant assessment. It was going to be a huge step, so Kat had spent yesterday afternoon deciding how to approach this meeting so she could boost the little girl's confidence. As she walked, Kat went through the little talk she'd prepared, about having enough self-belief to make anything happen, and about staying true to one's self. It sounded a bit pompous when she recited it to herself; maybe she'd follow Millie's lead and say what felt right in the moment. She would make sure Millie knew there was always a way back if things didn't work out.

It was hot already, Kat noted, glad that she'd chosen to wear a lightweight summer dress in her favorite shade of blue. She scraped her long dark hair back as she walked, tying it up high on her head. Today was going to be a scorcher.

She saw Luke as she walked around the back of the main building to the room where she held her therapy sessions. He was by the fence at the very end of the garden, swinging a hammer to knock in one of the fence posts. She wondered if he'd ever tried to get Ben involved with such a physical activity. Perhaps she'd suggest it—not that he'd take any notice of any of her ideas.

The morning flew by so fast once she'd started her sessions that Kat didn't realize she'd missed lunch until she'd finished writing up her notes. Glancing at the clock, she hurriedly filed her papers, hoping she'd still be able to get something to eat in the kitchen. As she walked toward the door, she heard a gentle knock. When it came again, more urgently, she opened the door. "Can I help you?" she asked.

To her surprise, it was Ben. He was stepping from foot to foot, looking nervous. "Are you coming with us to get my bike?" he asked gruffly.

"To get your bike?" she repeated, trying not to show her bewilderment. For Ben to come looking for her was a real step forward, and she didn't want to risk saying the wrong thing. "Well…when were you thinking of going?"

He shrugged, staring at the floor. "I said I'd only go if you came along."

Bet that went down well, thought Kat. "Then I wouldn't miss it," she assured him. "You just find out when and we'll sort something out."

"*He's* taking me."

She smiled at him. "You mean Luke?"

"You'll have to talk to him."

Suddenly feeling for Luke, whose efforts with Ben seemed to be getting nowhere, Kat took hold of the boy's hands, encouraging him to look up at her. "Well, if he wants to buy you a bike, perhaps you should be the one to talk to him about it."

"He's not really my dad, you know," he insisted.

Kat shrugged. "That's between you and Luke, but if you'd really rather I talk to him, I'll give it a go…just this once."

"And he'll buy me a bike?"

Sadness filled her heart. Luke was clearly trying to make amends to his son, but bribery, although probably a step up from the discipline he'd been trying to enforce, was not the answer, either. "That will depend on how well you behave, I guess," she said.

"And you'll talk to him today?"

"I'll try. If I see him then I'll tell him what you said."

Ben turned and walked away, his shoulders rounded, and Kat thought about the way he'd been on that first sea-therapy course, when he'd pushed the boundaries by swimming out too far, so full of mischief. That was the Ben she wanted to see again.

HAVING PUT AWAY all his tools and the spare wood in the shed, Luke headed for his apartment. Sweat ran in rivulets down his back and his T-shirt was soaked. Even his hair was damp and curly with sweat. He glanced right and left and increased his stride, keeping his head down.

"Excuse me…"

Freezing in his tracks, he looked up to see Kat, bright, clean and shiny with a high-swinging ponytail and wearing a blue cotton dress. "Excuse me," she repeated. "Ben asked me if I'd mention him going to choose a bike."

"He couldn't manage to ask me himself?"

"It's a start," she remarked. "You either take the chance, or start all over again and wait for another opportunity…not that I really think buying him presents is the answer."

Luke ran his hand through his hair, very aware of his unkempt appearance. "Every boy should have a bike," he insisted, stepping back in case a whiff of sweat blew her way.

"To be honest, I agree…about every boy needing a bike, I mean. In theory. But what about the other children here? Wouldn't that be unfair?"

"I spoke to Mike about it. He said it would be fine as long as it was a belated birthday present. Some of the other children have their own bikes here and there's plenty of space for them to safely ride around the grounds in their free time."

"The exercise will be good for him, I guess," Kat said. "And speaking of exercise, have you thought about asking Ben to help you when you're working…like today, for instance? I'm sure he'd enjoy it and maybe he'd start to admire your skills."

"Meaning he doesn't admire me now."

She raised her eyebrows. "You have to earn admiration, you know."

He chose to ignore that. "I suppose, since he asked you to speak to me, that he told you he wants you to come along when we go to get the bike."

"If you don't want me to—"

"Frankly, I don't, but if it's what Ben wants…"

Kat's eyes flashed, but instead of shooting him one of her biting remarks, she burst out laughing. "You're so touchy," she told him. "Let me know if you do want me to come with you. You'll have to talk to Ben about it yourself, though. I've already interfered more than I wanted to."

Once she'd walked away Luke headed off immediately, eager to get showered and changed before he bumped into anyone else.

It had made him feel awkward and out of his depth, standing there all hot and disheveled while she looked so cool and calm.

When Kat had mentioned him gaining Ben's admiration it had made him realize just how much he longed for it. If he had to bring her along on this outing as a first step toward that, then it would be worth putting up with her company for a few hours. He'd try to talk to Ben about it tonight, he decided, at Wayne's party.

As Kat walked away, she couldn't hold back her smile. He made her so angry most of the time, but there were occasions when she felt sorry for the guy. He'd looked pretty hot and stressed today, and embarrassed by his appearance. Mr. High and Mighty hadn't been quite as sure of himself as usual. She felt a small surge of affection for this version of Luke. And maybe going with them to choose the bike would be a chance for her to help them bond…and a chance to get on Luke's good side and persuade him that her animal therapy wasn't such a bad idea.

She'd start making plans right away, she decided, about what animals to get and where to keep them. There was a small shed behind the cottage; maybe she could clean that out. After all, how much space did a few rabbit hutches take up?

Kat finished her day around four and hurried out the front door thinking about her plans for the shed, so deep in thought that she didn't even notice Mike calling her name until he caught up with her.

"You're in a rush," he said. "Got a date?"

She slowed down and he fell in beside her.

"No, of course not." Her tone was sharper than she'd intended.

Mike laughed. "Why 'of course not'? Nothing wrong with a young, unattached woman like you having a date. Work isn't everything, you know."

"I love my work," she said.

"I know you do, and all credit to you for that, but leisure's important, too. Anyway..." He put a friendly hand on her shoulder. "It's Wayne's birthday party tonight, so you'll have to take a break from thinking about work."

"But I..." she began, trying to think up an excuse. Suddenly the party felt like too much too soon, and Mel hadn't officially invited her, after all...

"No buts. This party isn't optional. Everyone has to be there or else," he said jovially. "I'm on my way over there right now, as a matter of fact. Mel's persuaded Wayne to go to the races today with his brother, and when he gets back everyone will be there to surprise him. It's not every day you turn fifty."

Kat smiled. When he put it like that, what could she do? She didn't want to become known as Flight's recluse and a party would be fun.

"But I haven't even got him a present," she said.

"Wayne won't be bothered," Mike insisted. "And I think we have a spare card. I'll ask Gwen to bring it with her when she comes with the children. In fact…" He stopped in his tracks. "You wouldn't be able to give her a hand, would you? You need eyes in the back of your head to keep a check on that lot."

"Of course." Kat felt a whole lot happier about having a purpose; she'd imagined herself hanging around at the back of the room with no one to talk to. "I'd love to help— shall I give her a call?"

Mike shook his head, looking relieved. "No, I'll let her know you're coming. Six o'clock at school, okay? The party starts at seven and they're walking down, so that should be about right."

"Great," Kat said. "Tell her I'll be there, and if she does have a card then that would be perfect."

AN HOUR LATER, having given the shed no more than a cursory glance, Kat was rifling through her meager wardrobe. She was sure Mike had mentioned it was a barbecue, so she assumed the dress was casual. Trouble was, everything she tried on just looked wrong. In the end she decided on blue skinny jeans and a T-shirt with Head Full of Dreams emblazoned across the front. She was still wondering if it looked ridiculous as she locked the door behind her and headed back to Flight.

Gwen and the children were in the hallway already. "You look nice," Gwen said. "And thanks for helping. I really appreciate it."

"My pleasure," Kat replied, searching the gathered faces for Ben. "I was a bit worried about turning up on my own, anyway, and I'm not even sure where Wayne and Mel live."

"Well, we're all ready to go, I think. Oh, and here's the card. Do you have a pen?"

Kat scrawled her name on the card and put it in her bag.

"Where's Ben?" she asked.

Gwen looked puzzled. "I thought he'd gone with Luke."

"No… He wouldn't go with Luke. He'll be hiding in his room. I'll go and check."

"Luke told me he was going to ask him, so I just presumed… I'd be mortified if we left him behind."

Kat raced up the wide sweep of stairs. She heard Ben as soon as she reached the door and the sound made her heart ache. No child should be sitting all alone trying to hide their muffled sobs.

"Ben," she called, pretending she hadn't heard him. "I've come to get you. We're going to the party, remember?"

For a moment, there was silence. Then she heard the sound of a chair being scraped back. "Ben," she repeated. "Everyone's waiting for you."

The door opened just a crack and she saw his tear-streaked face peeping through the gap. "Come on," she urged. "It'll be fun— it's a barbecue, you know."

The door opened wider and with a warm smile she just took his hand and led him to the sink. "I'll help you get cleaned up," she said in a matter-of-fact tone.

Five minutes later they both ran down the stairs to find Gwen and the other children still waiting patiently.

"Sorry, Ben," called Gwen, "I thought you'd already left."

"*He* came to ask me but I hid in my room," Ben murmured for Kat's ears only, and again she felt a rush of pity for the man who normally drove her mad. He should have told someone he wasn't heading over with Ben, though; what if he'd been left alone all evening?

She said as much to Gwen, who nodded in agreement. "I'm just glad you realized," she said. "I suppose Luke presumed that when Ben didn't answer his knock, he wasn't in his room and must have left already. It's just a shame that Ben won't even give him a chance."

"Well, he did abandon him for nine years," Kat pointed out.

"In my view, you should never judge a book by its cover," Gwen said. "I mean, none of us know the circumstances, so perhaps we shouldn't judge Luke too harshly. Until we find out more."

Kat had the grace to blush. "I'm sorry if you think I'm too harsh. Luke and I haven't had the best start, I'm afraid…as you've probably noticed."

"Maybe you can make a fresh start tonight," Gwen suggested. She raised her voice above the children's chatter. "Now remember, kids, not a sound when we get there, not until Wayne comes in, and then you can shout as loud as you like."

CHAPTER ELEVEN

IT TOOK A lot longer to walk to Wayne and Mel's house than Kat had expected. It was still warm, despite the breeze that always seemed to blow along the coast, and she couldn't help wishing that she'd worn a light summer dress rather than jeans. Gwen had opted for some loose linen pants and a floaty cotton top; she looked cool and fresh and smart, Kat thought with a flicker of envy. When she mentioned it to Gwen, she laughed out loud.

"Isn't that funny?" she said, linking arms with her as they trooped along behind the children. "Because when I saw you, looking so young and fashionable, I felt like an old frump."

"No way," Kat exclaimed. "You look cool and classy. I don't suppose we ever think we've got it right, do we. Anyway, it's too late for either of us to get changed now."

The Whites' house, just past Tanners'

boatyard, was set up on a low limestone cliff so they never had to worry about flooding. Unlike Cove Cottages, thought Kat; at high tide, the water seemed to lap right up to the edge of the small front garden. Elsa had told her not to worry about it, as the sea never came any higher than that, but Kat guessed it could be a bit scary, especially on a wild and windy night.

"Wait until you see what Mel has bought for Wayne's birthday," Gwen said, ushering the children through the gate. Kat duly followed suit, encouraging the stragglers. Giggling and laughing, they filed through the door…except for Ben. He seemed very quiet and thoughtful.

"It's something really special, the present," Gwen continued. "And he doesn't have a clue about it. I can't wait to see the look on his face. Although…" Gwen frowned, her face falling. "After what happened to that poor young couple last night, it makes me wonder if a boat was such a good idea after all. Oh, sorry! I didn't mean to give it away. Come on, kids. You have to stay quiet. It's a secret, remember, and Wayne will be back soon. We need to surprise him."

"What young couple?" Kat asked, already knowing.

The children finally fell silent and she suddenly had Gwen's full attention. "They went out in a dinghy last night. Cast off right here from the jetty and they haven't been seen since. They were on holiday, I think. People never seem to realize just how dangerous Jenny Brown's Bay is until it's too late."

"I saw them," Kat said quietly. Icy fingers seemed to squeeze her heart and the breath caught in her throat.

Gwen stopped in her tracks. "What? You mean…"

"No, I didn't actually meet them. I just saw them getting in the dinghy. They were so young and in love. I can't believe…"

"Hey…" Gwen patted her shoulder. "These things happen, I'm afraid. Hopefully they just went farther than they expected and were forced to put ashore somewhere else. Morecambe, maybe, or even on the other side of the bay. There are lots of places they could have gone. I'm sure they'll turn up soon. Or perhaps they abandoned the boat and don't want to have to pay any extra so they've cleared off altogether."

Kat couldn't help worrying. For fate to

deny such a happy young couple their future was inconceivable. "Do you really think so?" she asked hopefully.

"I *know* so," Gwen replied determinedly, though Kat noted a resigned sadness in her eyes.

Once inside the spacious, open-plan house, Kat's attention was taken by trying to help Gwen keep the children quiet.

"Shhh, everyone…" Mel urged. "I can see his car coming up the road."

The room fell silent and the children all went to hide behind the furniture, while the adults gathered at the back of the room so Wayne wouldn't immediately see them when he came in. The door opened, everyone held their breath and Mel stepped forward.

"Happy birthday, love," she cried, flinging her arms around him.

"Some birthday," he groaned. "All my horses—"

Before he could finish, everyone jumped out, shouting "happy birthday," and Wayne spun around, disorientated. "What the…?" he began.

Mel reached up and kissed him on the cheek. *"Surprise!"*

"You're having a party, by the way," Mike said as he walked in with Luke.

"And these two have been getting your present ready for me," Mel explained, hanging on to her husband's arm, eyes glowing with affection.

Kat glanced at Luke, intrigued by the delight on his face. For a fleeting instant their eyes met, and then he gave her a huge wink. Embarrassed at having been caught staring, she turned away and busied herself with the kids, but Luke was having none of it. He materialized beside her.

"Have you seen Ben?" he asked.

He was standing so close that Kat could feel the heat of his body. "He was here just a minute ago," she said, annoyed at the way her voice came out in a kind of gasp.

"Probably trying to avoid me," Luke remarked drily.

"Oh, no…"

He shook his head before she could continue. "Spare me the sympathy vote. You know it's true."

"Do you still want me to come with you to choose his bike?" she asked.

"No point. I've decided that bribery is the wrong approach. As you pointed out."

"But you promised him. He's expecting to go now."

Luke huffed impatiently. "Yes, but he'll only go with me if you come along, and that's not quite what I had in mind."

Kat understood that Luke wanted to bond with his son one-on-one, but it wasn't fair to make promises to a child and not follow through. The last thing Ben needed was more inconsistency from the adults in his life. Before she could object, Mel made an announcement.

"Come on, everyone," she called, holding a blindfolded Wayne by the arm. "I want you all to come and see Wayne get his present from me."

Luke had disappeared from Kat's side, and she couldn't help feeling a bit disappointed. She just couldn't decide if she felt angry with him, sorry for him...or something else. Something she refused to admit even to herself. Everyone was always going on about what a great guy he was, but so far she hadn't really seen it, especially when it came to his treatment of his son. His parenting instincts were way off, as far as she was concerned. And yet, in his own way, he was trying very hard to make it work, and he obviously loved Ben; there was no doubt in her mind about that. She just wished he'd let the boy see that.

"Come on, Kat," called Gwen. "You're going to like this. Plus, I need you to keep an eye on the children with me."

"Of course," Kat said, glad of the distraction.

The Whites' house backed onto the sea and they all trooped across the garden with its amazing view of the bay and went down some steps carved into the limestone, winding up on the shore. The tide was up and a small motorboat bobbed on the rippling waves, firmly attached to a small jetty by a long, thick rope. It was blue and white with the name White Lady painted boldly across the bow. Mel led Wayne to the end of the jetty and pulled off his blindfold with a flourish. "Happy birthday, darling," she cried.

Wayne looked stunned. "For me? Really?"

"Yes…really." Mel smiled. "But before you thank me, you need to know that you have Luke to thank, too. I couldn't have got it without his help. He came with me to see it and he even painted the name on it for me just the other night."

"I thought you were being a bit secretive lately." Wayne laughed. "Thanks, Luke."

"And Mike," Mel added. "He helped us get it down here while you were out earlier."

"Thanks to you all, then," Wayne called, jumping onto the boat and almost losing his balance as it bobbed up and down on the waves. Everyone laughed when he had to grab the side.

"You sure about this, Mel?" teased Mike. "Doesn't look like he has any sea legs at all to me."

"Oh, he'll learn," Mel assured him.

Kat couldn't stop her mind from going out to the happy young couple who were possibly lost somewhere in the ocean. She hoped Gwen was right about them having been forced to go ashore somewhere else. It was too painful to think that a tragedy could have occurred right on their doorstep.

Mel grabbed her husband's arm and tried to yank him from the boat. "You can play with your new toy tomorrow. Now it's party time!"

When he pulled her to him and planted a kiss on her lips, everyone cheered. For a moment, Mel leaned against him, her eyes shining, and Kat felt a lurch of envy at their togetherness. Would she ever have that?

"Right, kids," cried Gwen. "You heard what Mel said. Who's ready for a party?"

They all rallied around her in excitement, but yet again, Ben held back.

"Hey, Ben," Kat murmured for his ears only. "Don't you like parties?"

He nodded. "Yes, but missing my grand-dad is making me sad."

Kat placed her hand on his shoulder, touched when he didn't shrug it off. "So where is he, your granddad?"

"He's gone," he said sadly. "To a funny place."

"And your grandma?" asked Kat.

The little boy looked down at his feet and Kat thought he wasn't going to answer. "Taking care of him," he eventually said.

Kat wanted to question him further but she sensed it would be too much. She had to go see Mollie Jackson, she decided, whether it was against the rules or not.

When she noticed Luke approaching them, her heart sank. His timing was totally wrong.

"Hey, buddy," he said, offering Ben a forced, way-too-wide smile. "You coming in to the party?"

Ben shrugged. "I might…" He looked up at Kat. "With her."

"We can go together," suggested Luke, his bright smile fading just a little. Something pulled at Kat's heartstrings.

"All the children are going now," she said. "I'm helping Gwen keep them under control. Why don't we all head up together?"

"Whatever," said Ben with feigned indifference. Kat saw the defensiveness in his eyes. He ran off, squeezing himself into the center of a group of children who were all pushing to try to get back into the house.

"He'll come around," Kat said, glancing up to see a set expression on Luke's handsome face.

He shrugged, pretending not to care—he and Ben were more similar than either of them seemed to realize. "He's *my* son," he said drily. "And I don't need you to tell me that."

"Fair enough," she responded, her cheeks burning. "But it might help if you changed your attitude and accepted some help."

"From you?"

"Outsiders often see things from a different perspective."

"As you've already said, he'll come around," he remarked in a clipped tone.

He held her gaze, and when she felt her heart quiver she hardened it instantly.

"And it won't be by trying to buy him with the promise of a bike," he said, turning on his heel.

When she spotted Ben watching them with a sullen expression on his face, Kat pulled at Luke's sleeve. He turned reluctantly.

"Look, I know what you mean, but going back on your promise will just make Ben more confused. He needs to be able to rely on you," Kat said.

"I don't need you to make my decisions for me," Luke snapped.

"And sulking won't help, either," she murmured as she walked away.

KAT'S REMARK STUNG far deeper than Luke had expected. She was right about the way he was behaving, he knew that, and yet it only made him want to dig in his heels. What was wrong with him? he wondered. Why did she always seem to bring out his worst qualities? Was he jealous because Ben obviously preferred her company to his? The thought made him feel childish and shallow; perhaps he should go and apologize. She was so strong, and he couldn't help but feel a grudging admiration for the way she was with Ben. She was so sure of herself, too, so sure of her methods and so comfortable in her own skin...

Following on behind the excited throng of partygoers, Luke contemplated going home before anyone noticed. He knew what Kat would say, of course: *only cowards run away, you need to stand your ground*. Now, how did he know that, he wondered, stifling a smile.

"Luke!" Mel called, pulling him out of his thoughts. He turned to her, noting her determined approach. What now? "Mike says you can sing and play guitar," she said, catching up with him. Her cheeks were pink with exertion; she just wanted everything to go right for Wayne's birthday, he could see that, and he admired her for it.

"I haven't performed for years," he said doubtfully. "And I was never very good. I just strummed a bit, and sang country music and ballads—easy stuff."

"Wayne has a guitar," she said, her eyes bright with excitement. "I bought it for him last year, but he's never even tried to learn to play it. It's a good one, I think—it just needs tuning. Please say you'll do it."

Luke's instincts told him to just say no and walk away but he felt himself faltering. "Well, I…" he began.

"Please," she begged, wringing her hands, and he couldn't help but smile. "It'll make the party," she insisted, pulling him through the door.

CHAPTER TWELVE

BACKGROUND MUSIC FLOATED out into the garden as Mel and Wayne's guests made the most of the rather unusual catering arrangements organized by their two sons, Jack and Joseph, who had come home from their summer travels around Europe for their dad's birthday, Gwen explained to Kat, and when they offered to be in charge of the food, Mel had reluctantly agreed. She'd planned a barbecue, so at first their new idea had met with her total disapproval, but as usual they'd worked their charm on her. She'd been forced to agree that Wayne did love fish and chips and the idea of a fish-and-chip van turning up was certainly novel. Her delight was evident when he spotted it in the driveway and grinned from ear to ear.

Gwen and Kat organized the children into a haphazard line and they chattered excitedly as they queued up for their treat. "Now, who wants fish and who wants chicken, kids?" Gwen called.

She was met by such a babble of voices that she ended up having to write down each child's order. Ben was hanging back again, and as Kat headed toward him, he retreated to the rear of the crowd. She found him sitting on a low wall all by himself.

"Not hungry, Ben?" she asked.

To her surprise, he nodded. "What…you *are* hungry?"

He nodded again. "Yes, but I don't want to see him."

"Who? You mean Luke?" Kat didn't quite understand. "Why? Where is he?"

"In the van."

Unable to believe what she was hearing, Kat went over to the fish-and-chip van, and sure enough, there was Luke, helping out.

She wriggled through the crowd of eager children to see him. "Ben said you were in there, but I thought he was imagining it." She laughed. "You look a bit hot, if you don't mind me saying."

"I'm just filling in a gap," he explained. "Someone's coming to relieve me any minute…hopefully."

"Well, despite the risk of being reprimanded yet again," she said, "I have an idea."

Five minutes later, Kat watched Luke leave the van carrying a newspaper-wrapped parcel. She slipped behind a sycamore tree, not wanting to interfere. Ben was still sitting on the wall looking less than happy, and when he saw his dad approach, he half rose, as if he intended to run off. Luke sat down beside him before he got the chance.

"Hi," he said. "I brought you fish and chips...or chicken, if you'd rather. I like both."

Ben ignored him and stood up, but Luke took hold of his sleeve. "Don't go...please. You must be hungry and these are extra. They'll go to waste if we don't eat them." When he opened the paper, releasing an appetizing aroma, Kat could swear she saw Ben's nose twitch.

"You might as well eat them," suggested Luke. "I won't hang around if you don't want me to."

THE LITTLE BOY shrugged and sat down. "Can I have chicken?"

"That's fine," Luke said. "I love fish."

They ate in silence, a companionable silence, Luke hoped, glancing down at his perfect, pint-size replica. "Good, aren't they?" he said.

When Ben nodded, a warm glow ran through him. Any response was better than nothing.

Eventually, Ben crumpled up his paper and glanced sideways at Luke. "Miss is over there," he said. "I saw her just before. Has she had fish and chips?"

"Well, I don't really know, Ben," Luke said, stamping out a prickle of annoyance. "Why don't you ask her? Do you want me to give her a shout?"

The little boy smiled up at him.

"Yes, please."

Luke's irritation evaporated as he took in his son's smile—the first one he'd ever directed his way.

"Kat!" Luke waved her over and she approached with a spring in her step.

"Have you eaten?" he asked.

She sat down beside them on the wall, shaking her head. "I'm going to get some in a minute when the line dies down."

"You are still coming with us to see the bike, aren't you, Miss?" Ben asked.

Kat shot a questioning glance at Luke, but he gave her nothing.

"You must call me Kat, Ben," she said, smiling. "We are friends, aren't we?"

"But you *are* coming?" His eyes were bright, expectant.

She took a breath. "If Luke is still taking you, then of course I'll come along."

"We'll see," Luke said. He still hadn't decided, but now wasn't the time to make promises to—or disappoint—Ben.

"But when?" Ben asked, glaring at Luke and refusing to let it lie. "You did say…"

"I know I did." Luke hesitated. "But have you earned a bike?"

"Well, I don't have one."

"And do you think that's a good enough reason?"

Ben went quiet. Then he looked up at Luke with accusation in his eyes. "You promised," he said quietly. "And that's a good enough reason."

Luke was speechless. He had promised, and he'd been looking forward to it, but he'd imagined it would only be the two of them, an opportunity for a real bonding session.

"I didn't promise to take Miss," he said.

Ben glared at him, unfazed, and Luke saw

himself in the boy's eyes. "You really want her to come?"

"I really want her to come."

Luke held his son's gaze for a moment more before turning to Kat. "Well? You heard what he said. Are you up for it?"

Kat hesitated, and Luke suddenly realized that he wanted her to say yes. What was going on here? Her eyes held his and he couldn't look away. "Well?"

She smiled then, a smile that lit up her whole face. "Yes," she said determinedly. "I am."

Luke glanced at Ben, pleased to see his delight. "Okay, so when shall we go?"

Before Kat could reply, Gwen appeared, striding purposefully toward them. "Oh, good," she said, smiling at Luke and Kat. "He's had his fish and chips. I wondered where he'd got to…"

"He's fine," Luke was quick to insist. "We've been making plans…haven't we, Ben?"

Ben nodded eagerly, but obviously too flustered to listen, Gwen didn't pick up on Luke's comment. "We're heading back to Flight now, Ben, and Hilda's going to look after you and see you off to bed. I'll be taking you home, but then I'm coming straight back here."

"It's not my home," Ben said, scowling.

Luke caught Gwen's eye and saw the concern that darkened her pleasant features. "It's home for now, though, Ben," he said brightly. "Come on—don't give poor Gwen a hard time. We'll sort out our visit to the bike shop tomorrow."

Gwen took hold of Ben's arm and tried to lead him off. "Did you enjoy your fish and chips?" she asked.

"I had chicken," Ben told her, resisting her attempt to try to draw him away.

"And was it nice?"

"Kind of."

"You need to do as you're told…" Luke began, but she raised her hand to stop him.

"Tell you what," she said. "Before we go home, we'll all go into the house and sing 'Happy Birthday' to Wayne. Who knows—you might even get a piece of birthday cake."

Luke thought Ben was going to flatly refuse, but it seemed that the birthday cake had too much pull. "Okay," he said gruffly. "If I have to."

As Ben disappeared into the house with the other children, Kat couldn't help feeling a bit hurt that he hadn't even said goodbye. "Ben has a lot more going on in his head than he lets on, you know," she said with a sigh.

Luke frowned. "Whatever is 'going on in his head,' it doesn't hurt to be courteous. That's what he's never been taught—basic manners, like simply saying goodbye and thanks. Maybe I *should* put the bike on hold. Let him earn it by his behavior."

"No," Kat responded automatically, letting out what was in her heart. "Can't you see that he's lonely, lost and hurting? Getting him a bike might make him feel cared about, at least. Especially since you promised it. How can he ever trust you if you break your promises?"

"He's been cared about all his life," insisted Luke. "Too much, I think. That's the problem."

"No one can be cared about too much," Kat said quietly. Luke's approach to Ben worried her; he seemed to have no understanding of what the boy needed.

"You don't know his grandparents."

"I know that something to do with his granddad has really upset him."

Kat turned to Luke, searching his face for a clue. But his expression was blank, almost angry.

"Jim had some health issues—he needed a lot of care, according to Mollie. In spending all her time with him, she's neglected Ben. So no big mystery, after all… It's as simple as that."

That didn't satisfy Kat. "I want to go and see Mollie," she insisted. "To talk to her."

"If anyone is going to talk to Mollie about Ben, it will be me," Luke responded, his tone firm.

Kat just shrugged and walked away. What was it with Luke Travis? One minute she sensed a kind of loneliness in him, a vulnerability that warmed her toward him, but in an instant he could be harsh and unfeeling. It seemed as if he wasn't sure how to act with his son, as if he didn't know how to love him and he was stumbling his way through the whole relationship thing.

Maybe his own life hadn't been easy. He'd already mentioned that his mother had died young and his father was strict, but Kat hadn't had an easy time, either, and she at least understood something of what Ben was going through in his new life. Luke wasn't a trained child therapist, though, so she supposed she should give him a break. He was just a manager at Flight who was struggling to cope with the son he'd never met—and who didn't want anything to do with him. Regardless, it was clear to Kat that Luke was floundering. But she had enough to do trying to help troubled children without having to deal with mixed-up adults. Oh, how she wished she'd never agreed to go with him and Ben to choose a bike; the best thing she could do was keep well away from Luke Travis.

Imagining Ben's face if she let him down, she knew she couldn't back out. Too many people had let him down already; that was the root of his problems. The boy was hurt, bitter, insecure and something else—something she was sure had to do with his granddad— and she intended to find out what that was, no matter how much it upset Luke…or Mike, for that matter. For Kat, the children came first.

LUKE WATCHED KAT return to the house, frustrated with how their conversation had gone. Ben was his son; surely that stood for something. The boy was a bit mixed up, but he just needed to learn some boundaries. Kat didn't know the Jacksons and she didn't realize just how much they would have spoiled their grandson. After the tragedy of Carly's death, followed by the failure of the business and having to spend all her time caring for Jim, Mollie had allowed Ben to run so wild that she'd been unable to manage him.

When *he* was growing up, with his dad in control of his behavior, there had been no gray areas. You were polite and respectful and you did as you were told...or else. That discipline had worked okay for Luke. But then again, he remembered with a lurch of regret, there had been no hugs or spontaneous kisses in his childhood, and definitely no declarations of love. Even when he met and married Carly, swept away by the fire and passion of the young, she'd ended up accusing him of being cold and distant. In fact, during their final fight, when they'd broken up, she'd told him he was incapable of showing love and affection. Perhaps that was true. Perhaps that was why their marriage had been so short-lived; he'd never thought of it like that before.

Here, though, at Flight, he'd felt as if he finally belonged somewhere; he had people who cared for him and a job that really meant something. Now it felt like it was tumbling down around him and all his values were being questioned, by others and himself.

He watched Kat walk off with her head held

high. He wanted to look away but was somehow unable to. Her back was so straight, he noted, her legs in those jeans slim and yet shapely, and her shiny dark hair swung in time to her steps. She looked proud and so sure of herself. He could admit that he admired that trait, and yet it also drove him mad; she was way too inflexible in her beliefs.

Mel's voice interrupted his train of thought for the second time that evening. "Oh, there you are," she said. "Come on—you have a guitar to tune, remember?"

The sinking feeling in Luke's stomach worsened. Why had he agreed to this? It had been years since he'd played the guitar and he was sure to be terrible. "I don't think…" he began, but she just brushed his fears aside.

"Don't be daft. It's just a bit of fun. Others might even join in the singing."

Luke rolled his eyes. "Oh, no, not karaoke!"

"Probably for the best," she agreed with a grin. "Come inside—you can have a bit of a practice in the spare room."

CHAPTER THIRTEEN

BACK IN THE HOUSE, the party was in full swing. Wayne placed a large bowl of punch on the table and waved a silver ladle. "Help yourselves," he said. "And there's wine on the other table if you want it."

"I've brought some beers, too," Mike announced, struggling into the room with a large box in his arms. Several guests flocked around him to help.

Walking in on the revelry, still seething at Luke's comments, Kat poured herself a large glass of wine and took a gulp. "Steady on," said Tim Ellison, a broad smile belying his stern tone. "Oh, no, I forgot—it's a party."

"Sure is." Wayne butted in, laughing. "You only get to be fifty once in your life, you know."

"Try being my age," Tim groaned and everyone laughed. Kat smiled at him. She liked Tim; he was very strict and proper during school hours and the results he got with the children at Flight were phenomenal. Out of school, though, he was a very different person who liked to chat and socialize. His wife, Tilda, had died four years ago, according to Gwen, who seemed to know everything about everybody. After that he'd thrown himself into his work and shown no interest in meeting anyone else romantically.

He turned to speak to Kat again as she took another sip of her wine. "Ah, rebellious, eh?" he asked. "There are enough rebellious children around here already without the therapists joining in."

Kat laughed. "It's nice to see everyone outside of work, isn't it?" she said and he nodded.

"Too true. I'm lucky if I even get down to the pub for a couple of beers nowadays. The fish-and-chip van was wonderful, don't you think?"

"The kids loved it, too," she agreed. "It's a shame they couldn't have stayed a bit longer."

"I think we'd have had our hands full if they'd stayed any longer…or at least Gwen would have. She'd already lost Ben before they left."

"I'm afraid that was my fault," Kat admitted. "I persuaded Luke to get him some fish and chips and they ended up having a bit of a moment when Ben got stubborn about leaving."

Tim frowned. "Difficult situation, that. Between you and me, I was as surprised as anyone when it turned out Luke had a nine-year-old son. I wouldn't have pegged Luke as someone who shirked his responsibilities."

"Perhaps he didn't," Kat remarked, feeling strangely defensive of him.

"Oh, don't get me wrong—I've known Luke a long time. He's been good for Flight and he's a decent guy. I was surprised, that's all. As you said, though, he must have had his reasons."

"Speaking of Ben…"

"Yes?"

"Do you think he's doing okay? With his schoolwork I mean."

Tim frowned, looking thoughtful. "He's a bit behind," he said eventually. "But I think it's more a lack of attention than a lack of intelligence. Reading between the lines, I don't think he attended school much before he came here. At least not recently. That's another reason why his social workers decided it would be a good move to send him to a specialized school. It was actually his grandmother who insisted on Flight. Personally, I'm not sure that meeting his father in this situation was the right thing for either of them."

"That's probably true," Kat said. "Luke could have just visited him if he'd been at another school, gotten to know him gradually... If he'd wanted to, that is."

"Maybe that's why Ben's grandmother insisted on it," suggested Tim. "So that Luke *had* to spend time with him."

"What kind of man wouldn't want to acknowledge his own son, though?" Kat felt so sad—for Ben, of course, but also, in a strange way, for Luke. He must have lacked something in his life to be so cold.

"Perhaps Luke never knew he had a son," Tim mused.

She shrugged, trying to forget about Luke Travis and concentrate on Ben; he was the one who really mattered. "Either way, he's going to have to try very hard to make up for lost time, isn't he?" she said. "That little boy needs a dad and some stability in his life pretty quick or he'll end up with more problems than he already has."

"Oh, I don't know... In my experience, tough times can sometimes make children stronger and more resilient. It never fails to surprise me how they turn out."

Kat was reminded of her own childhood; it had been far from normal, by most people's standards, and she'd done okay…hadn't she? Yes, she was alone, but she'd always believed that was by choice. Could it instead be because she was incapable of sharing herself with anyone, unable to commit to another person?

"I guess we'll just have to see," she said, suddenly drained.

"Well, now that we've put the world to rights, so to speak, I suppose I'd better go and ask Mel if I can do anything useful. Nice talking to you, Kat."

Kat smiled. "Yes, it's good to have a chat outside of work."

"Even though that was really all we talked about." Tim chuckled.

"To be honest, there's not much else but Flight in my life right now," Kat said, thinking how pathetic that sounded.

"Hey," Tim objected. "You're at a party, aren't you? Go and have some fun."

Tim went to look for Mel, and Kat wandered through to the main living area. Someone was twanging on a guitar and Mel was waving her arms. "Quiet, please, everyone!"

The gabble of noise in the room faded and she reinforced her plea.

"Hey, just quiet down for a minute." Finally, she had everyone's attention. "I want to introduce you to tonight's entertainment. Give him a round of applause."

Behind her the guitar player began strumming a country-music song and everyone clapped and cheered. When Mel stood back to announce the performer, Kat froze.

"Our own Luke Travis," Mel cried. "He took some persuading, but…here he is, singing some country songs and other stuff."

"I'm not saying it'll be any good," said Luke, but everyone clapped again anyway, and with a broad smile he strummed a tentative chord, following it more confidently with a popular country tune.

Kat stood in the middle of the audience watching his every move; who would have thought that Luke could play the guitar?

"Country roads…" he began, his deep, mellow voice taking her by surprise. Without thinking, she stepped forward, eagerly listening. Around her, people began swaying to the music and she joined in, her gaze transfixed. When Luke looked up and caught her eyes, her heart started banging in her chest; she wanted to look away, to appear indifferent, but something wouldn't let her. And then he smiled a warm, friendly smile just for her and her cheeks started to burn. Still, she held his gaze until the music died. Only then did she turn abruptly away, melting into the crowd and feeling self-conscious.

Standing against a wall at the back as his guitar sprang to life again, she carried on listening to his deep, soulful voice, taking in the lyrics that tore at her heartstrings. When he eventually stood up, announcing that he needed a break, clapping and cheering filled the room. And suddenly there he was, right beside her.

"You were brilliant," she said on impulse, her eyes shining.

"Thanks," he said simply. "I'm glad you liked it. Do you want to get a drink?"

She nodded, not wanting to sound like a nervous teenager. "Yes…please."

She followed him to the kitchen, suddenly wondering if he just wanted another go at her about Ben.

He got himself a beer and handed her a

glass of sparkling wine. "Look," he said. "This is a party, so let's call a truce for now."

"Agreed," she responded happily, touching her glass to his bottle. "Not that I've actually fallen out with you anyway—as I remember, it was you who got angry with me."

He nodded. "Point taken. I guess you hit a nerve when you mentioned wanting to see Mollie."

"I was only looking out for Ben…"

"I know. The trouble is…"

"What? What's the trouble?"

"Oh, nothing," he said. "Let's not talk about it tonight."

"Good idea. Anyway, I enjoyed your performance. You were really good."

"Thanks. It's years since I played. I don't know how Mel managed to persuade me."

"I guess you three must be very good friends. And the work you put into that boat!"

Luke grimaced. "Wayne just has to learn to sail it now… To be honest, I worry…"

Kat waited for him to go on.

"It's probably stupid, but I can't help thinking that maybe a boat wasn't the best idea."

"Because of the young couple who disappeared?"

Luke blinked in surprise, then nodded.

"It was a shock, and it makes you stop and think. We all get a bit blasé about the sea, and something like that happening brings home to you just how dangerous the bay can be despite how tranquil and serene it can appear."

"And that's why you worry about my sea therapy?"

"In part, I suppose."

"I am trained, though, you know," Kat told him. "I know what I'm doing. Communicating with the forces of nature is good for the kids—it brings them down to earth, makes them understand what's real. Learning how powerful the sea can be—and learning their limits around it—is part of that."

"I totally get that, but there are quicksands here that can catch someone unaware, and the tide sweeps around the edge of the bay sometimes without you even noticing it. You can get into serious trouble in the blink of an eye."

Kat shivered. "I can't bear to think about that young couple… They seemed to be so in love."

"You saw them?"

She nodded, her face crumpling. "I watched them get into the boat and cast off. She was so vivacious, laughing at something he said, and he took her in his arms... Sorry, that sounds as if I'm some kind of voyeur. They just looked so happy."

Luke put his arm around her, giving her a comforting hug, and it felt so right.

"They must have had a big effect on you," he said. "They'll be fine, though, I'm sure." His lips were against her hair and his body, so close, felt warm and strong. "I didn't realize you were such a romantic."

"I'm not," she insisted, pulling away. "Or at least I didn't think so."

"Well, I am *definitely* not romantic," he said and the moment evaporated as quickly as it had come. He dropped his arm and she suddenly felt cold.

Taking a sip of his beer, he looked at her with sadness in his eyes. "Love is just... Well, it doesn't last."

"What about Mel and Wayne?" she asked, unable to help herself.

"Now, they," he said, smiling, "are the exception."

"If there's one exception to your belief, surely there must be others."

"Ah, so you are a romantic after all. Have you ever been in love?"

Luke's direct question took Kat so much

by surprise that she answered automatically. "No. Never. You must have been in love once, though...when you were married."

He shook his head. "That was a big mistake. I did believe I was in love, fleetingly, but it was a total disaster. It won't happen again."

Kat had never seen Luke in this mood, and it was an opportunity to find out more about the relationship between him and his son. "And Ben?" she asked boldly. "Where did he fit into all this?"

When Luke frowned, she realized she'd gone a step too far. "Sorry," she said, her tone subdued. "Your private life has nothing to do with me, but the more I know about Ben's situation, the better I'll be able to help him."

"No, my private life doesn't have anything to do with you," he said coldly. "Anyway, I'm off to do another set, so I'll see you around later."

"I'm actually on my way out," she responded, wondering if she'd just missed her one chance to break down Luke's walls.

As Kat followed the shoreline back to Cove Road, she couldn't keep Luke off her mind. Tonight, for the first time since they'd met, she'd felt kind of close to him. But he had obviously erected a barrier around his emotions that snapped back into place as soon as he realized he'd let his guard down.

Remembering the feel of Luke's arm around her, comforting her, his lips against her hair, she felt a sudden rush of longing. She did want a husband and a family of her own...eventually. If she ever fell in love, she would want it to be like Mel and Wayne, a love that stood the test of time. But the unexpected feelings she'd had for Luke tonight were definitely best avoided: for the sake of her career, her heart and, most of all, for Ben.

Taking a deep breath, she turned her face into the wind. Luke was right. Perhaps some people just weren't suited to being in love and would always be unable to give their hearts completely. After the childhoods they'd each had, perhaps neither of them knew how to deal with love. No matter; her work was enough. The children whose lives she helped try to sort out kept her heart full.

The tide was sweeping in, rushing around the bay as darkness fell, the water sparkling in the moonlight, so beautiful and yet so dangerous. Had the young couple in the boat stayed out until the moon lit up the sea and sky with its eerie light? Had they held each other close in the bobbing boat, unaware of the danger that surrounded them?

Scanning the shore and horizon in the vague hope of spotting a clue, she suddenly remembered the silver heart he'd found in the flotsam and jetsam. Perhaps that necklace had once been given with love. She needed to find it a really good home, and somehow she felt that home wasn't with her.

CHAPTER FOURTEEN

IT HAD BEEN TWO days since the party, and still no one had seen a sign of the lost couple. Hope was waning, and a deep sadness fell over Kat every time she walked along the shore. Today she was running another sea-therapy course, however, and she needed to put her emotions aside.

As she got ready, she spotted the silver heart and chain on her dresser, shining in the morning sunlight. On a whim, she picked it up and dropped it into her pocket before heading out the door.

She had an hour before she needed to be at Flight; plenty of time to take the route along the shore to see if anything interesting had washed up for the children to find.

Kat walked slowly, poking around in the long pile of rubbish left by the sea. Dead fish stared at her from plastic-looking eyes and a large crab sat alone on the sand, abandoned by the tide. Three little balls brought a dash of color to the debris, and she was surprised to find a small plastic horse; probably some child's precious toy, she thought, lost while playing on a beach somewhere. There were pieces of driftwood, too, in mysterious shapes, battered by the waves as they traveled from shore to shore. The children were going to be so excited by these treasures. They could spend time guessing where they might have come from.

Pleased with her finds, she felt in her pocket for the silver heart, then rubbed its smooth surface as she coiled up the chain. She drew it from her pocket and stared at it, trying to imagine where it came from, and imagining the delight if a child found it.

On impulse, she threw it into the flotsam and jetsam. The chain tangled around a piece of driftwood, glinting in the sunshine. If the necklace was meant to stay here, in Jenny Brown's Bay, one of the children would find it…and if not? It would be washed away by the next tide to find another home. And if by some chance the sea failed to take it, she decided, she'd know that it was meant to be hers. Pleased at her idea, she started to hum as she headed for the pathway up the cliff. All she had to do now was collect the children.

Kat arrived at Flight just after nine. Everyone was filing out of the morning assembly and heading in different directions, the teachers walking quickly and the children giggling and chattering like all children did...except for one.

Ben was the last to leave the auditorium, and Kat watched as he walked slowly into the hallway. "You okay, Ben?" she asked, trying not to make it sound like a big deal.

He nodded glumly, shoulders hunched.

"Are you looking forward to my class today?"

His deep brown eyes lit up a little, and he nodded. "I want to look in the flotsam and jet—jet..."

"Jetsam," she said, finishing for him.

"I want to look in the flotsam and jetsam for something really special," he said. "Like magic."

"Well, we can only try," she said, thinking happily about the little horse and the silver heart.

Ben shrugged, scowling. "Magic never happens to me."

"Maybe it will today," Kat told him. "Magic happens to everyone sometimes... It's just that we don't always notice it. You always have to be on the lookout. Come on. The others will be waiting for us."

Sure enough, when Kat and Ben arrived in the spacious entrance hall at the bottom of the sweeping staircase, the others were waiting impatiently. Little Tammy Nelson ran eagerly toward her, blue eyes bright with excitement. It warmed Kat's heart to see the little girl so enthusiastic. Even in the short weeks she'd been counseling her, she'd seen such a difference in Tammy's behavior. According to Mike, when the little girl first arrived at Flight six months earlier, she would barely communicate with anyone. It was Gwen, he said, who'd made a difference by taking her under her wing and including her in everything she did to make her feel like she belonged. All Kat had done was talk to Tammy, about life and love and laughter, filling her in on all the other children at Flight and helping her to build normal relationships. Now she was becoming quite outgoing and enthusiastic.

"Will we be able to go in the water, Miss?" she cried, grabbing Kat's hand. "Pleeeease?"

"We'll see," Kat promised. "As long as the sea is calm and no one tries to swim out too far."

"Like Ben did last time," nine-year-old Johnny Cartwright reminded them, glaring at Ben.

"That was last time," Kat said. "He knows better now…don't you, Ben? And I'll tell you all here and now—if there is any sign of squabbling or troublemaking, we'll all have to come back to school. And no fighting, Johnny. Remember, we don't do fights here."

"Don't like fighting no more," he responded and she smiled.

"Glad to hear it. You must be finally growing up."

He fell into step beside her as they headed down the steep path to the sea. Ben ran ahead with Tammy and Jack, an eight-year-old who was new at Flight and completely out of his comfort zone. "I'm pleased you've stopped fighting," she told Johnny. "And will you do me a favor?"

He looked up at her with pride in his eyes. "Sure, Miss."

"I wondered if you might help Ben to settle in here. I think he could do with a friend."

Johnny shrugged. "He doesn't like other kids and we all think he's weird. He never talks to anyone, and his dad actually works here but he doesn't even talk to him. I asked

Ben about it and he just said he doesn't know him and to shut up."

"All the more reason to make friends with him, Johnny. That sounds very lonely for Ben."

"Well, I don't have a dad, but if I did, I'd talk to him all the time. He's lucky."

"Everyone's lucky in some ways, and unlucky in others," Kat said. "And all you children are lucky to get to go to the sea today, so please be nice."

"Okay," he said cautiously. "I guess I can try."

By the time they reached Cove Road, Kat was pleased to see that the two boys were walking side by side. Johnny was doing all the talking, but at least it was a start.

The first thing Kat asked the children to do was look for living creatures that were native to the coast: crabs, fish stuck in rock pools, sandworms and shells. They were all amazed by the varied species, each busy in their own lives, doing what they were supposed to do in so many different ways.

"Like all of you, really," she explained now, sitting on some rocks with the children in a semicircle around her. "Each one of you is from a different kind of life in a different kind of place—none of them right or wrong. As long as you take pride in who *you* are, never be critical of other people and always try to be kind, you will go on to be someone very special."

As she spoke, the kids suddenly seemed distracted by something just over her left shoulder. Ben's expression hardened, and she knew at once who was there. "I didn't know you were attending my therapy course today," she said, turning.

"I was just passing," Luke responded. "I heard what you were saying to the children."

"And?"

"And it made a lot of sense."

"Oh…" She looked up at him, and he dropped down beside her.

"Just because I think some of your methods are dangerous doesn't mean that I disapprove of your reasons," he told her. He was close, too close, and all the children were watching expectantly…except for Ben.

"Having a good time, Ben?" Luke asked. The little boy just shrugged, refusing to meet his eyes.

Kat jumped up. "Right," she said, her voice forcedly bright. "Isn't it nice that Luke could join us, kids? Maybe he'll learn a thing or two."

"I'm going to be someone," Ben announced out of the blue. "Someone special." He glared at Luke. "You're not special."

Luke's jaw tightened and Kat's heart constricted, but before she could intervene, he cut in. "I agree, Ben," he said. "I'm not special… but I know you will be someone special one day—in fact, you already are."

Ben didn't reply but his whole face brightened.

"Come on," Kat said. "It's treasure time. We're going to look for treasure on the beach, and we'll try and guess where the things we've found have come from."

"Can I come?" asked Luke. He directed his question at Ben.

The boy hesitated then gave a little nod. "I guess so…if Miss doesn't mind."

"Do you mind, Miss?" asked Luke, with laughter in his eyes.

"No, as long as you stay quiet and behave yourself," she told him sternly.

The children ran along the beach and Kat kept her eyes on both them and the sea. The tide wasn't due in for a while, but there were always other hazards to address.

"Follow the flotsam-and-jetsam line," she called. "And don't go too fast or you might miss some treasures."

Luke strode beside her. "Do you really think they'll find anything? And shouldn't you tell them to be a bit more careful? There might be glass, or even jellyfish, washed up by the tide."

"I said that you could come along, not criticize," she responded, her hackles rising. "If you don't like it, go back to Flight. Ben might be your son but he's in my care today. And they will find some treasures if they look carefully. I've already checked it out."

"What, you mean you've planted things?"

"No, of course not. I just scouted them in advance."

Remembering the silver heart, Kat realized she was stretching the truth; it did come from the shore, though, so it wasn't really deceitful. She just hoped Ben would be the one to find it; he so wanted some magic to happen, and it would give him confidence to find such a treasure.

"How are you doing, kids?" she called, hurrying to catch up.

"Look, look, Miss!" shrieked Tammy. "It's a beautiful horse!"

Everyone flocked around to see what she'd found, and Kat took the opportunity to suggest to Ben that he investigate the unusual pieces of driftwood farther ahead. Preferring to be on his own, Ben charged off, with Luke following behind at a discreet distance.

"And I've got a red ball," Billy announced, throwing it up high into the air and neatly catching it. "I think it sailed here all the way from Spain."

"I've found a crab," cried Robbie.

"I think that's the first demonstration of enthusiasm Robbie's shown since he arrived here last week," Luke said.

Kat glanced at him in surprise. "I didn't think you had much to do with the children."

"Not with their therapy or schooling, but I'm always in on the discussions with Wayne, Tim and Mike. We meet two or three times a week. Since I'm kind of in the background, the kids don't take much notice of me, so I keep an eye on how they're behaving as I'm going about my usual jobs and report back if necessary. It doesn't work with Ben because he's too aware of me."

"Kind of like a secret spy," Kat said. "I'd never have known."

"It's got massive claws!" Jack was jumping up and down.

"Well done, Jack," she called. "Careful it doesn't nip you, though."

Luke went to take a look. "Don't worry," he said. "It won't be nipping anyone anytime soon."

"It's dead," Jack announced.

All the children, including Ben, raced over to see the dead crab, and Luke eventually suggested that they should put it back into the sea that was its home. "Like a funeral," he told them.

"You'll have to say a prayer," Ben said determinedly, looking directly at Luke as if it was some kind of test.

Luke picked up the crab, took it to the water's edge and placed it carefully into the rippling tide.

"Dear God, please bless and take care of this crab and let it rest in peace in the place it loves."

Kat caught Luke's eye. "Thanks," she murmured, unexpectedly moved by the little ceremony. When he smiled at her, his smile was slightly crooked; it made him seem more accessible, that imperfection.

After half an hour of foraging, all the children had found some special items ranging from the colored balls and the horse to sparkling stones and strangely shaped pieces of wood. Only Ben hadn't found anything of his own. On Kat's suggestion, he headed back yet again to look around the driftwood; hopefully, she thought, he would find the silver heart this time. He walked slowly, his shoulders hunched despondently. Kat didn't have favorites when it came to the kids, but Ben needed more help than some of the others. Luke was trying, there was no doubt about that, but the mistrust built up after years of absence undone in an instant. At least Ben was accepting his father's presence now.

Watching Luke shadow his son, Kat realized he still hadn't quite figured out what Ben needed. Instead of hanging back, Luke should try to join in the search, be his son's friend and earn his trust. Sometimes, it almost seemed as if Luke was afraid… Perhaps he was.

Her heart tightened. Luke acted so tough and strict, but maybe underneath that show of bravado he, too, was a lost and lonely little boy crying out to be loved.

Gathering the other children, she shepherded them along the shoreline. Eventually, they persuaded her to let them take off their shoes and wade into the rippling foam that swished up and back down into the sea again and again. The tide was slowly starting to come in, but the water was still shallow enough for safety.

"Miss!" Ben jogged over to her, waving the silver heart in the air. "Look what I've found! It's magic, like you said."

"I don't know how he did it," Luke announced, a broad smile lighting up his face. "But he appears to have struck silver…with help, perhaps?"

"Actually, no," Kat objected. "It really was washed up by the sea. Well done, Ben. Why don't we start guessing where everything came from while we have our lunch."

"He didn't help me, you know," Ben said, glaring at Luke. "I found it all by myself… If it's magic then it might bring Granddad back. I think I'll give it to him."

"Your granddad doesn't need magic," Luke told him firmly. "You found it and you should keep it."

Kat frowned but said nothing. Giving was good; it would make Ben feel useful and needed. She would have to try to make Luke understand that, but now was not the time.

"It's yours, Ben," she said. "What you do with it is up to you."

The other children were screaming with laughter as they ran in and out of the sea. "All right, kids," called Kat. "I've got some towels here. Get your shoes on and we'll go have lunch." Tammy and Jack ran back to where they'd left their shoes, well above the waterline, but Johnny was still knee-deep in water. When Kat called to him he started yelling, screaming that he was stuck.

Kat raced toward him, trying not to panic. "I can't get out," he cried. "The sand... I'm sinking!"

She dropped to her hands and knees the moment she reached him, clawing at the sand that had him trapped up to the ankles. Suddenly he pulled free, knocking her facedown in the foaming tide. She clambered up, pushing her hair back from her face, to find everyone laughing at her antics.

"So this is a part of your therapy, is it?" Luke asked.

"What do you think?" she responded.

He raised his eyebrows, making the most of the moment. "Well, you did kind of do the same thing last time," he remarked with laughter in his eyes.

Kat blushed. "A bit of water never harmed anyone," she said lightly, wishing Luke Travis was a million miles away. Oh, why did he always seem to see her at her worst…and why did she care?

She mustered as much authority as she could. "Okay, kids, you've all had a good giggle. Now let's go and get lunch."

Ben fell in beside her as they all trooped back to the patch of grass where they'd left their bags. "That wasn't very nice of Billy, was it, Miss," he said.

Kat looked down at him in surprise. "No, it wasn't very nice."

"Did you see my silver heart?"

"It's beautiful. You were very lucky to find it."

"Do you think I'll be able to go and give it to Granddad soon?"

Kat swallowed the lump in her throat. "No harm in trying," she said.

"We'll have to get Mike to sort it out," Luke said, catching up to them. "He's in charge of that kind of thing, visits and such."

Ben nodded eagerly. "Can I go tomorrow?"

"Well, perhaps not quite that soon…" Luke said.

A frown creased Luke's forehead, and he

pushed impatiently at the lock of hair that fell across his eyes. He seemed to be deciding what to say next. At least he was trying, Kat thought. Suddenly, he smiled. "Perhaps we could go see that bike on Saturday," he suggested.

Disappointment flickered across Luke's face when Ben looked up at her. "Can we?" he asked, tugging at her shirt.

"It's not my decision, Ben," she told him, feeling awkward.

"But you will come with us?"

"That's not my decision, either. I will if your dad wants me to."

For a moment, Luke looked at her and then he shrugged. "If that's what you want, Ben, I guess that's what we'll do."

CHAPTER FIFTEEN

KAT WOKE EARLY on Saturday morning, as dawn was peeping through her window. All night she'd tossed and turned, slipping in and out of sleep. Was she getting too involved with Ben? The question hounded her; she cared about all the children she counseled, but Ben had found a special place in her heart. Or was it his dad who was getting under her skin? Either way, she had to stay professional. She'd woken up several times, determined to back out of the trip to town, but Ben needed to build up a relationship with his father and today would be their chance to start bonding. Plus, she couldn't bear the thought of disappointing him, of being yet another adult to let him down. And that truly was her professional opinion, she told herself.

Besides, maybe Ben would open up to her more today about his granddad and let her in on what was at the root of his problems. If she knew the circumstances she could find a way to help him.

Rummaging through her wardrobe, she settled on skinny jeans, a bright blue T-shirt that brought out the color of her eyes and a pair of comfortable, open-backed sandals, before applying a touch of mascara and a pale pink lipstick. Not that what she looked like mattered. Today was all about Ben.

Luke had offered to pick her up at the end of Cove Road, and she was there at nine, fifteen minutes early. The sun was shining, making the whole bay sparkle right up to where it met the cool blue sky, but a blustery wind made Kat pull her jacket more closely around her, and she took shelter behind an old wooden shed.

The shed had a faded sign on the front that she hadn't noticed before—EMM'S. It reminded her of her landlord, Elsa May Malone Evans—EMM'S without the Evans. They must be her initials. What had she used it for? Kat wondered, peering through the grimy window.

The shed was larger inside than she'd expected, quite spacious in fact, and it had shelves all around as if it had been a shop. An idea began to form, vague but definitely hopeful. She put it aside to focus on later and ran across to Luke's blue pickup truck, which was just pulling in on the other side of the lane. Ben was waving excitedly, and Kat smiled in response, waving back; she'd never seen him so animated.

"Morning, boys," she called, thinking how nice it was to see them so relaxed together.

She scrambled into the passenger seat.

"Right, then," Luke said. "Let's get this show on the road."

"Show on the road?" Ben repeated solemnly, confusion in his eyes.

Kat spent the next few minutes trying to explain what the phrase meant, which broke the ice nicely.

"So where's this shop?" she asked. "And what color bike are you going to go for, Ben?"

He and Luke replied at the same time, and then laughed at the mistake. "It's in Kendal," Luke repeated.

"Red-and-silver," cried Ben for the second time. "Or blue."

"Or yellow or green or—"

Ben cut off Luke in midsentence. "No, not yellow or green. It has or be red or blue, with silver. I get to choose, right?"

Luke nodded. "Yes, it's your belated birthday present after all," Luke said. "It *was* your birthday just before you came to Flight, wasn't it?"

Ben nodded, suddenly forlorn. "Granddad forgot it…and Grandma forgot my present."

"Maybe she was just busy," suggested Kat.

"She's always busy," Ben said. "That's why she doesn't want me to live with her anymore."

"That's not true, Ben. She just thought it would be better for you to be at Flight so you could do things like sea therapy…and get to know your dad."

"No point. He'll probably leave, too, once he gets to know me."

"Like your granddad, you mean?"

Ben scowled. "No…that's different."

"I'm not going anywhere, Ben," Luke insisted. "You don't need to worry about that." He lightened his tone. "In fact, all you have to worry about right now is which bike you're going to choose. You can ride one, right?"

That seemed to lift Ben out of his dark mood. "Course I can—you'll see."

Luke parked in the center of town, outside the bank, and they headed down the street toward the bike shop. Kat found it strange to

be walking along with Luke and Ben, strange
and kind of awkward. At first, she trailed behind them, but when Ben kept looking back
she moved up alongside him, matching his
steps with hers, which made him smile.

The bicycle shop had an old-fashioned fa-
cade, but inside it was strictly modern, with
dozens of bikes on display. A middle-aged
man came over to help them and Luke asked
to see what they had in stock that might suit
a nine-year-old.

Ben said nothing, but Kat could tell he was
excited. He wriggled from foot to foot, as if
he could hardly believe that this was actually happening. She caught Luke's eye and
he winked, looking almost as excited as his
son. This could be a big step toward forming
a healthy father-son relationship, she thought,
feeling good inside.

As soon as the red-and-silver bike appeared,
it was obvious that nothing else would do. Ben
rode it in small circles around the store, grinning from ear to ear, and Luke pulled out his
credit card. "I think this will have to be a
Christmas *and* birthday present all rolled into
one. You're sure this is the one you want?"

"Yes!" Ben cried, holding on tight to the
handlebars. "It's brilliant." He stopped pedal-

ing and looked pointedly at Luke. "Is it for all the Christmases and birthdays you missed, or just for this year?"

Luke's jaw was set, but Kat could tell he wasn't sure how to react. She felt an unexpected lurch of sympathy for him. Everyone made mistakes in life and at least now he was trying to make amends. She just wished she could get rid of the horrible feeling that Ben was only putting up with his dad so he could get a bike. Luke seemed to be about to respond to Ben's jibe, but he turned away abruptly and headed for the counter, clutching his wallet. When Ben proudly pushed his new bike out of the shop while Luke settled up, Kat took the opportunity to talk to the boy in private.

"It's a beautiful bike," she said. "Aren't you going to say thank you to your dad?"

Ben shrugged. "You heard what he said. He's only buying it for me to make up for what he missed. It's to make him feel better, not me."

"Maybe it's for both of you," Kat suggested. "Why don't you give him a second chance? I'm sure he's very sorry about everything he's missed. And it won't hurt you to thank him. Remember what we talked about with the sea creatures? Being kind is part of becoming someone special. He is your dad, after all."

"My granddad's more like a real dad," Ben muttered. "Or at least he was."

"So what happened to him?" Kat asked, tired of skirting around the subject.

Deliberately ignoring her, Ben turned his attention to his bike just as Luke appeared, looking pleased with himself. "Please, Ben," Kat murmured. "Just keep an open mind and give him a chance to make it up to you."

"Suits him, doesn't it?" Luke said, standing back to admire the gleaming bicycle. "I hope you have fun with it…son." The word came out awkwardly "Right!" he announced in a loud, jovial voice. "Better get it back to the truck. You can't sit in the back with it, though, you know."

Kat cringed at his clumsy attempt at humor. Luke had done wrong by his son, no doubt about that, but he was trying so hard. Catching Ben's eye, she gave him what she hoped was a pleading look.

"Thanks," he mumbled, glancing up at Luke. "For the bike and stuff."

"That's okay," Luke responded, pleased. "The 'stuff' hasn't come yet, though."

She gave Ben a little nod to show her appreciation, and when his lips curved ever so slightly in response, she swore to herself that she would go and talk to Mollie Jackson as soon as possible.

On the way home, Ben kept turning to peer out the back window of the pickup to make sure that the bike was safe. Kat and Luke exchanged an amused glance. All in all, it had been a satisfying day. In fact, she didn't want it to end just yet.

Leaving the gray stone buildings of Kendal behind, Luke drove back toward Flight, but when they reached the coast he headed in the opposite direction. Kat was about to ask where they were going, but decided to go with the flow instead; it was kind of exciting, like a mystery tour. Still staring at his new bike through the back window, Ben didn't even notice in what direction they were traveling.

They drove in silence for a couple of miles along the coast, breathing in the fresh sea air through the open windows, taking in the amazing views. "It really is lovely here, isn't it?" Kat said with a satisfied sigh.

Luke nodded, glancing sideways at her before looking back at the road. "Nowhere better," he agreed, then made a hard left. Ahead of them was a large empty parking lot right next to a wide expanse of beach; he pulled in and cut the engine. "How about some practice time and some lunch? Maybe even a little splash if you'd like."

"What…here?" Ben asked as they all got out of the pickup.

"Why not?" Luke carefully lifted the bike from the back of the truck. "There's plenty of space, no people, and it's nice and smooth for cycling."

"It's beautiful here," Kat said. "But why is such a nice place so empty?"

Luke shrugged. "It never seems to get busy here, unless there's a school holiday. I suppose it's a bit off the beaten track."

Kat nodded. "You mentioned lunch, but I can't see a café anywhere near."

"Who needs a café or a fancy restaurant," Luke announced, lifting a box out of the back of the pickup, "when we have lunch right here."

"But aren't they expecting Ben back at Flight?" Kat asked.

Luke grinned. "I squared it with Mike. He said I could take Ben out for the day."

"Hey, Ben," Kat called. He was already

riding his bike around in circles. "Guess what—we're having a picnic!"

As Ben rode toward them, the expression on his face said it all.

"You can have half an hour's practice before we eat," Luke told him, then pulled out two plaid blankets. He spread them out beneath a stunted tree on a grassy bank between the parking area and the shore and urged Kat to sit. For a moment, she held back and he frowned. "I don't bite...honestly. Okay, so sometimes I get a bit worked up, but I have my reasons. And you're not always so easy to get along with yourself."

Kat sank down beside him, smiling. "Thanks, Luke. For today, it's just lovely to see Ben so happy for once."

"You look happy, too," he told her.

She nodded, meeting his gaze. "Seeing Ben this way makes me feel happy. I love it when children start to heal."

"And you think he's healing?"

"I know he is," she said, feeling a glow inside her at the hope on Luke's face. "I realize I said I didn't think bribery was the right approach, but getting him the bike was obviously a good idea. You do have a lot of making up to do, after all."

"Nine years," Luke said. "I have no idea if he'll ever totally forgive my neglect or even come to care about me, for that matter, but I have a duty to him…"

"Duty?" Kat's eyes narrowed. "Is that how you think of it? What about love?"

Luke leaned forward, an earnest expression on his face. "Of course I love Ben—he's my son. Look, Kat, I am trying, but I don't even know Ben yet—not really. I want to do the right thing and help him grow up into a well-adjusted, decent human being, but to be honest, I'm floundering a bit. All I know is that he needs discipline. It's how I was brought up, you see, to follow the rules set by my dad. Rules are what make you a better man, he always used to say. Following them defines who you are."

"And you believed him?"

"Well…yes, I guess."

Kat put a hand on his arm. "Don't get me wrong—rules and discipline are important, but they aren't everything. Try to be his friend as well—talk to him."

Luke held her gaze. "For what it's worth," he said, "I think you were right about the bike. I offered to buy it on a bit of a whim and then I regretted it because spoiling him isn't the answer."

"One bike in nine years is hardly spoiling him," Kat pointed out.

"It's not just me, though. He's been spoiled all his life and I need him to get past that. That's what his behavior is all about."

"How do you know? How do you truly know what his life has been like up to now? If he was spoiled, Flight will help him outgrow it. You need to let him learn to love you back, Luke."

Their faces were so close that Kat could feel his breath on her cheek. "That's just it," he murmured, his eyes soft with a vulnerability she'd never seen before. "What if he never forgives me and never grows to love me? Perhaps I've already lost my chance with him."

On impulse, Kat moved closer. Cupping his jaw with gentle fingers, she touched her lips to his, and when his arms closed around her it felt so right. He smelled fresh, like pine, with a spicy undertone; she breathed in his aroma, drawing it deep into her lungs, wanting...*needing* more. And when his lips closed over hers, so soft and yet fiercely demanding, for an endless moment it felt as if they were one being, a part of the vast space and beauty that surrounded them...

But they weren't alone. With a surge of guilt, Kat pulled away in panic, looking for Ben. What were they thinking?

To her relief, he was still riding happily around in large circles, totally focused on controlling his bike.

"Sorry," Luke said, reaching out to tuck a stray lock of hair behind her ear. "Bad timing."

Kat jumped back as if she'd been stung. "Bad timing? Don't you mean completely inappropriate?"

"Actually...no," he said, smiling. "I'm taking that *sorry* back. It was bad timing, but I'm definitely not sorry. In fact, I'd like to do it again."

"No, Luke. We can't. Ben has enough to deal with. The two of us together...would just complicate matters."

Luke frowned. "I guess you're right. I can't regret it, though. I don't know what you do to me, Kat. Our relationship is..."

"Hot and cold?" she suggested.

"Something like that," he agreed, his brown eyes sparkling. "It was just the timing that was inappropriate, though, not the kiss."

When he reached out one finger to stroke her cheek her whole body trembled. "Ben is the one we have to focus on," she said, pulling reluctantly away. "We can't do this… It's not right. He's got enough problems as it is."

"Okay, point taken," he agreed, jumping up. "Now, how about this picnic? Why don't you set it out and I'll go and see how Ben's doing."

Kat watched him walk off across the sand, his brown boots leaving deep footprints; he walked so confidently, so tall and straight and true. The vulnerability he'd revealed had been real, though, she was sure of that, and he did seem to be genuinely trying to build bridges with Ben, even though his priorities were slightly off.

But from a romantic perspective, Luke had to be off-limits. Any kind of relationship between them could compromise her position at Flight and hurt her reputation. How could she have acted on that sudden whim?

It was a risk she wouldn't take again.

CHAPTER SIXTEEN

BEN HAD GOTTEN up especially early that morning to go and polish his bike.

A rush of pride overcame him as he gazed at the gleaming metal one last time before he went for breakfast; until he came to Flight, he'd always had a bike of his own, but never one so big and shiny.

He spotted Luke as he came out of the bike shed and froze. Yesterday had been a good day, even though he knew Luke was trying to buy his friendship to make himself feel better. If he truly cared about him, he never would have left in the first place. Ben had overheard his granddad and grandma talking about how selfish his dad was and how he was better off without him.

That was ages ago, though, before his mum died and everything had started to go wrong. Maybe if Luke had been around, things would have stayed good and Granddad wouldn't have gone weird.

To Ben's dismay, Luke saw him and stopped walking, shading his eyes from the bright morning sunshine. "Morning," he called.

Ben wanted to shout "morning!" back, to smile and walk beside him, but fear held him back. Luke might have seemed nice yesterday, but had he meant it? Or would he leave, too, once he got bored?

What if...what if...what if?

"Checking on your bike?" Luke asked.

Ben tried to smile, he did, but words just didn't seem to want to come out of his mouth. In the end, he just nodded.

Luke took a few steps toward him and Ben wanted to run off. He didn't know what to say to the stranger who was his dad; everything was so strange.

"I hope you still like it…" Luke said.

Wishing Miss was there, Ben shrugged. "Guess so," he said. Miss helped him because that was what she did—she helped messed-up kids. He knew he was messed up because he'd heard the social workers talking about it when they didn't know he was there. He was good at hiding and he knew lots of things from listening.

Ben hoped Luke would just go away, but he didn't.

"We had a good time, though…didn't we?" Luke insisted. "Yesterday, I mean, going for the bike and the picnic?"

Ben shrugged again, feeling awkward and unsure. "I've got to go now," he said.

Luke's face tightened and Ben could see that he was getting cross. "I bought you a bike to try and make it up to you, show you that I cared," he said. "But obviously it was a waste of time because you don't even seem to appreciate it."

His cross voice made Ben feel angry, too; he felt angry a lot nowadays. "I don't have to talk to you just because you bought me a bike," he announced defiantly, glaring at Luke.

"No, you don't," Luke agreed. "But you do need to be polite. All children should learn to be polite and respectful—surely your grandparents taught you that, at least."

The mention of his grandparents pushed him over the edge. He missed how they used to be so badly, and he wanted to see his granddad. "I hate it here," he yelled. "I want to go home!"

He was about to run away, but Luke grabbed his arm. Ben didn't fight him, even though he wanted to; he just looked at the ground.

"Look, Ben," Luke said. "Despite what you might think of me, I really do want us to be friends. I am your dad, and I know I've let you down, but I want to try and make up for that…if you'll let me."

Ben looked up at him. He wanted to have a dad and he wanted to trust Luke, but he'd already gone away once. If even Ben's grand-dad, who had promised never to leave him, could go…what would stop Luke? "It's too late," he said.

Luke's face went very pale and he let go of Ben's arm. He walked away without looking back, and Ben was glad Luke couldn't see the tears that rolled down his cheeks. He needed a friend, but *what if…what if…what if?*

KAT WALKED EAGERLY toward the wooden shed at the end of Cove Road. Excitement fluttered inside her. Last night she had phoned Elsa to ask her about the possibility of renting it, and the result couldn't have been better. Elsa had told her that she'd once used it as a shop, selling items from the sea: shells, interesting pieces of driftwood and other items that she'd sourced elsewhere. She'd told Kat she could use it for free if she tidied it up after Kat explained her unique twist on child therapy.

"And if there's any merchandise left in there, you may as well have it for the sea-therapy course you were telling me about," Elsa had offered.

There was even a key for the shed hanging in the cottage, and today Kat was going to open it up and take a look inside.

The key felt stiff in the lock, but after a bit of effort, it turned and the door clicked open. Inside was a faint, musty smell and clouds of dust floated up when she started to poke around on the shelves, but she could see that all it needed was a good clean. Just as Elsa had suggested, a number of items had been left behind: unusual shells, sea-horse-shaped charms, a bracelet made up of silver fish all linked together and weird pieces of driftwood, some of them huge. Kat placed some of the smaller trinkets in a tote bag to take home and clean. If she was to use the place to house animals, it had to be suitable for them.

The front of the shed, where the shelves were, could be left as it was. She'd let the children put the treasures they'd found on the shore there, as a proper sea collection.

The other side of the shed was wide-open, a nice big space where she could put cages and make pens. Her animal-therapy course might finally get off the ground, she realized with a surge of anticipation…though she still had to get Mike's final approval.

Still, he'd said she could start with a few animals, and once she had the place spick-and-span she'd do a risk assessment to persuade Mike to sign off on bringing the children to visit.

Locking the door again and making a mental note to get something to spray into the partially seized lock, she headed back to Number Three Cove Cottages with the tote bag over her arm. This afternoon, she intended to try to contact Mollie Jackson. Mike might not approve, and Luke certainly didn't, but she didn't need their permission; therapists were allowed to contact the students' family members to discuss their treatment and progress.

Thinking about Ben took her mind straight back to yesterday at the beach. Back to Luke. Her cheeks burned as she remembered that kiss; how could she have let herself make such an unprofessional mistake? Well, it wouldn't happen again, and to be fair, Luke had been the perfect gentleman about it.

In fact, apart from feeling a bit awkward, she'd enjoyed the rest of their outing. Ben had loved the whole day; that was the main thing. On the way home he had chattered on and on about his bike.

It was only as they arrived back at Flight that he'd withdrawn, but when she'd asked what was wrong he'd refused to answer. Luke had been more insistent, telling Ben he was being rude, and that he would not put up with rudeness. That had only made Ben sulk, which had put a disappointing hitch in their otherwise productive outing. Hopefully, though, that negative moment hadn't detracted from the overall progress Ben and Luke had made in their relationship.

After Kat dropped off the sea items, she headed to Flight, partly to check on what therapy sessions she had the next day and partly in the hope of seeing Ben. Most of the kids were playing outside, groups of them spread across the grounds, making the most of the beautiful day. Of course, she realized, heading around the back of the main building, Ben would probably be in or around the bike shed giving his new acquisition a loving polish or maybe taking it out for a ride. She cut across the newly mowed lawn, breathing in the aroma of cut grass and thinking how fortunate she was to work in such a beautiful place. Her other option had been a smaller school farther inland. It had been a huge step for her to return to the sea, as it held so many sad memories of her childhood gone wrong, but it was a step she was so glad she'd taken…even with Luke Travis to contend with. Anyway, she was sure Luke wouldn't be a problem anymore. They'd had their "moment" and gotten past it, and it had helped them see just how much they each cared about doing what was right for Ben.

As she'd expected, Ben was in the bike shed, kneeling and rubbing his fenders with a large rag. When she entered, he looked up, smiling. "Hello."

"Hello," she replied. "Still like it?"

His smile broadened. "I love it and I'm going to ride it in a minute. You can watch if you like."

"Thanks. Is your dad coming to watch, too?"

Ignoring her, Ben went back to his polishing, proudly rubbing the already gleaming metal. It was nice to see him so animated.

"I'm glad you've settled in so well, Ben," she said. "You do like living here, don't you?"

Kat waited for a response, trying to appear casual about it.

Ben frowned. "It's all right…but I liked being at home better. Especially when Granddad was…there."

"So where's your granddad now?" she asked.

"Don't want to talk about it," he responded, going back to his bike.

"Is it far, your grandparents' house? Maybe I could take you for a visit."

"It's not very far. High House Farm in Arkholme. It's not really a farm anymore, though, just a house with a field and a big garden. Granddad used to like doing the garden. Will you really take me for a visit?"

"I'll talk to Mike about it," Kat promised. "So why doesn't your granddad do the garden anymore, if he used to love it so much?"

Ben ignored her question, so she changed the subject. Asking about his grandfather directly was getting her nowhere. "I'd really love to watch you ride your bike… After school tomorrow would be good, if that's okay. And, Ben, if I let you in on a secret, will you promise not to tell anyone else just yet?"

Ben's eyes lit up. "A secret?"

She nodded. "Yes, a good one."

"What is it?"

"Well…you know how we do the sea sessions, on the shore?"

"Yes…"

"I'm going to start another type of session soon. With animals. I think I've found somewhere to keep them."

"So where are they now…all your animals?" Ben asked eagerly. "Have you got lots of them?"

Kat shook her head. It was silly of her to talk about the animal therapy when she didn't have any actual animals yet. But she couldn't hold in her enthusiasm, and she told herself it would be good for Ben to have something to look forward to. "No, but I'm going to start looking for some now that I have a place to put them."

"Can I help?" Ben asked, and she took hold of both his hands.

"Of course you can. You can help care for them and you can learn about them…and play with them."

Ben tilted his head. "Will you have a dog?"

"Yes," Kat said, suddenly decided. "In fact, I think that might be the first animal I get. But the dog will live with me… Oh, and I have another idea, too."

"What—what is it?"

"I thought that I might take some of you mudlarking next weekend."

"Mudlarking," repeated Ben, frowning. "What's that?"

"Well, it's a bit like the sea sessions we've been doing. You know, searching for special things around the shore."

"In the flotsam and jetsam?"

"Yes, that's right, except with mudlarking you go down on the shore just as the tide's going out and search for things in the sand. Sometimes they've been there for years and when the sea goes out it pulls away some of the sand and reveals them."

"So why isn't it called sandlarking?" asked Ben.

Kat laughed. "I guess some of the sand seems pretty muddy. And people do it in rivers, too, where they have muddy banks. Perhaps that's where it started."

"Okay," he agreed, appearing excited by the prospect. "I'll have to ride my bike first, though."

"You could ride it down the path to the beach," suggested Kat. "With me, of course."

The bell rang, calling the children into the dining room. Ben pushed his cloth into his pocket, taking one final look at his bike before turning to her.

"I'd like to go mudlarking," he said with a broad grin. "And don't worry—I won't tell anyone about our animal secret, but you will show me the dog first, won't you?"

"Of course I will," she called as he ran off across the lawn.

Hopefully she would be able to talk to Mollie this evening and find out what was really troubling Ben. There was something that worried him, deep down, something he wouldn't face up to; she'd seen it too many times before to miss the signals.

Kat finished her preparation for Monday's therapy sessions around one thirty, and she almost bumped into Luke as she ran out the doors. Her heart jumped when she saw him, and when he smiled at her the breath caught in her throat.

"You heading home?" he asked. "Fancy a a coffee first? I could do with a chat about Ben."

She glanced at her watch. "Actually… I have an appointment."

He looked at her imploringly. "It'll only take a minute."

Kat hesitated. Though she was determined to keep their relationship professional, her reaction to running into him didn't bode well. The feelings she had for Luke weren't acceptable, and too much time spent in his company could be dangerous. This was her workplace, and for them to ever be more than colleagues would be both ethically fraught and unfair to Ben. He had enough confusion in his life already. Plus, she and Luke still didn't agree on anything, including her methods of therapy; when Luke found out that she was going ahead with her animal venture he wasn't going to be happy. Cozy chats with him definitely shouldn't be on her agenda, but they had agreed to work together for Ben's sake.

"Okay, just a few minutes," she said. "I'll skip the coffee, though, if you don't mind."

They walked over to a bench near the front gates and sat, so close and yet so far apart. Her whole body tingled with his nearness but her tone when she spoke was cool.

"So what can I help you with?" she asked,

acutely aware of the sunshine on the bright green of the grass. Beyond the cliff top she could hear the sea crashing against the rocks, and way above them a single gull shrieked out its lonely cry.

"I thought I was really getting somewhere yesterday," Luke sadly admitted. "But this morning I tried to have a chat with him and he was…well, surly and uncooperative. He needs to learn to be more polite."

"You're disappointed," Kat said. "I get that, but you knew it wouldn't be smooth sailing. Give him some time and stop worrying about discipline and manners. Ben's confused about lots of things, but yesterday he showed some real progress. That's still meaningful, even if he was withdrawn again today. And I intend to try and find out exactly what's going on in his head. It's what I do."

Luke related the basics of his conversation with Ben, and she could see he was hurting. She was about to offer more words of comfort, but when she opened her mouth, he raised his hand to stop her.

"I know you're going to tell me that I should have dealt with it differently, but I do feel that, no matter what, Ben still needs to learn to be civil and acquire some basic manners. All kids do. Once he sees the rewards and consequences for good and bad behavior—"

"If you already know what I think, why are you even telling me this?" she interrupted.

For a moment, Luke was silent, contemplating her question. "Because you are supposed to know kids," he eventually said. "And I want you to explain to me exactly why teaching basic manners and decent behavior has somehow become lost with modern therapy techniques. All you seem to want to do is pamper kids, not teach them how to behave so that they can learn to deal with life."

"Basic manners and decent behavior haven't been lost," she told him. "Kids develop them through love and respect, not force. Children have to have discipline, of course they do, but they also have to know that they are loved and cared for. They need security, Luke, and I think a lack of security is Ben's basic problem."

"But I told you what his background was like," Luke insisted. "Doting grandparents who I'm sure bought him literally anything he wanted and a lovely home with gardens to play in. How could that make him inse-cure?"

"Security, emotional security, isn't always about money and possessions, you know," Kat said. "It's about knowing someone is there for you, that you have stability in your life…and that you're loved. It helps children develop confidence in themselves, and with-out that, they can't grow."

Luke just stared at her, his face filled with confusion and doubt. "But what if I don't have the capacity to provide all that love and security? What if I'm not capable of being a good father…? What if I let him down?"

"Did your father let you down?" There, she'd said it, the question she'd pondered over again and again.

Luke glared at her. "You're trying to coun-sel me," he accused her. "This is about Ben, not me. Was *your* life perfect?"

Kat stayed quiet for a moment. She usu-ally tried to avoid talking about her past. But she had to give Luke something. She wanted desperately to help him understand what she was trying to say. His relationship with Ben depended on it.

"My mother committed suicide," she said eventually. "When I was fifteen. I went into care and I've never forgiven myself for not stopping it."

She bowed her head and on impulse Luke reached out and gently took her hand. When she didn't resist, he held it firmly. "And that's why you went into child therapy?"

"I guess… Maybe I thought I had something to offer because I've been there myself. Anyway, this isn't about me. It's about you…and Ben."

Luke looked out across the bay. When he spoke, his tone was reflective. "My dad was tough but fair—an army man. He lived by the rules. It was just me and him, and we muddled along okay."

"Look, Luke—" Kat placed her other hand over his. "Muddling along is sometimes what you need to do to survive. Nothing wrong with that. You didn't have control over it when you were a kid. But life isn't just about rules. You need to learn how to love and be loved…and I think you're afraid of it."

To her dismay, Luke's tanned face turned a deep shade of red. He dropped her hand and jumped to his feet. "I already told you not to counsel me," he snapped. "I'm not one of your protégés and I won't have you questioning my upbringing. Stick to what you're supposed to, if you even know how to do that."

As Kat watched him rush off, all she felt was sympathy. Luke doubted himself, but he'd never admit it—he was terrified of fatherhood and failing, simple as that. Blaming her was just his way of avoiding the real issues.

He wouldn't be able to build a strong relationship with Ben until he faced those demons, she thought sadly. But there was still something she could do to help Ben. Kat headed around the side of the school, hurrying toward the path so she could go home and pick up her car to visit Mollie Jackson.

"Kat!"

She turned in surprise.

Luke was coming toward her with a determined step. He stopped right in front of her. "I couldn't let you go without…well, apologizing, I guess."

"It's okay." She smiled. "I suppose I did overstep the mark a bit. I had no right to try and analyze you like that."

"You were a bit off with your opinions, but I suppose once a therapist, always a therapist. And you can't always get it right."

Kat knew full well that she *was* right but

decided to let his comments pass. "Truce, then," she said, holding out her hand.

"There is one more thing," he said, not taking her hand. Her heart fell at the tone of his voice. "I was going to tell you before, but…" He took a breath. "I think it would be a good idea to keep the children away from the shore for a while. The young couple you saw… They've found the boat."

For a moment, Kat felt as if the earth beneath her feet was rocking.

Luke frowned. "You okay?"

Blood pounded in her temples. "Have they found…anything else?"

"No, not yet. The boat could have just gone adrift, though, you know."

"Oh, I hope so," murmured Kat, thinking of the love and joy she'd seen as the young couple had boarded the boat and put out so happily to sea.

"Still, it's probably best to postpone your sea sessions for a while. Until… Well, you know what I mean."

Her eyes filled with tears as she grasped his insinuation. "That's an awful thought."

Her hand had fallen back to her side and Luke reached out and took it. "Don't worry," he urged. "It is just a precaution, that's all.

For all we know, they just dumped the boat and went off somewhere."

Kat looked up at him, her eyes brimming, and when he tightened his hold on her hand, drawing her toward him, she leaned her head against his chest as if it was the most natural thing in the world.

"Oh, Kat," he murmured. "You are such a difficult person to know. One minute you are judgmental and tough, and in the next you're loving and caring, especially to Ben, and now you're showing me an emotional side I would never have believed existed."

Warmth flowed between them. She raised her head to look up at him and couldn't look away. His eyes were a deep and fathomless brown. He placed his thumb and forefinger beneath her chin, tilting her face up toward his. She didn't resist when he drew her even closer.

"Who are you, Kat?" he whispered, peering into her eyes.

The world seemed to stop. There was no one but the two of them, and when his lips touched hers, soft and tender, she found herself wishing that things were different. If only they'd met in another time and place, she could well have fallen in love with Luke Travis.

BEN RAN UP the stairs to his room two at a time. All the kids were supposed to tidy their rooms on Sundays, and as soon as he was finished, he wanted to go and ride his bike around the grounds before tea. Gwen had told him it was all right as long as he promised not to go outside the front gates. He saw Luke and Kat from his bedroom window as he grabbed his jacket, and he pressed his face against the glass to watch them, his bike temporarily forgotten.

They were standing very close together and he could tell that Miss was upset; he wanted to open the window and yell at Luke to leave her alone, but he didn't. He just watched him put his arm around her, holding her close as she pressed her face against him. And when he leaned down to kiss Miss properly on the lips, and she let him, a red-hot anger bloomed inside him. He wasn't going to let this man, the man they said was his dad, take *his* friend away from him. It was Luke who had to go.

A plan formed in his mind as he burst out of his room and ran down the stairs. If Luke had nowhere to live, Ben decided, then he would *have* to leave. There were no more staff bedrooms for him to stay in; he'd heard Mike telling someone that just yesterday.

The plan was set.

He just needed the right materials to put it into action.

CHAPTER SEVENTEEN

LUKE COULDN'T SEEM to get Kat out of his head. The way she'd rested her face against his chest when he'd told her about the boat being found had touched him in a way that made his heart ache. And that kiss... He wasn't used to feeling emotional, and he didn't like losing control of his senses like that. He needed to focus on being professional when he was in her company; she was in charge of his son's mental stability, and Ben needed their full attention, with no complications.

Anyway, he mused, heading back into the house shortly after their encounter, they didn't even see eye to eye on most points... except for wanting the best for Ben. And even then, they disagreed on what *was* best for him. All this alternative therapy of hers was just a cop-out, as far as he could see, a modern fad, yet he admired her passion for it. She genuinely cared for the kids, too, and tried to help them adjust and interact with others so they would grow into confident adults.

And he couldn't pretend that he didn't find her attractive. When she smiled, her whole face lit up. He shouldn't have kissed her, though; it was stupid and irresponsible when he knew there was no future for them. Ben came first, and Luke wasn't prepared to compromise his son's future or their fragile relationship. Still, remembering her warmth as he held her close and the feel of her lips against his, he knew he could never regret that kiss.

He was still thinking about Kat when he walked toward the dining room and saw Ben coming down the stairs, alone as usual. It worried him that the boy was always on his own. "Going for tea?" he asked. Ben nodded.

"Mind if I join you?" When Ben just shrugged, Luke fell into step beside him. "Everything okay?"

The little boy gave him a sideways glance. "Miss is my friend, not yours."

"I know that, Ben," Luke responded quickly. "But can't I be your friend, too?"

"Guess so…but *she's* not your friend."

"You're right. She's my coworker and she

looks after you, so we like to talk about that," Luke explained.

"You kissed her!" Ben's face was flushed with anger and his voice rose an octave as he made his accusation.

Luke froze; this was the last thing he wanted. "She was upset," he explained, his mind working overtime. Ben must have seen them outside the school. Oh, how could they have been so careless? "I was trying to comfort her, that's all." He could see by Ben's face that he was having none of it.

"*You* must have upset her, then. What did you do?"

"No… It wasn't me." Luke decided to tell him the truth. "Do you remember people talking about the young couple who went out in a boat and disappeared?"

Ben nodded, frowning thoughtfully.

"Well, they found the boat and Kat was worried, that's all."

"Because they didn't find the people, you mean?"

"Yes…but I told her they probably just accidentally let the boat get loose, so it floated off into the sea on its own."

"Do you think that's true?"

As he held the boy's direct gaze, something inside Luke flipped over. This was his son, his flesh and blood, and he knew he would do anything to protect him. "I hope so, Ben," he said.

Seemingly content with his reply, Ben walked in silence and didn't object when Luke accompanied him into the dining room.

"I'll get a table if you go for some sandwiches and orange juice," he suggested in such a grown-up manner that it made Luke smile. Yet behind the flush of pride he felt for his son lurked a niggle of worry. Ben had been furious about him kissing Kat; why would he drop it so easily? Was there something else, something he'd missed…or had Ben simply accepted Luke's explanation? Guilt flooded him as he thought about that kiss. It must never happen again.

Piling sandwiches onto a plate, Luke precariously balanced two glasses of orange juice on the side and turned to see where Ben was sitting. The expression on the boy's face as their eyes met across the room was brooding, and Luke's heart sank. So Ben hadn't really forgiven him at all… But why would he pretend?

KAT RAN DOWN the path to Cove Cottages. Her heart beat hard in her chest and her calf muscles ached, but it was better than thinking about the young couple…lost in the sea. She stopped for breath down on the shore, looking out over the sparkling expanse of water as if expecting to see them. The bay looked so beautiful and serene now, a sleeping beast about to awaken as the tide came rushing in. They couldn't be drowned; they just couldn't be.

The more she stared out across the bay, the more convinced she became that they must have accidentally allowed the boat to drift off. She imagined them drinking cocktails in a bar somewhere much farther round the bay, watching in horror as their boat came unfastened from its mooring and sailed away without them. Perhaps they'd rented it and panicked when they'd discovered it was gone, leaving town so they wouldn't have to pay. That must be it, she decided; the young man had appeared way too confident and sure of what he was doing with the boat to be any kind of novice sailor. They were probably miles away by now, giggling at their exploits.

Feeling better, she went into the cottage for a quick wash and change. She would think about that kiss with Luke later; it was Ben she had to concentrate on now. And yet

Luke's words still came back to haunt her: *Who are you, Kat?* Did *she* even know who she was? Perhaps, like him, she was incapable of truly loving and committing herself to anyone.

Was that why the young couple in the boat had affected her so much? Because she was envious of what they had? No, that couldn't be right; she'd just seen something pure and real in them, that was all, and she couldn't bear to think of it ending in tragedy. Truth was, she would probably never know what happened to them, and she needed to put them out of her head.

Still, she couldn't ignore the obvious lesson in their disappearance: that when you have a chance at love, you should embrace it with open arms since you could never know what might be just around the corner.

Finally, Kat was on the road to Arkholme. As the miles rolled by and she left the coast behind, Kat found herself becoming more and more excited to see Mollie Jackson…and maybe even Jim. Luke was convinced that Ben's life had been perfect and he was just spoiled and uncontrollable, but she knew it was way more than that. She hoped this evening would give her insight that could lead to a breakthrough with the little boy.

After almost an hour, the sign loomed out at her, announcing that she'd arrived in Arkholme. It was just a village, clean and neat and well looked after with a village hall and a pub and some lovely country properties and farms. The village store was still open, she noticed, as she pulled over to park on the street. She went inside, hoping to ask about High House Farm. She had to wander the aisles for a few minutes before a woman appeared from a door at the back. Kat grabbed a loaf of bread and made her way to the counter.

"One twenty-five," said the woman, and Kat handed over her money.

"I don't suppose you've heard of High House Farm, have you?" she asked as she took her change.

"Why, yes." The woman smiled. "The Jacksons' place, you mean."

"You know them?"

"Well, Mollie mostly… She comes into the shop. Not quite as much these days, since her grandson went away to school. The place is on the market now. Oh, I guess you've come to view it."

Deciding not to correct the woman, Kat simply asked for directions. To her relief, the farm was less than a mile away.

"Perhaps we'll be seeing some more of you," the cashier said as Kat took her leave. She smiled politely, closing the door behind her.

High House Farm had its own private drive with impressive grounds and gardens, just as Luke had described. Kat drove slowly, taking in her surroundings and trying to decide what to say when she knocked and the front door opened.

As it happened, she had no need to knock because Mollie Jackson was in the garden on her hands and knees weeding a flower bed. She stood awkwardly when she saw the car pull up, leaning on the wall for support, her hands black with dirt. "I'm so sorry to disturb you," Kat said, climbing out.

Mollie shook her head and smiled. "I'm glad of an excuse to stop, to be honest," she said. "How can I help you?"

Kat decided to jump right in. "I'm from Ben's school. I'm his therapist, actually. It's probably a bit unconventional of me to come here like this, but I wanted to talk to you about him."

Mollie heaved a sigh. "You'd better come inside."

The house had obviously once been quite grand, but now it looked run-down and a little sad.

"It's for sale, you know," Mollie told her. "We can't afford such a big place anymore, and it's way too much for me to keep up with the housework." She threw out her arm to encompass the messy hallway. "As you can see. So how is Ben?"

Taken by surprise at her directness, Kat froze; what to say? "He's fine," she said simply. "I just want to try and understand him a bit better."

"I've been worried about him," Mollie said, her face puckering a little. "But I thought it would be better to just leave him to settle. He's been through enough and he needed some stability in his life. I thought if I visited or tried to be more involved, it would just make him homesick and unable to move forward. Come through into the kitchen and I'll brew a pot of tea."

Kat followed the diminutive older lady into a large, airy kitchen, where, dismissing her offer of help, Mollie pointed to a chair.

Kat sat, watching in silence as Mollie brewed tea and poured it into two china cups.

"We tried to give him the world when he was small," she said wearily, sitting down at the table. "But after—after Carly died, everything seemed to go so wrong. Jim took it bad. He made some mistakes, the business suffered and eventually we lost everything. I think Ben would have been fine if… Well, money isn't everything, is it?"

"What happened, Mollie?" Kat asked. "With Ben's granddad, I mean. It's troubling him. I know it is."

Mollie clasped her hands together, her shoulders trembling slightly. "They were very close, you see, like father and son, really. When Carly died, Jim took it hard, as I said. We both did. He started behaving oddly, seeming at times almost to resent Ben for being here when she wasn't, snapping at him for no reason or just ignoring him. They used to have so much fun together. After the business failed and the debtors started knocking on the door, Jim got worse. He shut himself off, sometimes hardly seeming to know us anymore, and I was too busy trying to keep everything together to see just how badly it was all affecting Ben.

"When the school called to say he'd been skipping class and going into town, I tried to talk to him, to explain that his granddad still loved him but he was suffering from something called depression, which was an illness that made him feel sad all the time. For some reason, though, Ben seemed to blame himself for the way his granddad had changed. He started behaving erratically, becoming withdrawn and awkward, and he used to cry about his granddad being sad. It was only recently, since just before Ben came to Flight, that I came to realize Jim's behavior was more than just the grief and depression we'd believed it was. And then I understood why he'd acted as he did with Ben…"

Kat placed her hand over Mollie's. "Go on."

"He had a dizzy spell and he seemed to temporarily lose the ability to speak. It was frightening. The doctor sent him to the hospital for tests, and they found he'd had a slight stroke, probably not the first. The doctor told me that his odd behavior over the last months was more likely the onset of dementia brought on by one or more mini-strokes than simply depression. He's become much worse in the past few weeks. His dementia is now quite advanced."

"And is he here still, with you?"

"I'm looking after him for as long as I'm able. He has carers and he's at the day care center today—he'll be back soon."

Suddenly, everything became clear to Kat. Ben's insecurity, his hostility and inability to trust anyone were all rooted in the fact that after his whole world had been turned upside down, the granddad he believed in had let him down. And as was quite common in such cases, Ben had seen his granddad's rejection of him as a failing in himself, as if he was unworthy of his love. His bad behavior was just a means of getting a reaction from his grandparents—any reaction was better than no reaction at all.

"I'm glad you told me," she said quietly.

"I'm sorry I didn't talk to you sooner," Mollie replied. "I just thought Jim had depression, you see. I thought he'd get past it and everything would be all right. I didn't realize how deeply it had affected Ben until it was too late."

Kat took hold of her hands. "Well, now we both understand him a little better. For what it's worth, I think it would be good for

Ben to see you. He has a present he wants to give his granddad. I'll explain Jim's illness to him, too. Maybe hearing that the way his granddad acted wasn't because he'd stopped loving him will help him accept everything better."

Mollie's face brightened. "You'll arrange for me to see him?"

"I'll speak to Mike—we do sometimes take the children for home visits, so it may be possible."

"And Ben's father… Is he looking out for him?"

"Luke is trying his best, but Ben does seem to have a problem with him."

"I think that could be my fault," Mollie admitted. "Carly never wanted him to know about his son, but I took it on myself to tell him. Luke wanted to spend time with Ben but I talked him out of it. Carly was annoyed that I'd even told him about Ben, but I thought it only right. As far as she was concerned, they were over, and she didn't want him around Ben. I know it might sound selfish, but that's how it was and Jim always backed Carly up. We told Ben he didn't have a father of his own, but that it didn't matter because his granddad was going to be like a dad to him. But then…"

She stared down at her hands, moving her stiff fingers, and Kat followed her gaze, taking in her swollen arthritic joints with a lurch of sympathy. Here was a woman who had had more than her share of heartache, and it wasn't over yet.

"Then his granddad let him down," she went on. "So how does Ben know his father won't do the same thing? As far as he's concerned, Luke never even wanted him in the first place."

"I'll try and make Ben understand," promised Kat. "Please try not to worry. You have enough on your plate."

As they said goodbye, she thought Mollie looked a little more relaxed, so Kat leaned down impulsively and kissed her cheek. "I hope you get a nice new place to live soon," she said. "Somewhere easier for you."

"It won't be that easy, though, even when we do find somewhere else," Mollie said, sighing. "Because then there'll be the chickens to get rid of…and April, of course."

Kat frowned. "How many chickens do you have…and who's April?"

"Six chickens. They all still lay, but not

as much as they used to. And April—April is a sheep."

"You have a sheep?" Kat cried. "What… a pet sheep?"

"Here…" Mollie beckoned for her to follow her around the back of the house. "I'll introduce you."

They crossed the yard and came upon an old stone building, crumbling slightly and in need of new windows.

They stepped inside. "They were stables at one time," Mollie explained, pointing out the rows of stalls. "They're mostly empty now, though."

She opened a small door near the end; it creaked in objection and a loud bleating burst out from behind it. When a small, white-faced sheep trotted out, Kat stepped forward to control it, but Mollie just smiled. "She won't go anywhere," she said. "Will you, April?"

The sheep nuzzled up to Kat, and when she rubbed the backs of her long ears, April lifted her head for more. "She's just like a pet dog!" Kat exclaimed.

"That's the trouble," Mollie said. "The kind of house we're looking to buy wouldn't have any room for April, and I can't just let her go anywhere."

It felt to Kat as if this was meant to be. "I'll take her," she said, suddenly sure.

Mollie's face lit up. "Really? Oh, that's such a relief. She's getting a bit boisterous for me to handle, to be honest. She almost pushed me over yesterday when I tried to put her back in. What will you do with her, though? You're not going to send her to market?"

"Of course not. I'm starting animal-therapy classes with the children, and she's perfect."

"So Ben will get to see her?"

"He can help take care of her."

Mollie's tone became wistful. "I got her for Ben last spring when she was just a few days old—in April, obviously. It was when his granddad first went into what his doctor told us was depression. Ben was upset about Jim's behavior, and I thought that maybe having a lamb to feed and care for might be a distraction."

"And was it?"

"Sadly, no, not really. He was struggling with the whole situation, and getting him to look after April ended up being harder than feeding her myself." She looked up at Kat, her eyes bright with unshed tears. "He's had a tough time, what with his mum and all the trouble with his granddad. Ben must have felt so alone… He'd had everything before that— love, attention and everything money could buy. Money can't buy everything, though, can it? It couldn't save Carly. Eventually sending Ben away just seemed like the best thing to do for him."

They'd already been over this, and Kat didn't want Mollie to dwell on the subject; she had so much on her plate already.

"I've offered to take April in, but what about the chickens?" Kat said, hoping to lighten the mood.

"What…you might take them, too?"

"I can take a look at them, at least…if you want me to."

"Of course! They're in the orchard. I'll show you."

The chickens were all hybrids, the reddish-brown variety popular for their regular laying and lovely brown eggs. They were scratching around in the orchard, but when they saw their two visitors they came rushing over.

"So they're quite tame," remarked Kat.

Mollie smiled. "They are my friends," she admitted. "Sometimes I sit on the bench over there and just tell them my problems. Does that sound mad?"

"It sounds sensible to me," Kat told her. "But are you sure you want to part with them?"

"I have to, I'm afraid. I'll miss them, but I'll be happy knowing they're with you and doing some good, maybe even for Ben."

Kat took her hand and shook it. "Then we have a deal. I just need a few days to get their quarters sorted."

"Perhaps I could come and see Ben and bring them with me," suggested Mollie. "If you really think that's the right thing to do."

"He'd love to see you—I know he would. I'll have a word with Mike. I'm not sure how you'll be able to transport a sheep and six chickens, though."

Mollie laughed. "Oh, don't worry—I won't be loading them. Our next-door neighbor is a retired farmer and he's always helping me out. He'll put them in my Land Rover and you can unload them when we get there."

"Sounds like a good plan," Kat agreed. "I'll get your number and call you when I'm ready for them—and when I've arranged something with Mike."

"Don't leave it too long," Mollie said. "And

please do organize that visit with Ben. I really miss him."

"I know you do, and don't worry—he really is doing okay."

CHAPTER EIGHTEEN

KAT'S VISIT TO Mollie had opened so many
new avenues to explore with Ben, she could
think of nothing else as she drove back to
Jenny Brown's Bay. How hard it must have
been for him when his whole world had been
in upheaval. He'd had to cope with the death
of his mum without the support of his granddad, the person he was closest to in the whole
world. Although Mollie had obviously tried
with him, she'd had too much on her plate to
deal with the little boy's needs.

She'd seen it so many times before, the
confusion children went through when the
person or people they trusted weren't there
for them when they needed them most. And
so often they dealt with their insecurity and
loneliness by acting out or becoming withdrawn. With Ben it seemed to be both; he
could swing from retreating into himself to
being loud and angry. As was often the case,
she'd found, many of these children consid-

ered any attention from a loved one to be better than no attention at all.

The Jacksons had been wrong to keep Ben away from his father; she was sure of that. It was selfish of them to want to keep him all to themselves; surely every child should have the opportunity to know both his or her parents, if it was possible. And it had been cruel to Luke, too, though she still thought he could have tried harder. If she'd been in his shoes she would have insisted on seeing her son. If Luke had been around when Carly was killed and when Jim's health and business had begun to suffer so badly, maybe he could have helped Ben understand what was happening.

Pulling up outside Cove Cottages, she cut the engine and sat in her car for a few moments, still deep in thought. It never failed to surprise her just how cruel a place the world could be. Take the young couple from the boat, for instance. Could fate really have stamped so hard on their dreams?

No...

She put the thought out of her head, refusing to allow herself to get emotional about something that probably hadn't even happened.

Ben needed her right now…and perhaps Luke did, too. There was something quite endearing about the way he was clumsily trying to form a bond with his son. She had to talk to him about the Jacksons' problems; he didn't have a clue what was going on with them. In fact, he'd been quite arrogant in his insistence that he was the only one who understood Ben's situation. It was about time that he faced up to his mistake in not fighting to be in his son's life, but she wasn't sure he could do that unless he had the full picture. Then maybe he would agree with her that Ben needed love, not discipline.

The sun sank lower in the sky, drifting down to meet the shimmering crimson sea. As Kat climbed out her car, she felt as if she was coming home. She'd try to speak to Luke tonight, she decided. He might not like the fact that she'd interfered and gone to visit Mollie without telling him, especially after their moment of closeness…and that kiss. That was his problem, though; this was about what was best for Ben, not Luke.

She got back in her car and turned it around, driving through the village toward Flight. With a vague feeling of foreboding, she pulled into the drive, more certain than ever that she had to talk to Luke as soon as possible.

The hallway was empty, and her shoes made a staccato sound on the gleaming wood. She looked around uneasily. The whole building seemed unusually still and silent. Normally, keeping down the noise of chattering children was the problem.

The sound of a television floated out from the main sitting room as she headed down the corridor, and she peered around the door to see several children watching a film. They all sat transfixed and she quietly withdrew, pleased to see Ben there. He was at the back of the room and sitting by himself, but he was obviously enjoying what appeared to be a *Harry Potter* film. He might still be a solitary little chap, but at least he was settling in.

Kat felt like taking him in her arms and telling him she understood what he was going through, but she knew that wasn't the answer. She needed to draw him out carefully and make him *want* to confide in her. That was what Luke needed to do with Ben, too. She hoped he'd understand how careful he had to be in his approach.

Gwen called out a hello from the laundry room as Kat passed and came bustling out with an armful of linens. "What are you doing here so late in the day?" she asked.

"I'm just looking for Luke," Kat said. "Have you seen him?"

Gwen smiled, rolling her eyes. "Looking for Luke, eh? Now, there's a surprise. I didn't think you two got on so well."

"We don't really," Kat replied quickly. "It's just business."

"Ah, business—so that's what they're calling it now."

Kat's mouth dropped open and heat crept into her cheeks. Gwen laughed. "Only kidding... I think he's in his apartment."

Luke answered her knock right away. His hair was damp, dark and curly from the shower and his face glowed.

"You should have told me you were coming," he said, awkwardly wrapping his robe more tightly around himself. "Is it important?"

"*I* think so," she responded, hovering impatiently in the doorway.

He stood back, holding the door wide. "I guess you'd better come in."

She hesitated. "This is bad timing, isn't it? Seems like you're about to go out."

"I was meeting a friend in the pub, but I can cancel. Is this about, you know…earlier?"

"No, no. I just wanted to talk to you about Ben."

He ran his hand through his hair. "What's he been up to now?"

"Nothing. I… Look, how about we meet up at mine tomorrow after work… Sevenish okay for you?"

"It's a date," he agreed. "I mean…well, not actually a date, but…"

Kat smiled. "I know what you mean. I'll make us something to eat—just a snack, nothing special."

He took a step toward her. "That would be nice. And, Kat, about this afternoon…you know, when you were upset and…"

Heat rushed into her face and she looked away, remembering the feel of his body against hers and suddenly longing for him to hold her again. "What about it?"

"Ben saw us."

"What? You mean…?"

"Yes, and he said you were his friend, not mine. He did also say he supposed I could be friends with him, too, but he seems to think I might steal your affections away from him."

"Poor Ben," murmured Kat. "He's so confused."

She almost told him then, about talking to Mollie, but she hesitated, unsure. It wasn't a conversation to rush—it would wait until tomorrow.

"Confused...in what way?" Luke asked, frowning.

She wanted to reach out and touch his face, to walk into his arms, rest her cheek on his shoulder and tell him all the things that were circling inside her head: her confusion about her feelings for him, Jim Jackson's dementia and how difficult all the repercussions had been for Ben to deal with, her excitement about April and the chickens. "See you at seven," she said, turning away to avoid the temptation.

"Kat..."

She looked back, excitement fluttering inside her like a trapped bird. "Yes?"

"See you tomorrow," he said and closed the door.

CHAPTER NINETEEN

KAT HAD BEEN up since dawn, clearing away garbage, sorting out all the items left behind in Elsa's shed shop and making plans for her animal-therapy course. She couldn't wait to get this venture off the ground, but if she was honest, she was also trying to fill her head with anything other than her "date" with Luke.

Last night she'd talked to Elsa on the phone, intending to keep her filled in on her plans, but she'd ended up confiding in the older woman about talking to Ben's grandma and agreeing to take on six chickens and a sheep—without giving away any private information, of course. Elsa had been more than helpful when it came to the animals; she'd suggested that Kat should use the small plot of land behind the shed for both April and the chickens; the dog she still had her heart set on would of course live with her in the cottage. All she needed now was a coop to go in the fenced-off area she'd earmarked as a run for the chickens. There was already a small shelter at the back of the shed that could house April if needed, and the plot was big enough for her to run around in. The area behind it had gone a bit wild, but Kat was sure April would soon sort out the long grass, or else she'd hire someone to mow it.

Full of enthusiasm, she dusted and cleaned and washed the floors, dreaming up plans for rabbits and other animals. She still intended to use the front of the old shop for the children's sea treasures, and the more items she uncovered from Elsa's hoard, the more excited she became.

It was almost eight when she stopped to look at her watch; she had only half an hour to wash, change and grab something to eat before she needed to set off for Flight. Kat hurriedly locked the door behind her with a warm sense of satisfaction before running down Cove Road to the cottage. One of her sessions this morning was with Ben, but she didn't intend to try to draw him out about his granddad until she'd spoken to Luke; it wouldn't be fair. She so wanted to make Ben see how much he was loved, by his grandmother and his dad…even his granddad.

She was certain his love was still there; it was just masked by the older man's illness. She'd make Ben see it, eventually, and then she could watch his confidence grow. That would be her reward.

As she got ready for the day, her "date" with Luke tonight preyed on her mind. It was just a meeting, but she was still kind of looking forward to it. Lately, she liked being around him. But she was nervous, too. How would he react when she owned up to visiting Mollie? Kat had been on the wrong side of Luke Travis's temper before and she hoped she wouldn't bear the brunt of it tonight. She'd get him to relax first, she decided, with food and chat, maybe even a glass of wine, and she'd just slip it into the conversation. *Oh, by the way, I forgot to mention I saw Mollie yesterday...*

The first part of Kat's morning flew by. She had a meeting with social workers about a new child who was due to come to the school in a couple of days, and she spent some time afterward filling in the relevant paperwork. Then she headed off for her session with a young girl she'd been counseling since she arrived at Flight.

As usual, Tara, a twelve-year-old with

mouse-brown hair and freckles, knocked tentatively on the open door, moving nervously from foot to foot, her fingers locked in front of her.

"Morning, Tara," called Kat, pretending to write something down. "Come on in and sit down." She'd found out that the less attention she paid to her, the more relaxed and outgoing the painfully shy girl became.

"Morning," whispered Tara.

Kat looked up at her, smiling. "Have you done the work we discussed last week?"

"Couldn't do it, Miss."

"Did you try?"

Tara's silence spoke volumes.

"Well, perhaps I can help you with it now," Kat suggested. "I'll start to show you how it goes and then it's your turn. Now, five things I either like about me or I am good at."

Kat chewed the end of her pen thoughtfully, looking down at the blank sheet of paper in front of her. "I see what you mean," she said. "Can you help me out here?"

"You're pretty," Tara suggested.

Kat laughed. "Thanks, but I can't put that down, can I? Even if I agreed with you. Tell you what I can put, though—I have a nice wide smile and I have very blue eyes. Now it's your turn."

"I…" she began falteringly. "I have nice long legs and—and…I'm kind."

"That's great, Tara. I agree with you—you are sweet and kind and generous. Look how you help all the younger children. No one is perfect, but we all have good things about us and we should be proud of them. We have things we don't like, too, but we can work on them."

"What bad things do you have, Miss?" Tara asked, her voice a few notches above a whisper now.

"Well," Kat began, choosing her answer carefully. "For a long time when I was young, like you, I had very little confidence in myself."

"But you're confident now," Tara declared.

"I've had to work very hard at it," Kat told her. "And studying to do child therapy helped. It was a bit like you with the younger children—by helping others, you help yourself, too."

Tara beamed. "I think I know how to do that exercise now, Miss. Can I take it with me and try again?"

"Of course you can. Oh, and let's add something else."

"What?"

"Write down five things that make you happy, too."

After Tara's session ended, Ben came into her office.

"Hello," she said when he walked in. He grinned in response.

"Hello… Can we still go mudlarking this weekend?"

"Of course we can," she promised. "Sunday probably—just you, me and maybe a couple of the younger ones…like Tammy."

"Can we have a picnic…or cake at your house again?"

"I don't see why n—" Kat trailed off as she remembered that Luke had advised her to keep the children away from the sea for now. She was about to tell Ben it might be better if they waited until another weekend, but realized that would only bring up questions or make Ben feel insecure. She didn't want to explain to him about the lost couple—who might not have even drowned, for all anyone knew—and she certainly didn't want him thinking yet another adult was breaking a promise. She would simply scout the area before they went out, she decided. Not that she expected to find any sign of the couple. They were probably miles away from Jenny Brown's Bay by now, going on with their lives. That was what she would continue to tell herself.

She cleared her throat. "We'll have cake at my house," she told him, hoping that the compromise would satisfy Luke's concern.

"And what about *him*—will he want to come?"

"Luke, you mean? Why? Do you want him to?"

Ben shrugged. "Don't care."

To Kat, that was a yes; it seemed their father-son relationship was starting to get somewhere. The problem was that she'd agreed to take Ben mudlarking when Luke had asked her to keep the children away from the shore. "I don't know if he'll be able to come this weekend," she said thoughtfully. If she happened to see Luke, she'd explain then, but she wouldn't deliberately seek him out. "But we'll have a good time."

After all, what right did Luke Travis have to tell her what to do? She'd been responsible about the trip and that was enough.

Ben grinned. "Yes, course we will. I might

find something else magic, like the silver heart, to give to my gran when I see her."

"You never know what you'll find," Kat said.

"Mike said that I could see her soon. You'll have to hurry up and get the animals so I can show them to her when she comes to visit. We used to have animals at home—a sheep and chickens."

"That's great," Kat told him. "If you're already used to looking after animals, you'll be such a great help."

Ben looked down at his hands, his shoulders slumped. "I didn't… I mean, I wasn't very good at it and…"

"And what?" Kat asked gently when he fell silent.

"And I didn't want to," he admitted. "My gran got cross about it, but I—I was glad."

"Why did you want to make your grandma cross, Ben?"

"Because she made me cross…because she made everything different."

"Sometimes things just change," Kat said. "And it isn't always someone's fault. Things can happen for no reason at all—bad things and good things. If it's something bad, we have to do our best to get through it. I'm sure your grandma was doing her best."

Kat kept her tone light and casual. For Ben to have let out even a small part of his thoughts was a real breakthrough, but she knew if she made a big deal of it, he might clam up again. "Anyway," she went on. "You can make it up to her now, if you want to."

"I wasn't very nice to Grandma," he said abruptly. "She got me a lamb to love when Granddad went...different, but I wouldn't look after it."

"And why do you think that was?" Kat asked quietly, afraid of pushing too hard.

"Because I was cross..."

"Why, Ben? What really made you cross?"

He looked up at her with his father's eyes, deep, fathomless, dark velvet brown. "Granddad wasn't Granddad anymore and Grandma didn't help me—even when I skipped school she didn't care. And then she sent me here."

Kat leaned toward him, placing her hand on his shoulder, drawing it away again when he tensed against her touch. "Your grandma sent you here because she cares about you." Her voice was as gentle as she could make it. "She was so busy looking after your granddad, and she knew that here at Flight, you'd have people to care for you properly."

Ben's face darkened. "You don't know that... You don't know anything about us. My grandma wouldn't have sent me away if she cared about me. And my dad wouldn't have left me if he cared about me."

"That's not true, Ben," Kat began tentatively. "Listen, I went to see your grandma and—"

Ben jumped up, his face pale and expressionless. "You saw her and you didn't bring me? That's not fair! I thought you were my friend, but you're not. You're just like all the rest. None of you care." He was shaking.

Kat's heart sank. She should have stuck to her plan not to tell him about Mollie quite yet. She should have anticipated this reaction. "No, Ben, I went because I *am* your friend. Your grandma told me how much she loves you and how bad she feels for letting you down. In fact..."

"In fact what?" Ben's tone was sulky, but his stance had relaxed a fraction.

"In fact," Kat went on, taking the plunge, "she asked me if I'd bring April here so that she'd remind you of home. And you can help look after her."

"April…" repeated Ben. "Coming here?"

"Yes, and the chickens, maybe. Think how proud your grandma and granddad would be if they knew you were taking care of April here."

Ben shook his head. "Granddad stopped talking to me. He was funny and sad and different."

Kat took both his hands in hers, and he didn't pull away. "Ben, your grandma and your granddad have had a hard time lately, that's all. Your granddad is sick. He can't help that, or the way he acted—his illness caused that. He still loves you very much. He just can't show it. Your grandma loves you, too, but she's had so many worries that she's forgotten to tell you lately."

"I wish I'd looked after April for her," Ben said, his voice little more than a whisper.

"Well, now perhaps you can," Kat said. "It'll be a second chance to show her that you can do it…that you want to help."

"And Granddad really can't help being like he is?"

"No, Ben, he really can't help it—he wants to tell you, deep inside."

"And you'll always be my friend, even if *he* tries to take you away?"

"I'll always be your friend, Ben, and no one will take me away."

The little boy's face brightened, as if a tiny ray of hope had lit him up from the inside, and it pulled at her heartstrings. Kat had never been the type to keep a clinical distance from the children she counseled, the way some of her peers could; she always got involved with the children she was helping. But this was different. She was becoming close to Ben. Would she have driven several hours to visit the grandmother of any other child in her care? She couldn't help wondering if her emotional attachment to Ben was tangled up in her feelings for Luke. Clearly, she needed to sort that out. She couldn't let an adult relationship affect her professional behavior.

"Anyway, young man," she announced in what she hoped was a neutral tone, "I think it must be almost time for your next class. What is it today?"

"Art," he said. "I like art."

"Excellent. Why don't you do some animal pictures for me and I can put them up on the wall?"

The broad grin on Ben's face as he walked toward the door said it all.

Kat smiled all the way home as she thought about the progress she'd made with Ben. It was strange how it worked sometimes, child therapy; you could go for weeks without seeming to get anywhere, and then suddenly there would be a breakthrough. He'd actually let her in at last. For a moment, her interference had seemed like a big mistake, but in the end, it had paid off.

She'd frame her conversation with Luke tonight in terms of Ben's progress. Maybe that would stop him from getting mad about her visit to the Jacksons' farm. But she would leave the news about the animals for another day; there was plenty of time for that after he'd taken in everything else.

BY SIX THIRTY Kat had a pizza ready to go into the oven, and she'd set a salad bowl and potato chips on the table next to an open bottle of wine, with two flutes waiting to be filled. She'd been on a high all day after her successful therapy sessions, but nerves had begun to prickle as the clock approached seven. Was it fear or anticipation that made her feel so wound up?

She poured herself a glass of wine and went out into the balmy summer's evening to sit on the bench outside the front door. Seven o'clock came and went and she breathed a sigh of relief; perhaps he wasn't coming.

Sunshine glittered on the sea as the evening sun hung in a golden globe above the bay. Way out she could see boats, tiny in the distance; they reminded her with a sweeping sadness of the two young lovers setting out in such high spirits, and she took a gulp of her wine.

"Started without me, eh?"

The sound of Luke's deep voice brought a rush of heat to her cheeks. "Oh!" she cried, startled. "I didn't hear you coming."

"You were miles away. Mind if I join you?"

She moved to get up. "I'll pour you a glass of wine."

He held out his hand to stop her. "No, don't worry. I'll help myself."

When he returned with a full glass and sat down next to her she glanced sideways at him; her mouth felt dry and a pulse beat in her throat when he held her gaze. Ridiculously, she couldn't look away.

"So…" he said. "Is this a social meeting or just business? You said you wanted to talk about Ben?"

Suddenly she found her voice as panic hit; did he think this was a date after all? "Business," she said too quickly.

He touched his glass to hers. "Are you sure about that?"

Kat stood abruptly. "Of course I'm sure. I promised you food, though, so why don't you sit and drink your wine while I go put the pizza in the oven."

"Don't tell me..." A smile lit up his handsome features and Kat soared out of her comfort zone. Her heart started to thud and all she could think of was the feel of his lips on hers. "Buffalo mozzarella and sun-dried tomatoes?"

"How did you know that?" she cried, laughter bubbling up.

Luke shrugged. "I guess you just strike me as a sun-dried-tomato kind of girl... Either that or I may have seen the box sticking out of the bin over there."

Kat laughed, hurriedly going across to push the box farther down and close the lid. "Let's eat first and discuss...business later," she suggested.

"Sounds good to me," Luke agreed. "And I guess by business you mean Ben?"

"Ben is my business, and I think today I've made a breakthrough."

He raised his eyebrows. "Sounds interesting."

"When we've eaten," she insisted, buying time. Somehow she couldn't imagine Luke being ecstatic about her visit to High House Farm, and for now, at least, she didn't want to break the mood.

When the pizza was ready, she called him inside. They sat on Kat's two-seater sofa, sipping wine and tucking into the food she'd set on the coffee table in front of them. After another glass of wine, Kat felt relaxed and much less worried about what she was about to tell Luke, or about the questions she had for him.

"So how come you never had much to do with Ben until now?" she asked, suddenly feeling bold.

Luke stayed silent for a moment, turning his glass around and around by the stem. "I was never given the opportunity," he told her, his voice thoughtful and somewhat sad. "I was married, briefly, but we split and she neglected to tell me she was pregnant. It was Mollie who told me eventually, but she asked me to stay away. She made it sound like the right thing to do, and I guess I didn't need much persuading."

"And you never even tried to see him?"

Kat's tone held a hint of criticism and Luke's jaw tightened.

"Sorry…" she said. "It's not my place."

He looked across at her, his brown eyes crinkling softly at the corners. "It's okay… As you said, Ben is your business, so I guess it does matter. Look…" He shifted closer, and she could feel his breath against her skin. "I messed up. I'm not proud of it. I guess I was afraid of fatherhood—still am, frankly—so what kind of a man does that make me?

"I did go to the house to see him once—he was in the garden with Carly and his grandparents. It was all so perfect that I couldn't bring myself to let them know I was there. I just watched from afar then walked away. I felt like a failure—what could I offer a child who had everything? Shortly after that, I got this job at Flight. I felt as if I was doing something worthwhile, finally, and I hoped that working with the children here would ease my guilt about Ben."

"So you did feel guilty?"

Luke's face fell. "What kind of man do you think I am? Of course I felt guilty. It hurt so much, knowing I had a son but that I'd walked out of his life. Never even walked into it, really."

He dropped his head into his hands. "I've failed him, Kat," he groaned. "I talked myself into believing he wouldn't want me in his life, that meeting me would confuse him, when all the time I was afraid, and now..."

"Now?" she murmured, turning toward him, longing to stroke the hair back from his face.

His voice trembled. "Now I've been given another chance, but I'm worried I'll never be able to make things right between us. I love him so much, Kat, and I'm so ashamed of the way I've handled everything." He moved closer, his eyes dark with emotion. "Will you help me try and make it work, Kat? Please."

Her response was instant, from the heart. "Of course—of course I will."

When he slowly lowered his lips toward hers, a shiver ran through her whole body and then she felt the warmth of them and her heart exploded. "Oh, Luke..."

His arms tightened around her, his body pressing close as his lips worked their magic, moving, exploring, invading her senses.

"No," she groaned, panicking at the depth of her own feelings.

He held her away from him but he didn't let her go. "This is right, Kat," he said, placing his lips gently to her forehead. "*We* are right."

She relaxed back into his arms, drowning in his closeness, wanting nothing more than this moment. "But what about Ben?" she asked.

Luke tensed. "Ben can't know about us... not yet. It wouldn't be fair. I talked him down when he saw us yesterday, but he was upset and confused. I don't want to risk that again."

"Us," she repeated, trying it on for size. "Is there really an *us*, Luke?"

"Maybe," he said sadly. He released her and stood, walking across to gaze out the window. "There are so many things stacked against us."

"Like my job, for one," she said. "And professionalism aside, being together could compromise Ben's recovery. That's the last thing either of us wants."

"His confidence and security has to come first," agreed Luke. "I need to focus on that relationship before I can even consider...us."

Feeling awkward, Kat started collecting

the plates and tidying up. There was something between them that they couldn't deny, an attraction that neither of them could resist. For a few moments, though, it had seemed like more than that and it had given her a glimpse of a part of herself she had never experienced before. A part of herself she had to try to keep contained if she didn't want to end up with a broken heart. Suddenly her hand slipped and the cup she was holding flew onto the floor, smashing into a thousand pieces.

Luke materialized beside her. "Leave that," he insisted, taking hold of her hand and drawing her toward the door. "Let's go outside to clear our heads and get back to…business. Ben, I mean—let's talk about Ben."

They sat on the bench outside, watching the sun slowly slip toward the horizon. "I made a breakthrough today," she said, knowing that she had to tell him. "Ben talked to me about his granddad. You know he has dementia?"

"Dementia? What, you mean the disease?"

Kat nodded. "I'm afraid so."

"And he told you this?"

She hesitated. "Well, no, not quite—he told me his granddad was… I'm sorry, Luke, but I went to see Mollie. I should have told you."

His whole body stiffened. "Too right you should have…and after I asked you not to!"

"I'm sorry. It just felt like something I had to do, and I knew what you'd say if I told you my plan. It was worth it, though. That's the main thing. If we'd known his situation from the start, maybe we could have better understood what Ben's been going through. He thought it was his fault that his granddad turned away from him, Luke—that he did something to make Jim stop loving him. He's hurting inside. Even his refusals to go to school were all about getting attention from his grandma."

"And Mollie told you all this? Why didn't she say anything before?"

"I think she was just as mixed up as everyone else," Kat said, lifting a shoulder. "She regrets how she treated Ben. She wants to visit him and I hoped you might help arrange it."

Luke frowned. "Are you sure about that? You don't usually take note of my suggestions," he said curtly.

"Luke…" Kat tried to get him to look at her, reeling at how quickly the atmosphere had changed. He seemed to stare straight through her. "I'm sorry I went behind your back by going to see Mollie, but I would do it again. I know it will help Ben, and that's my job. If you didn't work here, I might not have even told you about that conversation. Parents aren't always involved in my treatment of their children because—because very often they are the cause of the problems. It's results that count, Luke... The children count."

"So did you see Jim?" he asked. "And if not, how do you know Mollie was telling the truth?"

Kat shrugged. "She had no cause to lie. His doctor diagnosed him with depression after Carly died, but it was only later, when he had a dizzy spell and went in for tests, that they found out it was dementia. He'd had a couple of small strokes, they think... Look, why don't you go and talk to her yourself?"

Luke stood, staring at her for an endless moment, his expression fathomless. "I might just do that. Anyway, I'd better be off. No doubt I'll see you tomorrow."

"And you'll arrange a visit?"

"I'll speak to Ben first and see what he has to say."

He took off down Cove Road and Kat watched him go, a dull ache filling her heart. For a moment, she'd dared to imagine they really could be an *us*; how naive was that? He was handsome, even charming when he wanted to be, and there was something about him she found hard to resist. But he had let his son down. Did that make him selfish, or had he learned from his mistakes? He obviously regretted how he'd handled things in the past, and he was trying so hard to be a good father, but she couldn't let herself forget how narrow-minded he often was.

She noted how his hair lifted in the breeze, and she took in his gait, tall and strong and sure. Despite her determination to focus on all the reasons she shouldn't fall for Luke Travis, she was sharply reminded of his lips against hers, his tenderness when he held her. He was right to put space between them, she decided, because if she spent too much time with him the idea of an "us" would be too tempting.

And then she thought about her animal project and her sea therapy and knew she still had far too much to do here to be chased away from her goals by a man. She would do her part to keep their relationship professional and avoid social outings. Tomorrow she'd apologize; not that she needed to, but if they were to move on, they needed a fresh start.

LUKE STRODE HURRIEDLY along the pathway back to Flight. What was he thinking, he wondered, to have allowed Kat to get to him like that? What an idiot she must think he was… This wasn't the first time he'd been carried away by a beautiful woman. It had been a total disaster the first time, and now the stakes were much higher: he had a son to think about.

And for Kat to take it on herself to go see Mollie Jackson was unforgivable. It was his job, not hers. *So why didn't you?* asked an inner voice. Tomorrow, he decided, he'd have a proper chat with Ben…or maybe he *should* try to get the truth from Mollie…not that he really believed that she or Kat were making anything up.

He paused to look out over the bay. The sun was disappearing into the sea and leaving behind a glorious trail of golden light. It was so beautiful and serene that it brought a warm feeling back into his heart. Perhaps he'd been too harsh with Kat. Perhaps she did have Ben's best interests at heart. Rationally, he knew she wasn't trying to make him feel inadequate. But he felt that way all the same.

They needed to get their relationship back onto a professional footing, that was all, and limit their communications to what was best for Ben.

How hard could that be?

CHAPTER TWENTY

LUKE FELT NERVOUS as he tapped out Mollie's number; it rang over and over in his ears and he was just about to put the phone down when she answered.

"Hello—Mollie Jackson."

"I, er…" He struggled to find the right words. "It's me, Mollie. Luke."

"Is it Ben? Is he okay?"

"He's fine—don't worry. I just… Kat said she came to see you."

"Such a lovely young woman," Mollie said. "She's organizing a visit for me and Ben."

"No, I'm organizing it. That's why I've called. How about Sunday?"

"That would be great. Jim will be at the day care center."

"I'm sorry to hear about Jim," Luke said. "I mean, I knew he was ill, but…"

There was a slight tremble in Mollie's voice as she replied. "We didn't realize he'd had a slight stroke until recently. In fact, the consultant told us that he'd probably had more than one. We thought he had depression when all the time... All the time it was the dementia getting gradually worse. It was tough on Ben, and I let him down. It was all just too much."

"Things happen," Luke said. "I, of all people, should know that. You can only do what you think best."

"Like we did when Ben was born, you mean?" Mollie asked sadly.

There was a momentary silence on the line. "At least you're trying to make amends now," Luke eventually said. "I'll see you Sunday."

"Thank you. Oh, and please remind Kat about April and the chickens. I told her I'd bring them when I came to see Ben."

"April and the chickens?" he asked, confused.

"Ben's pet lamb," she explained. "Well, she's a sheep now, but she's still a pet. Kat is taking her and the chickens for her animal-therapy course."

"Don't worry," he said. "I will *definitely* remind her about that."

Since their evening at Number Three Cove Cottages, Luke had seen very little of Kat, which suited him because his feelings for her were confusing. They'd both agreed that Ben came first, but their kiss was still so fresh in his mind that it was hard to try to forget it. Despite his reservations, though, he needed to have a word with her today; Ben had told him that she was taking him mudlarking on the weekend. It was so typical of her to dismiss his advice about keeping the children away from the shore, as if she was the only one who knew best. Apart from the regular dangers of the sea, there was now the risk of a child coming across the bodies of the couple from the dinghy. Until they were found, it would be better for the children to stay off the beach.

He headed for the room where she held her counseling sessions. The door was open and he went straight in and sat down, glancing at his watch. Eight forty-five. He knew she started at nine, so he had only a few minutes to wait.

If Kat was surprised to see him when she came into the room, she didn't show it. She just unpacked her briefcase, placed her papers on the desk in a neat pile and sat down opposite him with a forced smile on her face. "Well," she said brightly. "I'm sorry, but you weren't on my list of appointments today. I have ten minutes to spare, so whatever it is, you'd better keep it brief."

Luke decided to come straight out with it. "I rang Mollie and I've set up a visit for Sunday. Oh, and she asked me to remind you about April and the chickens coming with her."

"Ah, yes." The corner of her mouth lifted. "Don't worry—they're not coming to the school. I'm keeping them in Elsa's shed, so it won't affect you. Some of the children—obviously Ben, in particular—can come and see them there if they want. It'll be fun," she said. "You'll see."

"And another thing…"

She rolled her eyes at him. "Go on. What's complaint number two?"

He crossed his arms over his chest. "It's the mudlarking."

"I told Ben we could go on Saturday, so Sunday's fine for Mollie's visit, if that's what you're worrying about."

"I'm not worried about that…"

"You're afraid we'll stumble across the bodies of the couple from the boat, aren't you?" she cut in.

"It's a possibility, isn't it?"

"No one knows what's happened to them."

"Exactly." He took a breath and tried to make his voice calm and reasonable. "Look, I know you don't want to believe they drowned, but it's just not worth the risk of one of the children stumbling across something horrible. They'd never feel the same about the sea again."

Kat met his gaze across the desk, and to his surprise, Luke saw her eyes were brimming with tears. One slid down her cheek and she brushed it away impatiently. "Sorry, you're right. I don't want to believe it," she admitted. "And you're right that it would upset any child to come across a body or any sign of a drowning. Let alone these children, who are already struggling with insecurity and trauma."

Luke's irritation faded and on impulse he reached over and covered her hand with his. "I know how you feel," he murmured. "But we have to do what's right for them."

She let out a heavy sigh. "Okay...point taken, but it doesn't mean I'm accepting that the young couple is gone."

"So you won't take the kids?"

"Of course I'm going to take them." When he scowled at her she managed a smile. "Eventually."

"Thanks for that."

"No problem," she said. "I get your point."

He stood up from his chair, hovering indecisively before resolving to get everything out. "For what it's worth, I'm sorry I didn't believe you about Ben's problems stemming from his granddad's illness."

Kat held his gaze. "And I'm sorry, too," she said. "For going behind your back."

He held out his hand and she reached across and took it. Her grip was firm and warm, and it took all his self-control not to pull her to him. "Truce?" he said.

"Truce," she agreed. "How many is that now...about ten?"

Luke laughed. "At least ten, I think."

BEN WASN'T HAPPY about the mudlarking being postponed. He went into a sulk when Kat told him, which she ignored, and then he apologized and she promised to take him as soon as she could.

"Tell you what," she began. "Why don't you ask one of the carers to bring you over to help me get ready for the animals? I'll have a word with Mike if you like, get him to sort it out."

Ben brightened. "April really is coming here?"

Kat smiled. "Yes, she is, on Sunday hopefully, with your grandma, and you can help look after her. She'd like that."

"And will *he* be helping?" Ben asked.

"If you mean your dad, then no…not as far as I know. But why don't you want him around? I thought you and Luke were getting along now."

Ben shrugged. "He gets on better with you than me." His face clouded. "I saw you kissing."

Kat froze as panic gripped her. "It was just a friendly kiss," she said. "I was sad, and your dad was comforting me."

"Because of the people in the boat?"

"Yes, but I was just being silly. I'm sure they're fine." She ruffled his hair. "So are we on? Will you help me?"

Ben nodded. "I guess."

To HER SURPRISE, when Kat asked Mike about Ben helping her get ready for the animals' arrival, he was less than enthusiastic. "I've been meaning to talk to you, Kat," he said. "You're doing a great job with the children here—I couldn't be happier with your results, but…"

She waited for him to go on, alarmed by his concerned expression.

"I've had complaints."

Kat's heart fell. "What do you mean? Complaints about what?"

"Some of the children have complained to me that you've made Ben your favorite. It's not good for them and it's not good for Ben, either. I've looked into it myself, and I'm sorry, Kat, but you really must distance yourself from the situation. You need to cool your relationship with Luke or your job will be at risk. We're dealing with vulnerable children here, and total professionalism is a must."

Kat was mortified. Mike was right. She'd become too attached to Ben. It wasn't all because of her feelings for Luke, though.

"I understand," she said. "And you're right. I've let Ben get under my skin and it is unprofessional. He's a lovely boy and I became overly invested in his care. I see that now. But you're wrong about Luke. There's nothing between us now."

"So there was?"

"No…not really. We are aware that Ben's

needs come first, and since Luke is his dad and I'm his therapist, then there can't be anything between us."

"You have to treat Ben the same as you would any other child, Kat."

"I know," she said. "And I will. It's just…"

Mike sighed and urged her to go on.

Kat explained her trip to the Jacksons' farm and what she'd found out about Ben's background, then brought up Mollie's impending visit and the animals scheduled to arrive on Sunday. She gave him an appealing look as she finished, but she could tell he was less than pleased.

"First of all, you should never have gone to visit Mollie without discussing it with me. There are procedures we have to follow, you know that—paperwork to fill out. You could seriously compromise your whole career, not to mention the reputation of this school, by behaving so impulsively."

When she tried to speak he raised his hand. "And secondly, you shouldn't have built up Ben's hopes about helping you prepare for the animals without consulting me. I'm not going to say he can't go now—that wouldn't be fair to him—but you have to invite a couple of the other children along and make it an official outing."

Kat nodded. "Fair enough. Thank you for that."

Mike nodded. "You're welcome, but I'm not doing it for you—it's for Ben's sake. And thirdly..." His stern expression softened. "I'm glad you've come to some conclusions about Ben. I'm not condoning your methods, and you will be in serious trouble if you do anything like this again, but I won't pretend the results, in this case, aren't positive. You will take on board what I've told you?"

"Yes, absolutely," Kat promised. "I care about this job and about Flight and I won't compromise it any more than I already have."

"There's one more thing," Mike said.

"Yes?"

"Has it occurred to you that getting too close to Ben is placing a wedge between him and his dad? I realize it's an unusual situation for a boarding school, but you're not being fair to Luke, either. Their relationship can't grow."

Kat felt as if he'd punched her in the stomach. She lived for her job and she liked to think she put her all into it. To risk losing her job or even be considered less than good at it was unbearable. And as determined as she was to be more professional, she did care for Luke and Ben. It pained her to think she was coming between them.

"I'm sorry, Mike," she said. "I'll do it differently from now on."

Mike nodded. "Good. This job of ours carries a huge responsibility, and I won't entertain anyone who isn't totally committed."

Kat left his office in a daze. Mike's straight-talking had been a shock, and it had left her feeling less than good about herself, but she was determined to take his advice. She'd become too personally attached to Ben and the attraction between her and Luke hadn't helped; she had to stay more focused.

KAT COLLECTED THE children from Flight after lunch on Saturday. Taking Mike's directive, she'd asked Tammy and Lucy Bell along, too, and the three children ran on ahead of her down the steep path to Cove Cottages.

Once in Elsa's shed, all three children threw themselves happily into cleaning up and helping get April's area ready, taking pride in shaking out sweet hay in the makeshift rack they'd set up and putting down sawdust on the stone floor of the inside area. Ben was particularly enthusiastic, Kat noted with satisfaction while making every effort to be equally encouraging with the others. She'd already started repairing the fence around the yard behind the shed, and together they finished it, then stood back in admiration of their work.

"The chicken coop's coming tomorrow," Kat said, her voice rising with an excitement that rubbed off on the children. "And a local electrician is going to set up some lights."

By the time they headed back to Flight it was almost time for tea. "We'll have to apologize to Gwen for being late," Kat said. "And look at the state of you all—you're filthy."

To her dismay, Luke was standing on the front steps as they approached. Her heart fell when she saw the expression on his face. "Before you start, Mike knows all about it," she began.

"But as usual, you neglected to inform me," he pointed out.

"Run inside and get your tea, children," she said. "And tell Gwen I'll be in in a minute."

"It wasn't like that, Luke," she told him when the children had disappeared. "I don't need to tell you every time I do a session with Ben. The kids were helping me get the shed ready for the animals. Mike said it would be okay."

"You could have at least mentioned it to me. Out of courtesy. When the mudlarking was called off, I invited Ben to go bike riding with me to make up for it. I even went out and bought myself a bike. We arranged to set off at one thirty..."

When she saw the disappointment in his eyes, Kat's annoyance drained away. "Oh, Luke, I'm so sorry. You should have said." She couldn't bring herself to tell him that Ben hadn't brought it up at all.

"I didn't know I needed to."

"You don't. It's just—"

"That my son would rather spend time with his therapist than with his own father?" Luke said, finishing her sentence. "Mike told me about your conversation, by the way."

"I'm sorry I messed up your plans, Luke, and I've taken Mike's guidance to heart. I don't want to come between you and Ben. We were getting Elsa's shed ready for April and the chickens. It was all official—risk assessments and everything. I wouldn't have scheduled it this afternoon if I'd known about your bike ride."

Luke sighed. "I'm sure it was aboveboard,

and I know you weren't aware of my arrangement with Ben. He should have let me know he wasn't going to meet me. Have you met Elsa, by the way?"

Luke's sudden change of direction threw Kat off balance. "Um, no, not yet. Why? Do you know her?"

"She lived in your cottage when I first came here. I used to walk along the shore and we'd sometimes chat."

"I've only spoken to her on the phone, but she seems nice."

Luke's expression softened. "She is—nice and kind and caring. One of the few people who really seem to listen to what you say. And she's had her own share of troubles."

"She has?" Kat asked. "Sorry, I'm being nosy—it's none of my business."

Luke shook his head. "No, she wouldn't mind you asking. In fact, she's the person who made me aware just how dangerous the sea can be."

That surprised Kat even more. "What do you mean?"

"Elsa's husband disappeared one day shortly after they were married. He was walking the dog on the shore when the tide came rushing in and a heavy mist came down at the same time. He was lost for a long time, believed dead."

A rush of emotion overtook Kat, to think that had happened while Elsa and her husband were living in her cottage. "He wasn't dead, though…and he came back?"

"He washed up somewhere else, miles down the coast, I guess, but he'd lost his memory after a blow to the head. When he finally came back to Jenny Brown's Bay trying to piece together his life, he found out that Elsa had had his baby years before."

"What an amazing story," cried Kat. "And that was Bryn…the artist?"

"That was Bryn, and I have never seen a couple more totally in tune and in love."

"I guess that's what we all aspire to…" She sighed. "Well, most of us."

"Not you, Kat? Why is that? What are you afraid of?"

In the act of trying to think up a good reason, Kat decided to simply tell the truth. "I'm not afraid. I just don't think I'm cut out for love and marriage and the whole family thing…not yet, anyway… After the mess my mother made of it, I can't see it working for me, either. I suppose I'm scared of messing up, too. All I know how to do is help children who've been through bad situations. How would I go about creating a home where those situations don't occur in the first place? My work is all I need—it's rewarding and I can focus on children who really need me."

"A little while ago we talked about how maybe there could be an 'us' one day," Luke said. "So you must want more, on some level."

"It was a moment of weakness," insisted Kat, her heart racing as he stared at her, his eyes narrowed. "I don't need complications in my life...and as for you and me—there is no you and me, and there never can be."

"Because of Ben?"

"Yes, but not just because of him. Like I said, it's because of me and what I want out of life. Anything we may have felt for each other was a mistake. Two lonely people, that's all."

"Okay, suits me," Luke said. "After my last brush with love and marriage I don't think it will ever be for me again, either. Oh, and by the way..."

"'By the way' what?" Kat asked.

"This animal thing, the sheep and the chickens—hasn't it occurred to you that reminding Ben about his previous life with his grandparents might not be the right way to go? Won't it make him more unsettled than he already is?"

"Well...no," Kat responded, taken aback by his opinion. "I thought it would be good for him, a bit of home comfort. Besides, it's not for Ben alone. The animal therapy is for all the children, and taking in the Jacksons' animals is a great opportunity."

"I realize that, but I want to forge a *new* life for him, with me, not encourage him to dwell on the past."

Kat's heart sank. Luke meant well, she knew he did, but he just didn't get it. "Oh, Luke..." Once again, it occurred to her that his son wasn't the only one who could use some counseling. "Can't you see? You have to let Ben keep his memories, not forget them. He can definitely forge a new life with you, but you have to embrace his past, too."

Luke's face turned a dull red. "I don't need your fancy speeches," he said quietly. "You may think you know everything, but who's to say you're always right?"

"Mollie got the sheep as a lamb, for Ben to take care of. She thought it might distract him from all the heartache and problems surrounding him."

"And your point is?"

"He wouldn't look after it at the time, and he feels he's let her down. Taking care of April now could be therapeutic for him, make him feel better about himself."

For a split second, Luke's face crumpled, revealing, before his expression closed up again, a glimpse of the lost little boy he once was. Kat felt the urge to put her arms around his big frame and hold him. She wanted so badly, she realized, to show him how to love and be loved. But it wasn't her place. Especially not with Ben in the picture. But how else would Luke learn to be the father his son needed?

He let out a long breath. "I see where you're coming from. But I want to be there when the animals arrive."

"Sure," Kat agreed. "Mollie's bringing them when she comes to visit Ben. You can help settle them in if you like."

"I'm not sure that Ben would be up for that."

"I would, though…and in my professional opinion, I think it's important for the two of you to spend time together."

"You just can't stop with the good advice, can you?" he groaned.

"Not when I know you need it," she said, ignoring his glare.

CHAPTER TWENTY-ONE

AFTER HIS CONVERSATION with Kat, Luke felt marginally better about missing his bike ride with Ben. Still, it irritated him that she always had to be so…right about everything, giving him lectures on what his own son needed. Although he wasn't a teacher or a therapist, he thought he'd been at Flight long enough to have at least half an idea about what made kids tick. Routine and discipline were big on the Flight agenda, so he knew he wasn't wrong about how important they were. Kat's approach confused him, though he had to admit her explanations often made sense once he thought about them.

In his world, as a young boy, discipline and routine had been everything. He couldn't remember a single instance when his dad had done something spontaneous; not even a hug. Yet Luke continued to appreciate how confident his upbringing had made him, the comfort in having everything mapped out, neatly planned and orderly. Routine and self-discipline had even helped him through tough times in his life, like those difficult years after his divorce.

If he was honest, though, hadn't those qualities also contributed to his marriage falling apart?

Carly had been so wild and free, and that had appealed to him, but it had also caused stress and arguments. She'd often accused him of being too rigid and inflexible, and he'd struggled with her carefree ways.

And later, when he found out about Ben… Maybe he'd been so afraid of how disruptive a child might be to his carefully constructed life that he'd copped out. Luke felt a hot wave of shame course through him. And now? He still believed in the value of discipline—that wouldn't change—but was he hiding behind it? Was he guilty of being too narrow-minded when it came to figuring out how to raise his son?

He needed to break the mold. He decided to do something spontaneous for a change; he'd go and see Wayne at home, on his new bike. He worked with him most days but it had been ages since they'd had a proper chat.

Freewheeling down the hill into the village, Luke felt totally refreshed; the wind in his face was brisk and sweet, seeming to blow away all the complications that filled his head.

He jumped off his bike and leaned it up against the wall outside the Whites' house. He found Wayne in the back garden having a beer in the sunshine. "On your own?" he asked.

Wayne looked around, startled, but he recovered quickly, smiled and handed Luke a bottle from the cooler beside his chair. "Mel's gone shopping, so who knows when she'll get back. To what do I owe this impromptu visit? It's not like you to just turn up."

"No reason," Luke said, popping off the bottle top and taking a swig of the golden liquid.

Wayne laughed. "You always have a reason."

"I guess I just wanted to talk. It's difficult at work."

"Don't tell me," groaned Wayne. "This must be about Ben…or Kat."

"Well, yes, in a way."

"And what way might that be?"

"It's complicated," Luke admitted. "Sometimes Kat and I get along okay, but generally our views contradict each other. I'm really trying with Ben, but this fatherhood thing is new to me and Kat always seems to interfere when I'm about to make some progress. For instance, I arranged a bike ride with Ben, but when I went to meet him I discovered that she'd taken him off to get some shed ready for a bunch of animals she's getting from his grandmother...not that she knew about the bike ride, but—"

"Hey," Wayne interrupted, putting up a hand. "Slow down a bit. I do know she's keen to start her animal therapy and Mike told me about the shed she's preparing, but this whole bike business sounds like a simple misunderstanding. Is it the animals you have a problem with?"

"Well, no...not really, as long as she keeps it safe. I mean, I respect her expertise and dedication to her job, and the children love her, but I think she lets them get away with a lot. We've had so many disagreements about discipline and routine. I think it's important and she doesn't. But she doesn't get to decide, does she? Those are important values here at Flight, aren't they?"

"Well, yes, but perhaps more *routine* than discipline, along with a large shot of love. A regular routine builds children's confidence, so they know they have something to rely on. So many of these kids have had very little stability in their lives. The discipline is just a part of that. But it's not one-size-fits-all. Different approaches work for different kids."

Luke ran a hand over his face. "Okay. But we disagreed about her getting the animals from Ben's grandmother as well. Kat believes it will do him good to have something from his past to hang on to his memories. Personally, I think he should be encouraged to move on and start afresh. How could it be helpful to dwell on the very time and place where his problems began?"

"Well, you can believe what you like," Wayne said thoughtfully. "But one thing I have learned here at Flight is that the general attitude of all the therapists and carers is to never let a child forget his or her roots, but to try and help them come to terms with the things that have gone wrong with their world and face their demons."

"It makes sense, coming from you," Luke admitted. "I guess that's kind of what she was trying to tell me. Maybe I owe her an apology... It's hard not to let my emotions get the better of me when it comes to Ben."

"Maybe your feelings for *her* are getting the better of you," Wayne suggested, raising his eyebrows.

"No." Luke's denial was quick...too quick. "I mean, we're just colleagues. And besides, any kind of relationship would compromise her position as Ben's therapist. He has to come first."

"Go and see her," Wayne urged him. "Ask her to explain her methods and the reasons behind them—after all, she is an expert. And, Luke?"

"Yes?"

"Try to actually listen to her. I don't want to sound too brutal, but...you are a slightly confused, amateur dad."

"Thanks for that," Luke said sarcastically.

Wayne leaned forward, an urgent expression on his face. "Just talk to her, tell her how you feel and try to come to some kind of common ground."

Luke stood, then drained his bottle and put it in the bin. "Thanks for your wise thoughts," he said. "Seriously. I'll see you at work on Monday. You have that appointment with the builder, remember."

"Glad you reminded me," Wayne said. "It had slipped my mind."

Luke headed for the gate but he stopped and turned when Wayne called him back. "What's up?"

"They found a body on the other side of the bay today. It hasn't been identified yet, but it's pretty obvious who it might be."

Luke's first thought was for Kat; had she heard this? Was she okay? "That's terrible," he said. "Such a waste."

"I know." Wayne nodded sadly. "It really brings home the dangers of sailing, when something like that happens on your doorstep. You can never underestimate the sea."

"So beautiful and yet so treacherous," Luke said, looking wistfully out across the bay at the smooth serenity of the resting sea.

KAT STAYED UP LATE that night, working in the shed. It was so rewarding to see everything coming together, and now it was finally finished, thanks to Ben and the other children.

Her heart lifted when she remembered how hard they'd worked. When an image of Luke's sad face sprang into her mind she felt a prickle of guilt; was she coming between him and his son, as Mike had suggested? The trouble was that Luke seemed almost as mixed up as his son, and that would never help with Ben's stability.

She was awakened the next morning by the echoing, lonely cries of the seagulls. She jumped out of bed and went to look out over the bay, watching the big white birds slowly circling in the clear blue sky. They sounded so desolate, and that seemed wrong in such a beautiful place. The sea sparkled with a million diamonds, the sand shimmering as the tide ran back out into the ocean. Were the happy young couple still out there, she wondered, lost beneath the waves, or were they laughing together somewhere about abandoning their boat?

A heavy sadness descended over her as she headed out of the cottage half an hour later. There was so much beauty in the world and yet so much despair and confusion, too.

She glanced at her watch; she still had plenty of time to walk the long way to Flight and stop at the village shop for a paper; there might be an update in it on the couple from the boat.

"Morning," called the small, cheerful-looking woman behind the counter when Kat walked in.

"Morning," Kat responded, smiling.

"Terrible news, isn't it?" The woman's tone was hushed, confidential with a hint of excitement.

Kat's heart tightened. "What news?"

"They've found a body on the other side of the bay."

"A body? Who—who is it?"

The woman leaned forward, lowering her voice as if she was worried about being overheard. "Well, I don't know if it's been identified yet, but it's pretty obvious, isn't it? They should never be allowed to rent boats out to people who don't know how to sail them."

"He seemed to know what to do to me," Kat objected.

The woman's eyes opened like saucers. "You knew them?"

She placed her paper on the counter and fumbled in her purse. "No, I just saw them casting off, that's all."

As she headed up the hill toward Flight with a weight on her heart, Kat couldn't get the images from her mind, of the two young people, so happy and in love. Was it better to steer clear of commitment and avoid the inevitable heartache that came with it, or to grab love by the horns and ride out the storm? That poor young couple might have had their lives cut short, but at least they'd had something. At least they'd known love.

Not wanting to have to talk to anyone, she walked straight around the back of the building to her counseling room. She was staring at the ground, grappling with her thoughts, when two broad hands grabbed her by the shoulders, stopping her dead in her tracks.

"Whoa there," Luke said, holding her firmly. Kat looked up in confusion, and understanding crossed his face. "You've heard, haven't you?" His voice was soft.

With a heavy sigh, she let her head fall forward, and he wrapped his arms tightly around her as if it was the most natural thing in the world.

"It's so unfair," she cried, her voice muffled against his shoulder. "They had their whole lives in front of them and…" Suddenly she looked up. "How do you know it isn't someone else?"

"No," Luke told her. "It's too big a coincidence."

"But it's so unfair."

"Life is often unfair," he said. "Think of all the kids who've ended up here. But we have to deal with it." And then he kissed her, a sweet, gentle kiss that brought tears to her eyes.

"You know we can't do this," she said, pulling away. "We agreed."

"Okay, point taken, but we do need to talk. That's why I came here." He waved toward the door to her counseling room and they stepped inside. "I want to hear you out. About Ben and your therapy methods. We keep disagreeing even when we say we're going to make an effort."

Kat peered at him, stunned by his openness. He was usually so much more confrontational. She nodded. "You're right. Our bickering isn't fair to Ben."

Luke raised one hand to stroke her cheek. "No, it isn't fair to him," he said sadly.

"We both want the same things for him," she said. "We just have different ideas on how to get there."

Suddenly he smiled, lightening the moment. "Well, we should try, at least, to work those out."

CHAPTER TWENTY-TWO

SUNDAY AT LAST! Ben clawed his way out of sleep, excitement fluttering inside him. It had felt as if the week was going to last forever. Every night when he got into bed he'd been trying to remember April; she'd been small and sweet and needy when Grandma brought her home...and he had been horrible. He'd been so mad at her, though...and with Granddad, too. But Miss had said that wasn't Ben's fault, or his granddad's.

Reaching beneath his pillow, he felt around for the silver heart he'd found in the flotsam and jetsam. He wrapped his fingers in the chain and wished that it really was magic— then maybe it would be able to make his granddad like he used to be. But if it couldn't do that, maybe it could make his grandma happy. She was always sad, although there was a time he vaguely remembered when she used to smile and laugh and have fun with him.

Miss had helped him understand some of that stuff in a way he hadn't thought about before. She didn't *tell* him, though, and that was why he listened. She just talked to him and let him decide for himself. He didn't feel so cross anymore…not all the time, anyway. And he was looking forward to seeing April again. He would do his best to look after her…and the chickens, too.

Today he was going to give his grandma the necklace, and he couldn't wait to see her. He hoped Miss was going to be there.

AFTER MUCH REFLECTION, Luke decided to suggest to Kat that she should be with him and Ben when Mollie arrived at Flight. He was sorry when she refused, telling Luke that he needed to see Ben's grandmother himself and have a proper talk with her alongside his son. And, as she explained, Mollie's neighbor had offered to deliver the animals, so she had to meet him. "You, Ben and Mollie can come along later and settle them in," she told him.

When Luke turned up on his own to pick up Ben, the boy scowled. "Where's Miss? I want her to come with me, not you."

Fighting off an initial surge of irritation, Luke smiled awkwardly, cuffing his son gently on the arm. "You'll be all right with me," he said. "Kat has to settle the animals in."

Ben grunted in acknowledgment. "Will I be able to go there right after?"

Luke nodded. "Yes, and your grandma will probably want to come, too."

"But not you?"

"Of course me. Why don't you want me to come along, Ben?"

"Miss is my friend, not yours."

The expression on the boy's face was so hostile that Luke felt a heavy sadness settle over him; would Ben ever accept him or was it too late? "She might be your friend, but I'm your dad," Luke reminded him. "Your own flesh and blood. Kat is just your therapist. This is an important day for our…family." The word felt foreign on his tongue, and heat crept up the back of his neck.

"She'll want me to see the animals, not you."

Ben glared at him and Luke's heart tightened; it was like looking into his own face. "You are my son, Ben," he said with a quiet ferocity in his voice. "And I'm always going to be here for you, whether you like it or not."

"No, you won't!" cried Ben, surprising

Luke. He was used to his son giving him the cold shoulder, but this emotional outburst was unexpected. "You weren't here before, so how do I know you'll stay? Everyone goes away eventually and I don't want you to be friends with Miss because you'll take her away from me, too."

"I promise never to take her away from you," Luke said. "I can't promise she'll always be there, but I will. I always will."

Ben shook his head fiercely. "She's my friend and I don't believe you."

Luke's mouth set into a firm line. "Come on," he said, striding off purposefully without looking back in the hope that Ben would follow him. With a flicker of guilt he remembered his anger when Kat had tried the same tactic on the shore. "We're going to be late."

Sure enough, when he arrived at the door to the small sitting room that had been set aside for them, the boy was right at his heels. "You ready for this?" he asked, and to his surprise, Ben reached up and clung to his jacket. Luke swallowed the lump in his throat. Covering the boy's small hand with his own, he pushed open the door.

Mollie looked tiny, sitting in a huge armchair. "Your hair's gone whiter, Grandma,"

Ben pointed out and she laughed, supporting herself on the chair arm as she stood.

"And you've grown taller," she responded. "Now come and give your old grandma a hug."

Ben hesitated for a moment before running across to throw his arms around her. "Oh, I've missed you," she told him, and he squeezed her tighter.

"Can I come home now?" he asked. "I'll be good."

"Oh, Benny boy," she murmured. "I only wish you could, but it's…"

Sensing Mollie's distress, Luke stepped in. "We're doing okay here, though, aren't we, Ben?" he said. "And now you're going to have April to keep you company, too."

For a second, Ben appeared unconvinced, but then his face brightened. "I've got you a present," he announced proudly, pulling a silver heart from his pocket. Luke recognized it from that day on the beach. "Perhaps it'll be like Aladdin's lamp and make everything better."

Mollie took the silver chain from him, holding out the heart and rubbing it gently with her thumb. "Oh, I hope so, Ben," she said quietly.

"So, if I make a wish, do you think it might come true?"

"Only if you don't tell anyone what you wished for," he said, his face tight and serious as he watched Mollie frown with concentration. "Have you done it yet?"

"I've done it," she told him, returning to the chair. "Now, why don't you sit here right beside me and tell me all about what you've been doing with yourself, and then we'll go see April and the chickens."

KAT STRAIGHTENED AND restraightened the sea items on the shelves before going to inspect the animal quarters one last time. The rack was full of sweet meadow hay for April, the chicken feeder bulged with golden corn, and the wire fence outside had been checked and double-checked. All she needed now were occupants.

The truck, a large, bright red pickup driven by a burly farmer, arrived twenty minutes later.

Kat stood at the ready, a huge smile on her face. "You must be Steve," she said, grabbing his broad hand and shaking it as soon as he opened his door.

"The very same," the man said. "Now, where do you want these critters?"

Steve led April into the enclosure first, and she was happily exploring her new pen, already chewing on the green meadow hay, when Mollie's car pulled up. Steve was in the midst of unloading the crates of chickens, so Luke hurried across to help him. Ben jumped out of the back seat, hardly able to contain his excitement.

"Why don't you go and see April," suggested Mollie. She leaned on her cane in obvious discomfort, and as soon as Ben disappeared into the shed, Kat went over to talk to her.

"Are you all right?" she asked.

Mollie smiled. "Just tired."

"Did you have a good chat with Ben?"

The old lady pulled the silver heart from her pocket. "He gave me this," she said. "He told me to rub it and make a wish, like Aladdin's lamp. If only real life worked like that."

"He found the silver heart in the flotsam and jetsam, so who knows what it is or where it came from… Perhaps he's right," Kat offered.

Mollie slipped it back into her pocket, a thoughtful, serious expression on her lined face.

"Is something else bothering you?" Kat asked.

Mollie placed a frail hand on her arm. "Look, I really appreciate all you have done for Ben, here at Flight—I wanted you to know that. But there's something else I need to talk to you about before I leave."

"Why don't we go see what they're up to, and I'll make you a nice cup of tea in my cottage after."

Mollie shook her head. "Oh, no, don't worry about that—they gave us tea and cakes at the school and I need to get back for… I'll just go in and see the animals and perhaps you and I can have a chat out here afterward."

"Sure," Kat said, suddenly jittery. It was the serious expression on Mollie's face, she supposed.

Seeing Ben play with April made Kat's heart hurt. He seemed so happy.

"She's a Masham," he declared, looking up at her with a broad smile. "That's why she's so small…right, Steve?"

The farmer nodded. "They're a small breed, Mashams."

"She's beautiful," Kat agreed. April must have made a real impression on Ben when she was a lamb, even if he'd refused to take care of her. The scene reconfirmed what Kat was already aware of: that what troubled children put out to the world was not necessarily what they were feeling inside.

"Can I name the chickens?" Ben asked eagerly as the mishmash of hens emerged cautiously from their crates.

"Course you can," Mollie said. "I picked them up from all over the place—that's why they're all so different."

"Perhaps you should get some of the other children to help you," Kat suggested.

"Well…they are Ben's chickens," Mollie reminded her.

"I'm going to call the two gray ones Cuckoo One and Cuckoo Two," Ben announced before Kat could say anything else.

Mollie smiled proudly. "That's clever. They're Cuckoo Marans, so you got that right…and the little brown-and-black one is a Welsummer."

When Ben went over to check out the rest of the chickens, Mollie turned to Kat. "It's so nice to see him like this," she said. "He was in a very dark and unmanageable place when I…when he came here."

"He still has his moments," Kat admitted. "But I can already tell that the animals will work wonders. Anyway, what was it you wanted to talk to me about?"

Kat followed Mollie back outside, sitting down beside her on a bench at the edge of the lane.

"The thing is," Mollie began slowly, as if searching for the right words. "As I said, I really appreciate all you have done with Ben, but no matter how much his behavior improves there is no way he can come back home to us."

Kat's stomach twisted painfully. She understood this was a possibility, of course, and Ben wouldn't be the first child she'd worked with who was unable to return to where he'd come from. But for some reason this hurt more than she was used to. "Why not?"

"My Jim is in a bad way," Mollie explained. "He takes up all my time…and my arthritis is rapidly getting worse. I know I'm never going to be able to take care of Ben again, and it's breaking my heart. So I want the next best thing for him, and that is his father. I want Luke to have full custody."

"And you've told Luke this?"

Mollie nodded. "I spoke to him earlier, and

I've had a long conversation with Ben, too… He thinks the world of you."

Kat nodded slowly. "He's a great boy and I'm only too pleased to be of help."

"He needs to develop his relationship with his father, though—properly bond with him, I mean."

"We're working on that," Kat said, alarm bells pinging.

Mollie hesitated and then she took a deep breath, as if determined to say her piece. "The thing is…after talking to him, and to Luke, it seems to me that as long as you are around, he is never going to accept Luke into his life."

"But I'm Ben's therapist," Kat cried. "And we get on so well… I've made so much headway."

"That's true," Mollie agreed. "But perhaps it would be better if he changed therapists… so that he can move on with his life and gain some security with his father."

Before Kat could respond, Ben raced out of the shed, reciting the names he'd settled on. "Rosie and Snowflake and Goldie—what do you think?"

"They're great names, Ben," Kat told him, sadness settling on her heart. Ben was doing much better than when he'd arrived, but he still had a way to go. Changing therapists could cause a huge setback.

KAT SPENT THE next few days stewing over Mollie's suggestion. She thought she'd made progress on stepping back into a more professional role with both Luke and Ben, encouraging them to bond. Surely Luke didn't want her out of Ben's life. She needed to talk to him, but the animals kept her busy and he'd made himself scarce since the weekend. She wondered if that was by design.

After April arrived, Ben had taken his responsibility toward her seriously, coming down to Elsa's shed as often as he could to see to her and the chickens. One of the carers or teachers would drop him off on their way home, and Kat would see him safely back to school. It worried her a little, after what both Mike and Mollie had said, to be spending so much time alone with Ben. But he still hadn't become very close with the other children, and he rarely brought a companion with him, despite her encouragement. Luke didn't object, though, and Ben seemed happy and grounded when he was feeding April or mucking out her stall, so Kat decided to let things lie for now.

To her surprise, Luke turned up at the shed the following Saturday. She'd seen him briefly at Flight over the course of the week, but their conversations had been brief and polite. Whenever Kat had tried to draw him into a deeper discussion, he had made an excuse.

"Hello," she said in a forcedly casual tone when he walked in the door. "Did you want to see me about something?"

He shook his head. "Not really. I just wondered how things were going."

"Good," she said. "Ben's doing great." She paused, realizing this was her moment to tell him what was on her mind. "Do you know what Mollie said to me?" she blurted. "Did it come from you?"

"Sit down," he urged, sitting beside her on the ancient wooden bench. He took hold of her hand, allowing it to rest in his lap. "We talked, Mollie and I, and she spoke to Ben, too, on her own. I didn't interfere."

"But you knew she was going to tell me I shouldn't be his therapist anymore, that I was holding Ben back from forging a proper bond with you?"

He nodded briefly. "Yes, and maybe that's true. I want what's best for Ben, and we need to get on the same page as soon as possible if this custody thing is going to work. When Mollie told me her plan...frankly, I was terrified. Still am." He took a deep breath. "What if I can't cope? But I was pleased, too. Kat, I want this to work so much. I know I have to step up, and part of that is making sure he gets the help he needs. I believe he needs you in his life for a little while longer." He looked into her eyes, picking up her other hand and gripping it tightly. "*I* need you in my life for a little while longer...or even a lot longer if I'm totally honest."

"Oh, Luke," she murmured, drawing closer despite her reservations. "You know we can't do this..."

He dropped her hands and stood up. "You're right. I'm just getting carried away by the moment."

"Maybe we should listen to Mollie, though," Kat said sadly. "Maybe I should take a step back. Not seeing Ben will be unbearable but doesn't that clarify the truth? I've become way too attached to him, I can see it now, and it isn't helping you, either."

Luke's reaction was sincere. "No, he needs

you, Kat. And how will he feel when he thinks you're letting him down, too? He'll never forgive you."

When Kat dropped her head into her hands, Luke placed a comforting palm on her shoulder.

"It's a chance I have to take," she said, looking up at him through tear-filled eyes. "Mike has already pointed out that it can't go on like this—I am way closer to Ben than I should be as his therapist. It clouds your professional judgment to get too close to a child—you start to think with your heart instead of your head. That was drilled into us at the very beginning of our training. But apart from that, my relationship with him is creating a wedge between the two of you, and that's not fair."

The door suddenly swung open and they both turned toward it in surprise. "Hello!" Ben called as he stepped inside, but the smile left his face when he saw his dad.

Kat noted Luke's discouraged expression.

"Hi, Ben," she said, keeping her tone light. "Your dad and I were just having a chat. Why don't you get to work on the chores in here, and he'll walk you back to Flight when you're done."

"No!" Ben snapped, his cheerful mood replaced by anger. "I want *you* to take me."

"But Luke's going that way, and it will be good for you to spend some time together. He wants to take you, Ben. In fact…" She glanced at Luke uncertainly, and the vulnerability on his face made up her mind. "In fact, I'm going to insist on it. Look, I need to talk to you about something, and I guess now is as good a time as any."

"What?" Ben asked sulkily.

Luke was shaking his head at her but Kat ignored him. "I love being your therapist. It's the job I'm trained to do, to help you—you know that, don't you, Ben?"

He shrugged. "Yeah…"

"Well, I just wanted you to know how pleased I am with how well you've been doing. So well, in fact, that before long you probably won't need me anymore…and I'll have other children who need my help."

"But you're my friend. *I* need you to look after me."

The expression on the boy's face pulled at Kat's heartstrings, but she knew she had to follow through, for Ben *and* Luke's sake. "I'll always be your friend, Ben, you know that, but what I'm trying to say is that you have your dad to look after you, too. He'll always be there for you, even if I can't be."

"I will, Ben. I promise you that," Luke insisted.

"And that's why the two of you need to become good friends," Kat added.

Ben's face was red. "I hate you!" he yelled. "Both of you! I want to go back to live with Grandma."

"Your grandma can't look after you right now, Ben," Kat said gently, longing to pull him into her arms. "And I'm not going anywhere right now anyway. I just wanted you to understand things. It's important for you to get to know your dad, to give him a chance."

For a moment, Ben just glared at her. "If you leave me, I'll hate you forever," he said in a dauntingly cold tone. He turned to Luke. "Come on…Luke. I want to go back to school now." Kat fought off tears as she watched them walk away, Ben a small replica of his dad. As soon as they disappeared from view, she gave in to the huge wave of misery that engulfed her. And then she made her decision.

WHEN SHE SAW the email waiting in her inbox, Kat froze. She'd regretted making her application ever since she'd sent it over two weeks ago, even though she knew deep down that it had been the right thing to do. Luke had thought her timing was wrong when she'd tried to explain to Ben that things might change eventually, but she'd wanted to and make him understand how important his dad was in his life…and always would be now.

She'd tried to talk to Ben again the next day, assuring him that she wasn't going anywhere just yet and that she would always be his friend. He came around a little, but she could sense his distrust. That, she realized, was the price she had to pay if he was to have a future with his dad.

She stared at the subject line, afraid of the message's contents, knowing it could change her life. She clicked it open and read it hurriedly.

Dear Ms. Molloy,
Further to your application for the position of child therapist at St. Mary's College, we would like to ask if you would be available to attend an interview at two thirty on the fourteenth of August. Please confirm this appointment by ringing Mr. P. Maguire at our office.

We look forward to your response.
Regards,
C. Downs

Would she go for the interview? She'd sent off her application on a whim after the scene in the shed. Staying here was not an option; she was the resident child therapist, and there was no one else. She thought the world of Ben, but he still needed counseling and her presence was holding him back from bonding with Luke.

Luke…

Being around him was tough, too. Kat knew they couldn't pursue a relationship but she couldn't resist him, which would inevitably put a strain on Ben if she stuck around.

Since the day she'd told him she might not be his therapist for much longer, Ben had come to care for April and the chickens less regularly and very often with another kid in tow. Kat had had little opportunity to speak to him and he hadn't turned up for his counseling sessions. When she'd checked in with Gwen about it, she said she'd given him permission to stay in his room because he wasn't feeling well. Kat didn't even know if he and Luke were getting along any better.

To her surprise, Luke turned up at her cottage around lunchtime; it was her day off, and she'd spent the morning cleaning out the chickens and making some improvements to April's outside area.

"Hi," he said awkwardly and she stood back from the door to let him in, motioning him through into the kitchen. He loomed against the sink, larger than life, and her heart skipped a beat.

"I wasn't expecting you."

"Don't sound too pleased to see me," he responded with a smile.

A flush colored her cheeks. "I didn't mean it like that. I've hardly seen you, that's all... How are things?"

Luke shrugged. "Put the kettle on and I'll fill you in. How are things with you anyway?"

"I'm applying for a new job," she said, turning away to fill the kettle at the sink.

He frowned. "Isn't that a bit extreme?"

"Not really." She pushed the plug into the outlet and switched it on before turning to look at him. "What other option do I have?"

"It shouldn't have to be like this, Kat," he groaned.

"It shouldn't, but it is. A little boy's future

depends on what we do now. Has he been better with you?"

Luke's warm smile made her feel better about her decision, though it made her heart break even more. "Oh, yes. It's still far from perfect, but he talks to me now, really talks to me."

"That's good," she said, meaning it.

"Kat… Don't you think leaving Flight is a bit extreme? Surely we can work something else out. Mike doesn't want to lose you—I know he doesn't."

"I've spoken to Mike about my decision, and, yes, you're right—he doesn't want to lose me, but he agrees it's probably for the best."

Luke stepped toward her. "And do you think it's for the best, honestly, deep down?"

"I think it's best for Ben."

"What about us?" he asked quietly. "Is it the best thing for us?"

"Could there ever really be an us?" she asked with a sudden rush of longing.

Their eyes met and the depth of the emotion in his made her gasp. He stepped toward her and his spicy, masculine aroma made her head swim.

"Perhaps," he said and his lips curved into

the crooked smile that was becoming so familiar to her. "Perhaps you moving away and getting a new job is the answer. We could still see each other, but it would be on neutral ground. And later, when Ben is more settled emotionally…who knows. At least we'd have a chance." He was standing so close to her that Kat could barely breathe. Could they make it work? The truth hit hard.

"Ben comes first," she said. "You need to have time together with no distractions. Give it six months or so, and then…"

"Then what?"

"Then…maybe," she told him, stepping into his arms just one more time.

For a moment, he simply held her, and she rested her face against his chest. His arms around her felt so safe and strong and warm that she never wanted to leave their embrace. They held on to each other as if they were drowning, consumed by an emotion that was way more than desire, an emotion that made her question her decision. Perhaps they didn't need to wait so long. It was that very question that made her pull away; she mustn't weaken; it wasn't fair.

"We can't do this, Luke," she said. "We have to stick to what's right."

"I know," he responded, touching his lips to hers.

She drew him closer, drowning in his kiss for a final, endless moment before stepping determinedly away. "Maybe one day," he said.

"Maybe," she promised.

CHAPTER TWENTY-THREE

BEN CHECKED OUTSIDE the front door—all clear. He didn't need to wait for someone to walk him down the pathway to Cove Cottages; he was perfectly capable of going by himself. He'd been mad with Miss for ages, but he missed the time he spent with her. Maybe if he did an extra good job cleaning up after the animals she'd still be his friend and want to keep on looking after him.

He walked quickly along the drive and through the gates, hoping no one would notice him. When he reached the steep pathway that ran from the cliff top to the bay below, he started to run, trying to control his flying legs while reciting the chickens' names in his head. It was hard to remember them all, and he didn't want Miss to think he'd forgotten already.

By the time he arrived at Cove Road his breath was coming in gasps and he slowed to a walk, suddenly uneasy. She might have gone out and left the shed locked up; he hadn't thought about that. What if he couldn't get in to see April? He'd have to sit on the step and wait until she came back. That wouldn't be so bad. Or perhaps he could go onto the beach and do some mudlarking all by himself, seeing as she hadn't kept her promise to take him yet.

He spotted Kat's car at the end of the row of cottages, covered in a film of sand from when the wind blew it in from the shore. It always seemed windy down on the shore; he liked that. He kicked up piles of sand into clouds as he walked toward her house.

The front door was open, so she must be home. He'd take her by surprise and make her jump, he decided. She'd laugh afterward because Miss was always laughing...or at least she always used to be, before he got angry with her.

He heard the hum of low voices as he peered around the door. Who was there?

Then he saw them and his whole world turned on its head.

They were staring at each other, Miss and... him. Ben wanted to shout at them, to tell him to leave her alone, but somehow he couldn't get any sound out. Suddenly *he* was holding her and kissing her and she was holding him back. They were together, like a couple, and there was no room for him. That was why Miss didn't want to be his friend anymore, Ben realized: she liked his dad better. Oh, how he wished his dad would go away forever. Then Miss would like him again.

He didn't remember running back to Flight. He just knew that he had to do something to stop them, something to make *him* go away. The good idea came into his head as he ran down the hall. He crept into the kitchen, sure of what he would do.

Alice was at the stove, stirring something in a pan. She glanced at him and smiled. "What are you up to?"

He shrugged and smiled back. "Just playing."

When she turned her attention back to her cooking, he seized his chance, grabbing the box of matches from the shelf in the corner and hiding them behind his back. Just in time.

"Are you playing all on your own?" she asked, looking back at him again.

"I'm going down to see to the animals soon," he said and fled out into the hallway.

When she didn't follow him, he started to breathe again.

His next piece of good luck came when he tried the door to Luke's room and it opened. He quickly spotted a waste bin full of paper. Perfect. If Luke had nowhere to live, he'd have to leave Flight.

The paper lit easily, flaring up satisfyingly into bright orange flames. For good measure, Ben used a chair to push the bin under the curtains. When the flames curled up the flowered fabric, starting to roar, he fled, afraid of what he'd done but still glad he'd done it.

The hallway was quiet as he slipped back into the main building through the door that connected to the annex, shutting it firmly behind him. The smell of burning filled the air, and he paused. What if the whole house caught fire? It was only Luke's room that he wanted to destroy; he hadn't thought about it spreading. What if someone got hurt?

In a panic, Ben started to run. He had to tell someone before the flames got too bad. "Help—there's a fire!" he yelled over and over.

The alarms began to scream so loud that he couldn't think. Smoke crept toward him, curling around his legs. His chest hurt, and it was hard to breathe…

Ben struggled down the corridor toward the entrance. Through the window, he saw the fire engines arrive in a melee of flashing blue light and noise. *He* was there, hollering his name. "Ben! Ben! Ben!"

He reached the doors, finally, and ran outside into the garden to hide, curling up under a bush on the damp earth, sucking in the great gasps of cool, fresh air.

It was a long time before it was over. The noises had just about died down when Luke found him. He just held him, squeezing him tight without saying anything at all. It was all kind of strange, as if it was happening to someone else. Then a fireman and a policeman came and took Ben into the front hallway where the fire hadn't reached.

"We know you took the matches, son. Tell us why you did it," said the policeman. Ben looked into his pale gray eyes and told him the truth.

"Miss said she couldn't look after me anymore because she might be going away, but I saw them and now I know she was lying."

"Why don't you just tell us exactly what you saw," the policeman suggested.

"They lied!" Ben shouted. "He's taking her away from me! They don't want me anymore, and I hate them both."

"But what did you actually see them doing, son?"

Ben huffed. How could he make them understand? "He was kissing her and she was kissing him back. So I had to make him go away. If his room's all burned then he'll have to live somewhere else."

"Oh, Ben…" Luke's voice sounded choked and his eyes were all wet. "I was saying goodbye to Miss, that's all."

The fireman gave him a stern look. "Well, your plan appears to have worked out—your dad's room is badly damaged and we've had to close that part of the school because of the smoke. You're lucky the fire didn't spread past the annex—and that no one got hurt."

Ben folded his arms across his chest, glaring at them all. The fireman didn't scare him. He was glad that Luke would have to go and live somewhere else.

He felt something else, though—a tiny prickle when he thought about Luke's voice calling him, or the fact that he'd just held him instead of telling him off.

Ben didn't like that feeling. It was strange

and uncomfortable. He reminded himself of what he'd seen. What he knew was the truth.

Miss and Luke loved each other.

And Ben had done what he had to do to make sure he'd never be left alone again.

CHAPTER TWENTY-FOUR

KAT HEADED TOWARD Mike's office, her heart thumping as she thought about what had happened in the last twenty-four hours. She had nothing to say in her defense; Ben had seen her and Luke kissing, so he'd gone and set fire to the school. And Mike had already given her a warning about being unprofessional.

On top of the consequences for her career, it was over with Luke. In fact, it had never even started. What had they been thinking? Maybe they hadn't been thinking at all.

She'd have to hand in her resignation, of course; she hoped St. Mary's would still consider her for their opening once word about this got out. Could she even ask Mike for a reference at this point?

Suddenly, the reality of leaving Flight, not only the school, but also Ben and Luke, overwhelmed her. She let out a gasp. Luke's face sprang into her mind, his soft brown eyes, his crooked smile…and his expression as he lowered his lips to hers. Maybe if she'd left sooner, she and Luke could have tried to be together. If she had stopped being Ben's therapist, kept her distance from Flight, could there have been an "us"? Now she'd never find out.

As far as Ben was concerned, she'd totally let him down, and this would be a huge setback for him. She didn't blame him for making the connections that he had; she could see how that kiss must have appeared to him, after she'd told him she wouldn't be looking after him for much longer. The bitter irony was that she'd made her choices to help Ben and Luke form a real father-son relationship. Now that would be harder than ever for them.

Mike was waiting impatiently, his disappointment obvious. He launched into his tirade as soon as she sat down, and all Kat could do was put up with it. Every word was true.

"So?" he asked eventually, his face closed and stern. "What do you have to say?"

Kat hesitated. "I'd say…that you have every right to be angry with me. I'm ashamed that it has come to this. You knew, of course, that I was thinking of leaving—to give Ben and

Luke a chance—and now I guess I'll have to speed things up a bit."

"And where do you stand with Luke? You do realize that this has been traumatic for Ben?"

"Of course I do," Kat cried. "And there is no 'me and Luke'—we've already hurt Ben too much. I have an interview at St. Mary's College, to teach in their child-therapy program. I know I can't expect a glowing reference from you, but—"

Mike held up his hand. "For what it's worth, Kat, I'm sorry that this had to happen. You are a good therapist but you got distracted from what was right. You behaved unprofessionally, but in your defense…in your defense, it was only human. If you're not planning on working directly with children for a while, I won't do anything to hold back your career."

"Thanks, Mike," Kat said. "And I'm sorry, too. I've loved my time here and I was really looking forward to doing my animal-therapy classes."

"Will you stay at Cove Cottages?"

"I—I hadn't thought that far ahead," Kat said. St. Mary's wasn't too far from Jenny Brown's Bay, but the idea of staying so close to Luke and Ben was acutely painful. "Anyway, I'll give you fair notice. One month, isn't it? I guess you'll want it in writing?"

"Yes, thanks," Mike said. "But for Ben's sake I think it would be better if you wrapped things up here by the end of the week. Oh, and one other thing, Kat…"

"Yes?"

"It might be best if you brought the sheep and the chickens to Flight. It would be good for Ben to keep on helping with their care, and the other children seem enthusiastic about the animals, too. I thought the small paddock at the back of the buildings might be suitable—there's a shed that just needs a bit of cleaning up."

The idea of the animal therapy continuing without her was like a kick in the gut, but Kat knew in her heart of hearts that it was the right thing to do. "Who will look after them when I've gone, though? And supervise the children?" she asked, her voice breaking.

"Luke will have to take them over," Mike said. "And maybe your replacement will be keen to carry on in your footsteps."

"What…you've already replaced me?"

"Look, Kat," Mike said gently. "After our talk recently, I had to be prepared for the worst-case scenario—not that I expected a fire. I didn't advertise for the position, but I do keep a list of previous applicants. I have someone who said they'd take the job if it became vacant."

"Then I guess you can give them a start date," she said sadly.

Kat left Mike's office, her spirits low. It was over; everything was over. The job she loved, her relationship with Ben…and whatever she'd had with Luke. Her plans had burned up in that fire, too; her animal-therapy classes would never get off the ground now, at least under her direction.

She tried to console herself with the hope that, with her departure, Luke and Ben could repair their relationship—maybe even let it thrive. If that worked out okay, maybe this would all have been worthwhile. Children had no control over their circumstances, and every child deserved stability and love. She'd had neither, which was why she knew how important they were.

LUKE SAW KAT leaving Flight as he ran up the stairs to Ben's room. She looked so sad that he longed to call out to her, to try to make things better. Instead, he forced himself to keep on walking, knowing that to offer her comfort would just complicate matters for everyone.

When Ben explained why he'd started the fire, Luke had never felt so guilty. The repercussions of his and Kat's relationship, if you could even call it that, were heartbreaking on so many levels. Yet, if he was totally honest, he couldn't regret it.

Luke thought back to the sheer terror he'd felt when he'd learned Ben was still inside the school. And the unfamiliar burst of joy and relief when he'd found him in the garden and held him tight for the very first time, telling him he wasn't angry and it would all be okay. In that moment, love had overruled discipline; perhaps Kat had been right all along. And when he'd gone to see Ben later that night, after the boy had had time to reflect on his actions, Ben had apologized and given him a hug. It had made Luke feel as if, somehow, all this heartache and everything with Kat had been worthwhile.

Today Kat was leaving for good, and he felt terrible about that. But he and Ben were going for a walk together, down to the shore. Just the two of them, father and son; that was a good feeling.

The sun was high in the clear blue sky, and

a warm breeze caressed their cheeks when they stepped outside. Seagulls swooped and soared and shrieked overhead as they started down the steep pathway together.

"I love it here," Ben said. "The sea and everything, I mean."

"I love it, too," agreed Luke, seeing his surroundings through fresh eyes. "It's beautiful and wild and free."

"That's what Miss used to say," Ben remarked quietly.

"Are you still angry with her?"

Ben looked down at his feet, scuffing his toes on the tarmac. "I thought she was my friend and you were going to take her away from me...but she didn't really care about me, either."

Luke welled up, unable to speak or breathe. This was wrong; everything Kat had done was for Ben. "You mustn't think like that," he said. "Miss is a good person and all she wants is what's best for you."

"She wants you to be her friend, not me. That's why she was kissing you. And I burned your room because I thought it was your fault." Suddenly he stopped, taking hold of Luke's hand and looking up at him. "I'm glad now that you didn't have to go away... Bradley says that I might have to, though."

Luke frowned. "What do you mean, Ben? What did Bradley say?"

"That they might send me to prison."

"Oh, Ben..." Luke drew his son toward the low wall at the side of the path and sat down beside him, gazing out across the vast expanse of sea and sky. "No one is sending you anywhere. You have to believe that."

"Bradley Simmons says that starting fires is called ars— He says it's called arson and I'll have to go to prison for it."

"You have my word that you are definitely not going to prison," Luke said. "You made a mistake, that's all—a misjudgment. You weren't trying to hurt anyone. The fire people and the police know that, I've spoken to them myself, and they're not going to punish you at all. They told me so."

When Ben's face brightened, Luke smiled and tweaked his son's nose. "So you have to stop worrying...right?"

"Right," agreed Ben. "I'll try."

"Good," Luke said. "And, Ben, don't be too hard on Miss. She really does care about you. Grown-ups mess up, too, sometimes. I certainly have. Just because people sometimes make the wrong decisions it doesn't mean they're bad."

"Like me with the fire?"

"Yes, in a way. You thought you were doing the right thing, but it turned out not to be, and I thought I was doing the right thing when I left you with your mum and your grandparents."

"And that was wrong," Ben said.

"Yes, Ben, it was very wrong, and I want to make it up to you."

Suddenly Ben grinned, seizing the opportunity. "So can we go mudlarking?"

CHAPTER TWENTY-FIVE

LUKE LOOKED DOWN at the top of Ben's shining blond head as they walked hand in hand toward the shore. He was proud that his son had finally turned to him, but the satisfaction rang a little hollow. He missed Kat. She'd given up so much for him and Ben, and he had misjudged her. They needed to talk, to clear the air between them.

"So can we go mudlarking, then?" Ben pleaded.

Luke hesitated; the tide was on its way out, gently draining away, and the bay looked so serene. He needed to work on being less rigid if he wanted to build his relationship with Ben; he saw that now. What harm could there be in having some fun on the beach? He would be there to keep Ben safe, after all.

"Okay," he agreed, the rush of joy he felt when his son's hand tightened around his overruling his doubts.

"Yes! I'll need a spade," Ben cried, his

tone high with excitement. "And a bag...and a towel to dry my feet if I have to take my shoes off."

"All right, we'll just nip back to school." Luke couldn't see why Ben would need to take off his shoes, but he smiled; the boy's excitement was infectious.

KAT REACHED NUMBER Three Cove Cottages, feeling hot and disheveled and discouraged after her meeting with Mike. She ran up the narrow staircase, throwing open her bedroom window to take in the glorious view that never failed to raise her spirits. A gentle, calming breeze wafted against her skin as she sank onto the window seat, and even the seagulls seemed quieter today, as they made lazy circles in the clear blue sky.

Her mind went back to the happy couple on that summer's evening, setting out in their boat across the bay, heading for an adventure that had surely ended in tragedy. Was life always so tough? Did fate always throw obstacles at you or did some people really just fall in love and stay together for all their lives? The young couple were certainly a reminder to seize love with both hands for as long as it lasted. With her and Luke it was different, though; there were way more important issues at stake than their own happiness.

Kat tore her eyes away from the window, feeling restless. Perhaps a walk on the shore would clear her head.

The tide was rushing out as she set off. A fierce danger lurked behind the beauty of the bay, she was well aware of that, but still she felt as if she belonged here. This place had become home to her, and the thought of leaving made her heart hurt.

But it was time for her to focus on what else life had in store for her: new challenges, new mountains to climb. The trouble was, it didn't feel as if she'd climbed the present mountain at all. In fact, she felt like a failure. The only good that could come out of this now was a proper bond between Luke and Ben.

She sat on some rocks, watching the tide recede. The sea was magnificent yet scary and it pulled like a magnet, as if trying to draw her in to its murky depths. The water retreated, leaving behind the flotsam and jetsam that the children so loved to search in, and she felt a terrible sadness creep through her whole body. What of her sea sessions and the animal therapy she'd just been starting?

What about her dream? Would she be able to carry it on somehow in her new role at the college? Knowing the answer, she started to walk again, following the edge of the tide as it rushed back out to sea.

BEN STARTED DIGGING as soon as he and Luke reached the sand, his face bright with anticipation at what he might find. "Here's a crab," he called. "It's alive."

"Put the poor thing back," Luke told him. "We're looking for treasure, remember. Let's go a bit farther along the shore—there's a cove just beyond those rocks."

Ben ran ahead, waving his bucket, his small feet making imprints in the smooth, shining sand. On impulse, Luke followed them carefully, matching his steps, his huge feet covering the boy's every footprint. He'd never thought he would come to this moment, when he and Ben would finally feel like father and son, and it was all thanks to Kat. She'd sacrificed a lot for the hope that Ben might make room for him in his heart. As much as he loved his son, though, without Kat there would be a void in Luke's life. That was the price he had to pay.

When he rounded the ledge of rock, he

saw Ben, jumping from foot to foot. "Can I dig here?"

Luke put his bag down on a flat rock. "Good a place as any," he said.

For over half an hour Ben dug, dropping to his knees to unearth any item that came to light: small pieces of pottery and plastic and a mass of seashells, but no real treasure. He sat back on his heels in despair. "Nothing," he moaned. "I've found nothing."

"Don't give up yet," Luke said with a smile. "You have to be patient and keep on trying. You can't find treasure every time."

Ben jumped to his feet. "Come on, then," he called, grabbing his spade. "Let's try around the next corner."

Luke shook his head. "It isn't a corner—it's a cliff edge that goes into the next little cove. Hey, wait for me—we have to clear away all these bits and pieces you found first."

"But we can just leave them where they are, can't we?" Ben asked, already racing off. Luke shrugged, following in his son's wake, but when he rounded the rocky outcrop there was no sign of Ben.

"Ben!" he shouted, but all he could hear was the rush of the tide and the lonely cries of the gulls. He shaded his eyes, scouring

the empty stretch of sand and stones, but of
Ben there was no trace. Panic set in and he
broke into a jog. Ben must have gone farther,
into the next cove, perhaps; he was so keen
to find treasure. As Luke headed into yet another cove, he fully expected to see Ben, en-
thusiastically digging. His panic rose when
yet again the stretch of sand was empty…and
then he saw something on a flat limestone
shelf. "Ben," he called, relieved. "What are
you doing?"

It wasn't until he was closer that the truth
dawned. It wasn't Ben slumped on the rock.
Bile rose in Luke's throat and he retched. He
had to find Ben…and he had to do what was
right for this poor, unfortunate person whose
life had ended in the merciless sea.

KAT WALKED SLOWLY along the shore, her bare
feet sinking into the sand. It always lifted her
mood, feeling the soft, golden sand squelch
between her toes, and she certainly needed
a lift right now.

"Dad! Dad!"

She heard the cry in the distance, high-
pitched and panicky. It sounded like Ben…
Or was that just her wishful thinking? Hurriedly, she headed around the end of the rocky

ridge to the next stretch of sand. The coastline was made up of coves that had been battered out by the relentless tides wherever there were no limestone cliffs to hold back the sea.

"Dad!" the voice came again. Now she was certain.

"Ben!" she yelled. "Ben? Where are you?"

"Here!"

Following his voice, she ran behind a jumble of boulders and saw him at once. Where was Luke? "Ben, it's me," she called. "Over here."

He raced toward her and her heart turned over. "Are you okay? Where's Luke?"

Tears coursed down his cheeks as he threw himself into her arms, burying his face against her chest. "He's gone. I'm all on my own and...and I haven't found any treasure."

"I'm sure your dad wouldn't leave you on purpose, Ben," she said, hiding her fear. There was no way Luke would have left Ben alone unless he had no choice. "Let's go and find him together," she suggested.

He flashed her a shaky but grateful smile and they headed on along the shore. "We'll find him," she said. "You'll see."

LUKE HEARD THEIR voices on the breeze before he saw them. The two people he loved most in the world, together. The word circled inside his head. He did love Kat; he knew it with no shadow of doubt. With all his heart and soul and mind he loved Kat, but it wasn't enough because Ben's stability came first. The voices became louder, calling his name.

Adrenaline surged through him. They mustn't come here…mustn't see… He started to run. "Ben! Kat!" he yelled. "Go back!"

Kat was staring past Luke, and he saw the realization dawn on her face. He felt a jab of pain at her anguished expression. "Come on, Ben," she urged, trying to draw him away, but he resisted, staying still until Luke reached them.

"I thought you'd left me," he said.

Luke placed both hands on his son's shoulders. "I will never leave you—I told you that. I'm sorry we got separated. It was an accident. But, Ben, something's happened here, and—"

Kat started crying, and Ben looked up at her. "What's wrong, Miss?"

Luke met Kat's eyes and nodded grimly. "Do you remember when I told you about the couple on the boat, the ones who were lost at sea?" he asked Ben.

The boy nodded.

"Well, I'm afraid…I'm afraid…" He didn't know how to go on. What was he supposed to say? How could he explain? Maybe he'd been right about himself all along. He wasn't cut out to be a father.

Kat wiped her eyes and crouched in front of Ben. "What Luke's trying to say is that a very bad thing happened, but he's going to help make sure the…the girl won't be alone."

Ben looked between them, and a sad understanding crossed his face. Then his eyes flickered with pride. "And he protected us, too, didn't he? Didn't you…Dad."

Luke swallowed and managed a nod before sweeping Ben and Kat into his arms. They held each other like that for a moment, drawing on each other's strength.

Luke pulled away first, grabbing his phone from his pocket. "I'm going to call the police," he said. "And then let's go home."

Luke gave the dispatcher the details and without another word the three of them set off as one, heading back along the beach, their arms about each other and their thoughts on the poor young girl who could finally be laid to rest. "That's why you wouldn't let me go mudlarking, isn't it?" Ben asked as the row of cottages came into view. "In case we found her."

Kat nodded, squeezing his shoulder. "I'm afraid so."

The police had said they'd stop by the cottage to speak with Luke, and while they waited for them to arrive Ben sat quite still, deep in thought, sipping the hot chocolate Kat had made him. "What if you two die?" he suddenly asked.

Kat caught Luke's eye, motioning for him to answer, and he placed his hand on Ben's shoulder. "Everyone dies eventually, Ben," he said. "Flowers, plants and animals, as well as people. It's natural—we are born, we grow up, we grow old and then we die. How we live our lives when we're here is what really matters."

Kat placed her hand on Luke's arm, a rush of emotion flooding over her. When had he become so...caring? Or maybe he'd just allowed what had always been inside to finally come out.

Ben turned to look at her, his eyes as wide as saucers. "I'm sorry for being angry with you," he said.

"And I'm sorry to have to leave you and

Flight," Kat responded. "But I will always be your friend."

"Will you be my mum?"

The question caught Kat totally off guard and she looked desperately at Luke, her eyes brimming with barely contained tears.

"I think I can hear a police car," Luke said. "Go and look out of the window, Ben. You might be able to see it."

Kat gathered up the mugs and went to wash them, staring into the soapy water. She'd always believed that marriage and kids weren't for her, but now one small, lost boy was calling her whole life into question.

Luke spoke to the police in the sitting room, explaining what had happened; after he left with them, to show them where the body was, Kat tried to talk to Ben. She knew this must have been a shock for him. She was just grateful that it wasn't he who had come across the body. "You okay, Ben?" she asked.

He nodded slowly. "It was sad, wasn't it, Dad finding her there? But he did good, didn't he?"

"It was very sad and he did really good."

"Will I die one day?"

"You've got your whole life to live first, so

you don't need to worry about that for years and years."

"And are you still going to leave?"

"I have to, Ben. It's for the best."

"But I'll still be able to come and see you?"

Kat bit her lip. "I hope you will sometimes, when I get settled. But what about your dad? Aren't you afraid anymore that I might take *him* away from you?"

"Dad's okay. I think he loves me now."

"Of course he loves you, very much…and so do I."

"So if you're not going to be my therapist anymore, why can't you be my mum? You already love my dad—I know you do."

To Kat's relief, Luke came back just then. She jumped up and walked toward him. "Did everything go okay?"

"Yes, they're getting on with proceedings. I need to get Ben back to school…and, Kat?"

"Yes?"

"Thanks…for finding Ben, I mean. I was so worried he'd think I'd let him down again."

Kat shrugged. "I'm just glad he was okay. He was a bit lost and scared, but I think he knows now that you won't leave him."

Luke held her eyes in his for one endless

moment. "He's forgiven you, too… I'm sure of it."

Kat felt the pressure of tears and held them back determinedly. "It's early days yet," she said, afraid of the flicker of hope that rekindled suddenly inside her.

CHAPTER TWENTY-SIX

THE SUN WAS slipping down behind the far horizon, turning the sea to gold, when Luke came back from dropping Ben at school. He stepped in through the door, looking slightly awkward.

"How is he?" Kat asked.

"He's amazing. He seems to have taken it all in stride."

"I think the little talk you gave him about death did the trick," she said. "Perhaps you're the one who should be a child counselor."

Luke came closer, stopping right in front of her, so close that she struggled to breathe. "I've been thinking," he said. "Ben seems to be okay with both of us now, so…"

"So…what?"

"Maybe you could go and talk to Mike, make him see that you should keep your job at Flight."

"No, Luke." She reached out and placed her hand on his arm. "It's too late for that. To be a good child therapist you have to be totally professional. I'm way too involved with both of you to make it work."

Suddenly he smiled. "Fair enough. But if you're not Ben's therapist, you don't have to be professional around him…or me, for that matter. I've had a long talk with Ben—he's sorry about the fire, and he knows now that it was a terrible thing to do. He trusts me, Kat, finally—he knows that I love him and he wants you to love him, too."

"You know I do. That's why I can't be his therapist anymore. It's why I have to leave."

Luke took hold of both her hands, drawing her toward him. "But you could be my wife," he murmured. "Marry me, Kat. I love you, I love your passion and your determination, and I love the way you smile and the way you wear your heart on your sleeve. Please, Kat…"

Stepping into his arms, Kat placed her fingers across his lips. "But what about the things you don't like about me, all the issues we've had…and what about Ben?"

"I misjudged you," he said. "I was stuck in my selfish ways, feeling sorry for myself. It took love to make me see how wrong I was, love for Ben and love for you. I want us to be a family, Kat—you, me and Ben. Please say you'll marry me, Kat. We can take our time, give us a chance to really know each other. I'll wait forever as long as I know that you'll be my wife."

He closed his arms more tightly around her, looking deep into her eyes, his lips a delicious moment away from hers. Suddenly, everything became crystal clear. All she needed was to take a leap of faith. Love and happiness were so elusive and sometimes so short-lived…

"Oh, Luke," she said. "I love you, too. We'll have to tread carefully, though, with Ben, before we can become a proper family."

"So you're saying yes?"

Taking the leap, she raised her lips to his. "Yes," she said. As his mouth claimed hers she felt his heart beat against her chest.

"And you'll be a mum to Ben?" he asked.

This time it was she who pulled away, smiling blissfully up at him. "Just try and stop me," she said, threading her fingers through the thick curls on the back of his neck to draw his lips back down to hers. "Life is way too precious to waste one single moment of happiness."

* * * * *

Get 2 Free Books,
Plus 2 Free Gifts—
just for trying the Reader Service!

Love Inspired®

Get 2 Free Books,
Plus 2 Free Gifts—
just for trying the
Reader Service!

HOMETOWN HEARTS ♥

YES! Please send me **The Hometown Hearts Collection** in Larger Print. This collection begins with 3 FREE books and 2 FREE gifts in the first shipment. Along with my 3 free books, I'll also get the next 4 books from the Hometown Hearts Collection, in LARGER PRINT, which I may either return and owe nothing, or keep for the low price of $4.99 U.S./ $5.89 CDN each plus $2.99 for shipping and handling per shipment*. If I decide to continue, about once a month for 8 months I will get 6 or 7 more books, but will only need to pay for 4. That means 2 or 3 books in every shipment will be FREE! If I decide to keep the entire collection, I'll have paid for only 32 books because 19 books are FREE! I understand that accepting the 3 free books and gifts places me under no obligation to buy anything. I can always return a shipment and cancel at any time. My free books and gifts are mine to keep no matter what I decide.

262 HCN 3432 462 HCN 3432

Name	(PLEASE PRINT)	
Address		Apt. #
City	State/Prov.	Zip/Postal Code

Signature (if under 18, a parent or guardian must sign)

Mail to the **Reader Service:**

IN U.S.A.: P.O. Box 1867, Buffalo, NY. 14240-1867
IN CANADA: P.O. Box 609, Fort Erie, Ontario L2A 5X3

* Terms and prices subject to change without notice. Prices do not include applicable taxes. Sales tax applicable in NY. Canadian residents will be charged applicable taxes. This offer is limited to one order per household. All orders subject to approval. Credit or debit balances in a customer's account(s) may be offset by any other outstanding balance owed by or to the customer. Please allow 4 to 6 weeks for delivery. Offer available while quantities last. Offer not available to Quebec residents.

Your Privacy—The Reader Service is committed to protecting your privacy. Our Privacy Policy is available online at www.ReaderService.com or upon request from the Reader Service.

We make a portion of our mailing list available to reputable third parties that offer products we believe may interest you. If you prefer that we not exchange your name with third parties, or if you wish to clarify or modify your communication preferences, please visit us at www.ReaderService.com/consumerschoice or write to us at Reader Service Preference Service, P.O. Box 9062, Buffalo, NY. 14240-9062. Include your complete name and address.

HHBPA17

Get 2 Free Books,

Plus 2 Free Gifts—

just for trying the Reader Service!

YES! Please send me 2 FREE LARGER-PRINT Harlequin® Superromance® novels and my 2 FREE gifts (gifts are worth about $10 retail). After receiving them, if I don't wish to receive any more books, I can return the shipping statement marked "cancel." If I don't cancel, I will receive 4 brand-new novels every month and be billed just $6.19 per book in the U.S. or $6.49 per book in Canada. That's a savings of at least 11% off the cover price! It's quite a bargain! Shipping and handling is just 50¢ per book in the U.S. and 75¢ per book in Canada.* I understand that accepting the 2 free books and gifts places me under no obligation to buy anything. I can always return a shipment and cancel at any time. The free books and gifts are mine to keep no matter what I decide.

132/332 HDN GLWS

Name	(PLEASE PRINT)	
Address		Apt. #
City	State/Prov.	Zip/Postal Code

Signature (if under 18, a parent or guardian must sign)

Mail to the **Reader Service**:
IN U.S.A.: P.O. Box 1341, Buffalo, NY 14240-8531
IN CANADA: P.O. Box 603, Fort Erie, Ontario L2A 5X3

Want to try two free books from another line?
Call 1-800-873-8635 today or visit www.ReaderService.com.

* Terms and prices subject to change without notice. Prices do not include applicable taxes. Sales tax applicable in N.Y. Canadian residents will be charged applicable taxes. Offer not valid in Quebec. This offer is limited to one order per household. Books received may not be as shown. Not valid for current subscribers to Harlequin Superromance Larger-Print books. All orders subject to approval. Credit or debit balances in a customer's account(s) may be offset by any other outstanding balance owed by or to the customer. Please allow 4 to 6 weeks for delivery. Offer available while quantities last.

Your Privacy—The Reader Service is committed to protecting your privacy. Our Privacy Policy is available online at www.ReaderService.com or upon request from the Reader Service.

We make a portion of our mailing list available to reputable third parties that offer products we believe may interest you. If you prefer that we not exchange your name with third parties, or if you wish to clarify or modify your communication preferences, please visit us at www.ReaderService.com/consumerchoice or write to us at Reader Service Preference Service, P.O. Box 9062, Buffalo, NY 14240-9062. Include your complete name and address.

HSRLP17R

READERSERVICE.COM

Manage your account online!

- Review your order history
- Manage your payments
- Update your address

> ***We've designed the
> Reader Service website
> just for you.***

Enjoy all the features!

- Discover new series available to you, and read excerpts from any series.
- Respond to mailings and special monthly offers.
- Browse the Bonus Bucks catalog and online-only exculsives.
- Share your feedback.

Visit us at:

ReaderService.com

Get 2 Free Books,
Plus 2 Free Gifts—
just for trying the
Reader Service!

Love Inspired ® HISTORICAL

Get 2 Free Books,
Plus 2 Free Gifts—
just for trying the Reader Service!

Get 2 Free Books,

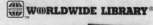